Tears in the Clover

a collection by
Greg J. Grotius

Author of *Places in the Woods*

authorHOUSE®

AuthorHouse™
1663 Liberty Drive
Bloomington, IN 47403
www.authorhouse.com
Phone: 1 (800) 839-8640

Published by AuthorHouse 12/20/2016

ISBN: 978-1-5246-5553-2 (sc)
ISBN: 978-1-5246-5551-8 (hc)
ISBN: 978-1-5246-5552-5 (e)

Library of Congress Control Number: 2016921011

Print information available on the last page.

Author's Note

Tears in the Clover is a collection of three stories that I had chosen to be my second published release. I had first intended to place a note under the front title saying that it was a trilogy, which I believed to be acceptable even though the three stories were not directly related. However, it was decided that I would just call it a collection and felt that the title would be enough to tie the stories together in a relative way. In saying this, the title is what I want to describe next in order to fill in the reader with my intention, which is, at best, a little contemplative. I didn't intend to display a confusing title for my readers.

The English language has allowed a single word to have more than one definition. My intention was to use the word Tears as in the meaning of rips in the clover. The other meaning is a tear from one's crying eyes. This enforces the use of a double entendre of tears meaning either rips, or crying tears. I decided to leave the title as is but felt like I needed to explain. At the same time, tears from one's eyes can also be tied into the themes of the stories due to the nature of the story themes. The clover is a three-leaf clover noting that there are three stories in the collection.

The similarity in all three stories is that they all have a traditional source of conflict, tribulation, tension, and the need for resolution of problems for the main characters. I do hope that my note has helped to enlighten the readers as to the correct pronunciation of the title as well as the double entendre that can very well be conceived in understanding the title's possibilities.

Acknowledgements

I would first of all like to thank my wife, Teresa, for having patience and physically helping me through the writing of this book. I am grateful to the people in my life whose personal lives and situations had inspired much of the writing in *Tears In The* Clover. I also want to thank those persons who had answered questions from me about certain aspects of description that were included in the stories herein. I am forever grateful to my nephew, Zachary J. Hunt, for his cover artwork. And last, but not least, I am very thankful to a representative of The Alamo Steakhouse and Saloon in Gatlinburg, Tennessee, who provided me with certain visual details of the restaurant which I incorporated into one of the stories.

Tears In The Clover Disclaimer

In regard to any references to a specific area of the globe, I want to apologize for any misrepresentation of that particular region and/or establishment. I did my research extensively and tried to describe a given site to the best of my ability. Any characters that I created are fictional and if seemingly depicts a story that is similar to an existing person's, it is merely coincidental. All people, places and things that are portrayed within the pages of this book, I will duly note that the story is strictly written in the utmost respect.

Contents

The Catalysts

Introduction

What lies in the outer reaches of all of our lives? There are traditionally surprises of one sort or another. Some things are good, and others, not so good. The scenarios can be comprised of the unexpected or the unexplained. During the blessed long life that I have experienced, I have seen a myriad of circumstances that I was determined to accept or get through in order to survive in the world in which I live. That is what most people must do if they expect to go on instead of withering away, allowing bad elements to take hold and destroy them. We are all a part of the picture. Whether or not we decide to endure pain and suffering is totally up to us, therefore, the whole picture eventually makes some sense based on self-awareness and action.

Tears in the Clover is an extravagant example of what I perceived to be a picture painted in lives of people who do not necessarily ask for what they have received. As you read each story, and eventually, all three, you will see that the plight of each individual is so very different. A common ground is not necessarily what I had in mind when choosing the stories that I did in writing this trilogy. It is a trilogy in the sense that the main characters or secondary characters hold different senses of value in their lives, but in retrospect, all are trying to survive in their own unique way. The first story is an example of a person who had encountered situations and lives her life in a way that she follows her emotions and dreams despite obstacles that was set out in front of her. The second is based on a dream that I had, and when I had awakened, did some research of a true-life event in history that fell into the atmosphere in which my dream represented itself. The characters are fictional, and some of them encounter a very surreal experience throughout the piece of work. The third and final story is based upon a friend's journey to recover what he had seemed to lose in his personal life. I feel that these stories will keep the reader on their toes and hope that he or she is crimping the pages of the book in interest.

Goodbye and Hello

By

Greg J. Grotius

Prologue

Winifred reached the dome in a little over ten minutes. Her striking red hair blew rapidly under the brown, fur-like headband that protected her head and ears from the cold wind that began to blow at that level of the Smoky Mountains National Park. She stood alone and absorbed the continuous ridges of mountains that cascaded the Appalachians. The season was close to the end for those who wished to hike to the dome, for the road to the dome was closed to the public in early December. Winifred Palmer was a natural beauty. If one were to face her as she stood looking out from the front of the dome, one would see a beautiful free spirit. Her brown eyes squinted at the late afternoon's hazy sun. She smiled a rich pleasing smile, showing dimples and light freckles. Her nose wrinkled in the center at times when she reacted to the chilly breeze that hit her face. As the scene entered her memory path, she thought of the road ahead that she must take. There was much ahead for this thirty-year-old woman who wanted no more out of life than to live it to its fullest. She had left much behind. Winifred not only left a family and a job, but she left all of her past experiences to be lost in the waves of time. A new life for her meant all things new would be her quest. She wanted to leave the past behind, but deep in her consciousness, she had wondered if this task would be possible.

1

He had gone out on her multiple times. Fifteen times, to be exact, and three of those times with the same woman. Chad Palmer had no reservations in calling Winifred at closing hours from the Fine Wining Emporium and telling her that meetings with the owner were of major importance. Those excuses were freely accepted by his wife, as she had spent evenings tending to their two children, Adrian, age 6, and Kira, age 8 boy and girl respectively. Both children were revered as future geniuses by their parents.

Chad Palmer was not a despicable man but had possessed a way with ladies. He was very handsome with short dark hair and stood around six-foot-three. His current and previous experiences with Winifred's work schedule had left him a virtually lonely man who fell into a situation of seeking more from life. He did love Winifred, but an occasion that helped jump start his extra-marital activities was a company dinner that his wife was not able to attend. After sipping on three martinis and waiting too long for dinner, a lovely lady at his table had sparked a conversation.

"Don't you just love long and drawn-out dribble?" she asked him. She was referring to speeches and company sales projections for the upcoming year.

"Oh, yeah." he answered, "and I'm sorry I had to be one of the speakers. Just something I have to do as the vice-president." He smiled at her. "I've seen you around but where?"

"I carry the load of arranging purchasing for Nicktown Liquors out of Iowa. Seen you before too. Must have been on the road. The Emporium had come to visit our store, and I believe you were present. Cora Shandling." She held out her hand and Chad gently shook it.

"Chad Palmer," he said as he retrieved his hand, snapped both his fingers in unison and pointed towards her. "That's it," he said. "Nicktown is that huge store chain that's like a warehouse of liquor."

"That's the one. It's a candy store for alcoholics." She laughed and Chad returned a laugh.

Dinner had finally started being served when their conversation had begun to subside, but it didn't end. They looked at each other and smiled while chewing on the grilled chicken.

"A little dry--don't you think?" she asked.

Chad smiled as he was eating and shook his head. "Just a bit," he answered. As the evening progressed with unfortunately more talk and endorsements, the two of them talked of going somewhere else for a drink. That never happened.

After the function was over, they merely left together in his car, drove straight to a hotel, and went to bed. The love making in Chad's mind was something to behold. It was very exciting to him even though he felt rather guilty. After an hour or so, he drove her back to her car. They talked about getting together again, said their goodbyes, and departed from one another. They never saw each other again. Chad had met several clients in the past year after the one night affair with Cora, all of whom with he had had sexual relations.

The children adored their father. He had spent quality time with both of them that Winifred, a dedicated social worker who worked 60-70 hours a week, could not even hope to spend with the children. For weekday afternoons and early evenings, the parents had hired a baby sitter whose references were checked out thoroughly by the Palmers. Sarah Morning was indeed a very reliable sitter. She had been the Palmers' employee ever since the children had been nearly infants. So, since Winifred was not able to be with the children as much as she would have preferred, her relationship with them was somewhat distant. Chad Palmer had spent Saturdays working early mornings--working on agendas on the sales for the wine business of which he was vice-president. The Fine Wining Emporium sold regionally-produced wine directly to the public and to liquor stores in a number of surrounding states around Wilmington, Missouri. His later mornings consisted of attending Kira's dance practice and recitals. He had enrolled Adrian in Spelling Bee training, which had begun when the boy was age five. It was not uncommon for the children's Saturdays to be spent with their father, ending with lunch and ice cream or an occasional movie at the theatre.

Winifred despaired at the absence of a normal family life. She had worked herself to near exhaustion; and, in spite of the fact that she loved her job, she had become overwhelmed in the past year. The number of cases assigned to her was taxing to her sleeping patterns. Some nights she could not sleep at all, for she invariably took her work home with her. Her specialty was abused spouses. The case that most bothered her was that of Kathleen Wicham. Kathleen had been in and out of the hospital a few times due to the beatings caused by her husband, Carl. There were also numerous times when Kathleen should have been at the hospital, especially those times where the injuries were so severe. She had once had her head opened up with a belt buckle, and—in a state of shock, Carl had banded her head tightly to help stop the bleeding and told Kathleen to keep her head elevated. The reason he did not allow her to go to the emergency room was that this type of injury would surely cause suspicion by the hospital and, eventually, the police. Carl had once pushed her off their balcony, and she fell through the tool shed roof.

She had a dislocated shoulder and cuts all over her face and arms. The reasons for these outbursts of anger usually revolved around her inability to have his dinner ready on time as he walked through the door from work, or rather, after several drinks following work. He had once beaten her badly for dressing up nice for work and wearing make up. Kathleen had briefly worked as a receptionist at a law firm, and Carl had made it clear that if she couldn't dress as nicely for him that she didn't need to be working. He had made her quit.

Winifred had pleaded with Kathleen to leave this man, and it was always the same answer. 'He would track me down and kill me.' This infuriated Winifred to no end. She had decided that the case of Kathleen Wicham was very hairy indeed. She had wished that she could send her off somewhere to a safe haven. This, however, was against the social work code, and intrinsically unethical.

June 5th

"They were at the Heritage Restaurant--together, Winny," Sharon Sikes said indignantly. Sharon was Winifred's best friend. The two ladies were having coffee at Springs International Coffee House.

"It could have been one of his associates, Sharon," said Winifred. "Besides—I have complete trust in my husband. He's a wonderful father. He'd never do anything to jeopardize our family."

"Ughhhh. Okay. She was an associate. Does one cradle an associate's shoulder while sitting on the same side of a booth?" Sharon retorted.

Winifred looked bewildered. "He had his arm around her?" she asked.

"Well—not the whole time, just occasionally."

"I've made up my mind. I won't say anything about it—unless he doesn't say something about a woman associate first."

"That a girl. At least you're on your guard. Listen. I gotta get to a boring meeting with the Writer's Club. Publishing is such a chore nowadays. You promise you'll call me if you find anything out."

"I promise," Winifred said. She raised her right cheek and squinted her right eye. "Do ya think? Never mind. I know what your answer might be."

Sharon jumped from her seat. "Love you." She bent and lightly kissed Winifred on the corner of her mouth.

"Love you too. Don't die of boredom," said Winifred. Sharon wisped herself away as if being drawn away by a wind. Winifred stared down into her too-strong coffee that she held and mechanically slammed it on the table somewhat gently. *You wouldn't, would you, Chad?* She was suddenly depressed, and it seemed to have little to do with her earlier session with Kathleen Wicham.

2

Carl Wicham had walked through the front door more inebriated than usual. His friend and co-worker, Charley Beals, had kept buying Carl shots of tequila on top of his personal pitcher of beer. After the fourth shot, Carl actually objected to any more hard drinks from Charley. Carl had gone to the restroom, only to come back and find another shot by his mug of beer at the bar where both men sat. "Charley," Carl said. "What did I just tell you? Thanks, pal, but I gotta drive home. You're only drinking tequila, but I'm also drinking beer."

"Oh—you'll be fine driving," said Charley. "I'm at seven shots. That will only be five for you."

"But I'm drinking beer. Are you deaf? I'll drink this one, but that's it. Promise?"

"I promise," Charley said as he smiled."

"Okay. Down the hatch." Carl downed his shot in one gulp. He looked at his pitcher of beer that had about two beers left in it. "Charley—you're welcome to the rest. I gotta go."

"Not stoppin' ya. Sure. I'll drink your beer."

Carl got down from the barstool and drifted right into a table where two ladies were sitting. Both ladies picked up their glasses of beer in time, but one had spilled some on herself. "I'm so sorry, ladies. It's that guy's fault." He pointed at Charley who was laughing hysterically.

The lady who spilled her beer looked at Carl with a smile. "No harm done," she said. "If I'd have drenched my shirt, I might have been pissed."

"Again—my apologies."

Carl didn't remember the ride home very well. He did remember almost running a red light as he had slammed on his brakes. There was luckily no police around. There was also a driver that came from his left in the cross lane that laid on the horn a few seconds. In the back of his mind, he realized that he couldn't drive as well as he had hoped, not with all that alcohol in his system, and he felt lucky to be at home. As he entered his house, he smelled food. Good smelling food. "Where's my darling?" he said loudly. "You've been a good girl, Kat."

Kathleen was in the kitchen and came out when she heard his voice. She had felt disappointed but didn't show it. "Welcome home, Carl. Been drinking, I see."

"So what?" he said. "What's for dinner, doll?"

"Lemon pepper chicken breast, zucchini with tomatoes, onions, and new potatoes. Sound good?"

"Oh, baby. It sure does. See what a little cooperation does for our relationship?"

Kathleen finally produced a smile. She shook her head. "I have to ask. What in the world did you drink? You're more tipsy than usual."

"Oh—that damn Charley kept buying me tequila shots—and even after I told him I had enough."

"Well—you were a good man."

Carl rushed to Kathleen. "You bet I was, darling," he said. He kissed her passionately. Kathleen thought the kiss was too hard and was barely able to kiss back.

She was laughing under the kiss.

"What?" he said. "You think I'm a joke?" He slapped her hard on the face.

"Damn it, Carl. Why do you have to hurt me?" She began to cry.

"I'm sorry, Kat. You didn't deserve that. You fixed a wonderful dinner. But why were you laughing?"

"Because I couldn't breath, Carl!"

Carl began to laugh, and laugh hard. "Heh-heh. It was a pretty smothering kiss, wasn't it?"

"I couldn't even kiss you back." Kathleen laughed. They both laughed in unison. "Come on, Carl. Let's eat."

"No argument there, hon." He still let out a few chuckles. He slapped her on the butt on the way into the kitchen.

"Quit that, Carl." She smiled.

"You know, baby. You have a beautiful smile," he said.

"Thank you, Carl. It's nice hearing compliments."

"Oh—I can be sweet when I want to be."

During their meal, Carl kept eyeing Kathleen. At one point he raised his eyebrows up and down.

"What?" she asked as she smiled..

"Damn. You are so cute. The way you said 'what.' Do I have to spell it out for you?"

"Tonight, Carl? I mean—you're so drunk."

"This meal'll sober me up. Yes—tonight."

"Okay. I need to shower."

"I think I'd rather have you dirty. Heh heh."

"Oh, Carl—you are bad." She laughed. "Uh—can **you** take a shower?"

Carl belted out with laughter. "Yes, honey. I'll take a shower. I probably smell like a goat after working that damn line all day." He took the last bite of his dinner and stood up. "I'll be right back." As he walked through the hallway, he glanced at the telephone. *Should I?*, he asked himself. He did. Carl picked up the phone and hit redial. The line rang. The receiving party picked up.

"Palmer residence." He slammed the phone down.

Kathleen could hear Carl stomping back down the hall to the kitchen. She was beginning to do the dishes.

"Okay, Kat. What the hell are you calling her for?"

"What. What—what?"

Carl went to the sink where she stood, picked up a dish and broke it over her head. "I told you I didn't want you to call that social working bitch again," he said as Kathleen fell to the floor.

Her forehead was streaming blood. "Carl," she screamed. "What the hell is the matter with you?" She cried a painful cry. She was in torment.

"What's the matter with me?" he asked. "What's the matter with you? You can't do anything that I tell you. Why did you call her?" he screamed to the top of his lungs.

"For your information, asshole, I called her to tell her that I was going to make things right between us. That I was going to fix your dinner and make you happy. That's why I called her." She sobbed uncontrollably.

Carl stood dumbfounded. He knew not what to say. Deep in his mind he knew that he treated his wife poorly. He hated himself, and he hated how his father had treated his own mother. He cried at the sight of Kathleen lying on the floor holding her head. He didn't want her to cry anymore. "Oh, baby. I'm so sorry."

"Don't 'oh, baby me, you louse. I'm a person. I want respect. I want to live my life not being afraid of you. Is that too much to ask, Carl?"

"No. It's not. I'm sorry. I screwed up." He immediately got a fresh dish towel and wet it down with cool water.

"Not my new dish towel, you idiot. Get an old one."

Carl scrambled through the drawer to get an older towel. He found one and got it wet and squeezed it. He knelt down on the floor and held it against Kathleen's wound. "Okay, baby. It's going to be okay."

Kathleen's crying began to subside but her head ached horribly. She vomited up her dinner. Carl quickly cleaned that up. There was no love making that evening, but only broken sleep for Kathleen and plenty of snoring from Carl's side of the bed.

June 6th

"Thank you for calling, Winifred. I have to be careful calling you from now on," said Kathleen.

"Why?" Winifred asked. "What happened, Kathleen?"

"Well—everything was going fine, even though he was drunk when he got home." Kathleen had omitted the part about the slap but would explain to her later. "He was sweet as can be—and frisky. He loved the fact that I cooked a meal as I told you I would do." She sighed. "We were planning on making love after dinner—then things took a turn for the worse. I didn't see it coming, Winifred." She began to cry while rubbing the top of her head where there was a bump.

"What did he do?" Winifred asked.

"He must have touched the redial on the phone and found out that I called you."

"I was wondering who had called and hung up on me. We got rid of our CALLER ID for the time being. Go on."

"He rushed into the kitchen while I was washing dishes, picked up a dish and broke it over my head. It hurt."

"That son-of-a-bitch."

"He asked why I called you, and I told him. He began to change his behavior when he got his answer. He actually began to cry as I was crying on the floor. He helped clean off my head from the blood and was very apologetic."

"Well wasn't that sweet. You don't need this, Kathleen. He's a ticking time bomb."

Kathleen let out a laugh. "I called him an asshole, Winifred. Heh heh."

"Well—good for you. Listen, Kathleen. Listen very closely. We have a petty cash account at the agency. If I could somehow get you the money.."

Kathleen interrupted her. "No, Winny. No. I don't want to get you into trouble."

"I can maybe figure something out. I don't know what. We're not supposed to help people out monetarily. It's against regulations to use any more than one-hundred dollars at a time for emergency situations. There's also a bail-out-of-jail allowance, but that doesn't help."

"No. I won't hear of it. I do want to leave him, Winifred. I do. Can I come and talk to you today? I'm going stir crazy. I don't want to be alone."

"Honey, come by anytime. I have two cases before noon but I should be back soon after. Stop by and we'll have lunch. Okay?"

"Okay, sweetheart. I'll see you around noon."

"It's a date, baby. And—put some ice on your head."

"I think I've emptied the ice maker." Kathleen laughed.

"See you at noon. Bye."

"Bye, Winifred."

After they hung up, Winifred thought. *Perhaps Chad could help her out. That way the funds won't be coming directly from me.* She decided then and there that she would ask him.

Little did Winifred know that three cubicles down from hers sat Karen DuPont. Karen didn't like Winifred, and she had just heard an ear full. Karen was jealous of Winifred. She knew that Winifred would usually get the best cases. Winifred was very attractive and everyone liked her. Karen was a little overweight and had not made much of an impression at the agency. She only had five cases and Winifred had numerous ones. *This could be **your** ticket out of here, **Mrs.** Palmer,* Karen thought.

12:10 pm

"So—where would you like to go to lunch, Kathleen?" Winifred asked.

"Oh, Winifred. Why don't you pick."

"No. This one's on me. You need a treat."

"Okay," Kathleen said as she smiled. "How about Dante's on The Walkway?"

"Dante's it is. Just give me a moment to let the boss know that I'm leaving for a couple of hours." Winifred got up from her chair and walked toward Ms. Arnold's office.

"What a sweety," Kathleen said to herself.

In Karen's cubicle, she dialed a number. "Hello, Cameron? This is Karen," she said quietly.

"Hi, baby. How are you.?"

"Oh—I'm fine. Listen, Cameron. I need a favor."

"Anything, Karen. I'm a bored laid-off machine worker. Whatcha need?"

"Could you possibly be at Dante's on The Walkway--pronto? There's some eavesdropping that I'd like you to do."

"Sounds mysterious. Who will I be looking for?"

"An attractive red-headed girl with freckles. Her name is Winifred. She'll be sitting with a trampy sort of girl named Kathleen. She is small build with long, dark brown hair. Not too bad on the eye as you guys say, but she will look a bit haggard. Her husband abuses her."

"That's a shame," he said.

"What I want you to listen for--are details of money. About what it would cost to send the abused girl away from her husband. I'm sure they'll be sitting outside since it's a beautiful day."

15

"I can do that. In fact, Dante's sounds like a good lunch for me."

Karen spoke even more quietly as she heard Winifred walk to her desk. "Get going. They're getting ready to leave. I'll take care of you for this one. Bye."

"Bye, darlin'," Cameron answered. Cameron Cole and Karen once dated but became good friends. She had broken it off since she had little self esteem, and Cameron also got on her nerves as a boyfriend. Karen smiled and thought, *You are one devious woman, Karen.*

Dante's 1:05 pm

"He was being so sweet, but." Kathleen hesitated.

"But what?" asked Winifred.

"He had laid a kiss on me before dinner. He was kissing me so hard that I could barely breathe. I-I began to laugh. He thought I was laughing at him and he slapped me hard across the face. What do you make of someone like that, Winny?"

"A very disturbed individual—that's what. The man suffers from low motivation. He needs a psychiatrist. He has no ambition to better himself. The very nature of his being revolves around eating, drinking, and making your life miserable. You asked me—and that's what I make of him."

"But—he has emotion. I saw it last night and I've seen it before."

"Of course he has emotion. He's not evil incarnate. He just has no business being married to anyone until he gets thorough help. But—you see, Kathleen—that's not going to happen. He won't stoop down from his insane selfish pedestal. So—you listen and listen carefully. You will end up dead, darling, if you don't leave that bastard as soon as possible. He's prone to doing the worst before things get better."

Kathleen held down her head revealing a cut on her scalp that Winifred could see. "You're right, dear friend. What would it cost to get me away from here?"

"I can have you booked on a flight out of Wilmington no later than Friday, the 9th, for around twelve-hundred dollars to either coast that you desire. There's a flight leaving for San Diego on Friday. What do ya think?"

"That sounds wonderful, but I don't want you to jump through any loopholes to get me there."

"I'll do what I think I need to do to get you there, Kathleen. What do you say?"

"Okay. Okay. But don't you get into trouble. I'll never forgive myself. I love you, Winifred."

"I love you too, baby. That's why I'm willing to do whatever it takes to get you to safety."

"He might come after you first."

"Do you think I'm afraid of him? No. I've been doing these cases so long I'm oblivious to fear of crazy husbands." Their lunch had arrived.

Cameron had heard nearly the whole conversation. He sat one table over from Winifred and Kathleen. The spiciest parts that he had jotted down was the price of the flight and that Winifred mentioned that 'I'll do what I need to do to get you there, Kathleen.' Cameron Cole's life was boring. He had no job and no prospects in sight. His lack of ambition was another deep-seeded factor why Karen had dumped him. The little assignment that Karen DuPont gave him was exciting to him. He finished his sandwich and beer, paid for his meal, and left the restaurant.

3

"Are you crazy, Win?" Chad Palmer asked. "I can't help her out. She just needs to file a restraining order and be done with it. Besides, you and I could both get into trouble if the agency found out that we helped her. No. Absolutely not." He fidgeted with his reports for work and placed them in order. His demeanor was not only detached from being a caring person, but he was abrasive to Winifred.

"I thought that you would understand, Chad. Perhaps I was wrong," she said indignantly.

"Okay. There's something else that I have to say. **You** are not someone who should be helping someone out that is outside of the family. You are not a good mother. On a good night you might be home at 6:00. How many nights have you gotten home just before the kids go to bed?" he asked.

Winifred put a look on her face that could kill. "How dare you! I work my ass off while you tromp around with your elite associates—if that is in fact what you're doing."

Chad exploded. "What? What are you saying, Win? I have a very important job."

"And I don't?"

"I'm not saying that you do not." He calmed. "But—what were you insinuating with that last comment?"

"I happen to know that you had dinner with a woman."

"What woman?"

"What woman?" Winifred retorted. "The woman at The Heritage restaurant? You had your arm around her." She tapped her foot on the floor. "Another associate I guess."

"Yes. Yes she was." He hesitated. "We discussed the upcoming year's promotional campaign." Chad was a good liar but his facial reaction that Winifred observed looked sort of desperate.

"Okay. But what about the touchy feely thing that was going on and the fact that you both sat on the same side of the booth?" She raised her eyebrows and bit her bottom lip while exposing a grin.

"Who? Who's telling you this? That meddlesome Sharon? Must have been. She's the only friend that you have."

Winifred's face turned red. "Oh. That sucked, Chad—and you know it."

"Ok. It did suck, but isn't it true? You barely have time for other friends not to mention your own family." He gave that desperate look again.

"You are pathetic. And don't turn this back around on me," Winifred screamed. "What is your **associate's** name?"

Chad's mind froze. "Jessica," he said.

"Jessica who? She does have a last name, right?"

Chad regained his calmness and gave a last name. "Solomon— Jessica Solomon." It was all that he could come up with.

"So—if I called the Emporium and asked to speak with a Jessica Solomon, she'd be available. Right?"

Chad was suddenly caught. He could not think. Through all of the years of their marriage, he was finally speechless. He didn't say anything but looked at Winifred with a serious look as if to say *you've got me.*

"Oh-ho-ho. So—it is true. Chad," she said with composure. "I know I haven't been there for you and the kids, but the deception. You could have talked to me."

"It's true," he said. "There is no Jessica Solomon."

"I assumed as much. Okay. She can't be the only one—and I'm not going to badger you by asking who else." Winifred began to cry. She walked from the living room and ran up the stairs.

"Mommy. What's wrong?" Kira asked. "I heard you screaming."

Winifred knelt down. She lovingly caressed her daughter's hair. "Nothing, baby. Daddy and I just had an argument is all. Go back to your room and go to sleep." She kissed Kira's forehead. "Go on."

Kira did as she was told. "Night, Mommy."

"Goodnight, darling. See you in the morning." Winifred retrieved a duffle bag from her bedroom closet, stopped and thought. She quickly decided not to run out in the middle of the night and that the living room couch would be very peaceful. Most importantly, she had told her daughter that she would see her in the morning.

Winifred had awakened on the couch at 6:15 the next morning. She did not sleep well. In fact, she had fallen asleep sometime after 3:00. She had done much thinking and decided that she could never forgive Chad for his unfaithfulness. Kathleen Wicham was also on her mind. She had wondered how she could help this woman get away from her abuser. She was determined to help Kathleen in any way that she could. Upon awakening, she had searched the room with her eyes. She glanced at the coffee table and saw a piece of paper with handwriting on it, and then turned on the light beside her to read it. Next to the paper was an envelope.

> *Dearest Winifred,*
>
> *I know that I have not been the husband that you expected me to be. I still love you but things have not been quite the way that they should. You do not deserve what I've done. I know that your job is very important. The bottom line is that I have been unfaithful. We will talk this evening.*
>
> *Please accept what you'll find in the envelope. It's what you wanted.*
>
> *Regards,*
> *Chad*

She quickly opened the envelope. What she saw was not what she had expected. She had expected money for her problem case with Kathleen. Chad had gone one step further. She held in her hand a one-way ticket to San Diego California. She knew that stricken with guilt, Chad must have purchased an on-line e-ticket to help Kathleen. "Thank you, Chad," she said quietly. *I still don't forgive you for what you've done, but this **is** a noble gesture,* she thought.

8:15am

"Why didn't you stick around a while longer, Cameron?" Karen asked. "They may have had more to say,"

"You told me to listen for their names, talk of an expense, and other incriminating statements," Cameron responded. "Besides, I thought Ms. Palmer's comment of doing anything she can to get Wicham out of here was sufficient."

Karen tapped her fingers on the desk. "Okay. Alright then. But remember I'm paying you for this." She waited for a response but Cameron said nothing. "Gotta go. Here she comes," Karen said, whispering. Winifred had come into the door walking to her desk.

"What?" Cameron asked.

Karen hung up the phone. *That dumb ass,* she thought. *'What?'*

The day began as many others for Karen. There were no calls until around 11am. Winifred's phone rang and rang. Then she heard the call for which Karen was waiting; and of course, she could only hear Palmer's responses.

"Diamond Social Services—Winifred speaking. May I help you? Yes. Morning, honey. How are things? … Oh, Kat. That's perfect. He'll be out of town until next Monday? I have something awesome to tell you but I need to stop by. Well—let's just say that things are falling into place. Can you come by my place at 4? Great. No. The money's not an issue at this point. Okay. See you, love. Bye."

3:45pm

Karen DuPont checked the computer for nearly every avenue of all petty-cash accounts that she could muster. She had finally found the total of petty cash available amongst all employees, and then divided the total by the number of social workers. She wasn't for sure that all employees were allotted the same amount. She did know that her own personal account was $2000.00. Going by that amount, she assumed that all petty-cash account amounts were similar in dollars. When the office began to show signs of slowing down and agents were out on assignments, Karen slipped into Winifred's cubicle, and also slipped on a pair of latex gloves. She got on the computer and did a search from the START menu. She typed in petty cash. No results for petty cash had shown. Karen thought for a moment and searched again. She then typed in Winifred's cash. She was pleased to see the results in the Excel program. She clicked on it and this is what came up.

CASH ALLOTMENT - WINIFRED PALMER - JUNE 2012

DATE	ACTION	CREDITS	BALANCE
1-Jun			2200.00
2-Jun			
3-Jun			
4-Jun	Fuel	44.79	2155.21
5-Jun	Bail money - Robert Laughlin	200.00	1955.21
6-Jun			
7-Jun			
8-Jun			

Within the employee's Excel cash page Karen clicked on 8-Jun. She typed in Kath Wicham under the ACTION, 1200.00 under the CREDIT column and then 755.21 under BALANCE. There it was; the newly revised petty cash report. Karen's adrenaline was flowing, her pulse was racing, and sweat covered her brows. She saved the information, exited Excel, and quickly got up from Winny's chair and raced back to her own cubicle. Just then, the door opened to the vacant office. In walked her boss, Cynthia Arnold.

"Any good today, Karen?" asked Cynthia.

"Yes, ma'am. I put two homeless children in foster homes, and they've already received prospects for adoption."

"Good. Very good," exclaimed Cynthia. "You're on the ball as always. I do have one suggestion, honey."

Karen hated to be called honey—especially by her boss. "Yes, ma'am. And what is that?"

"Perhaps you need to spend more time in the field. Visit some abuse shelters, soup kitchens—things of that sort. You do very well in researching from the office; but if you don't get out more, this stuffy office will cloud your brain. Just a little constructive criticism. I hope you don't mind."

"Of course not, Ms. Arnold. Any advice from you is most appreciated." Karen did not like advice but had to, for her job's sake, carry out the façade of accepting constructive input.

"Thank you, Karen. I'm glad we're on the same page. I'm getting some coffee. Want some?"

"No thank you, ma'am. I was just about to call it an evening."

"By all means. Get some rest and I'll see you next week. Unless you need to be here on Saturday. If I were you, I'd call it a weekend."

"A weekend it will be," answered Karen. Before she left, she thought again about what she did. *I should change it back. No. Winny's days of glory are over. Step aside, Palmer. I'm the next one to be promoted.*

"Oh, Winny. This is too good to be true." Kathleen hugged Winifred tightly.

"I'm gonna miss you, Kathleen," Winifred said. "I'm so happy that we could help."

"I'll miss you too," said Kathleen as she released Winifred.

"Now—of course you cannot go out there empty handed." Winfred took an envelope out of the inside pocket of her sport jacket.

"Winny--I can't take any more from you."

"I insist, Kathleen. It's a jungle in California. You'll need a little extra to get you started."

"Winifred. I have some money," Kathleen said. "A couple thousand dollars."

"Do you know how long that would last you in San Diego?" Winifred asked. "About one or two days. An apartment will cost you at least a thousand, and they usually want a deposit for at least that much. This is 10, 000 dollars, Kath." She forced the envelope into Kathleen's hand.

Kathleen had tears in her eyes. She accepted the money. "Are you rich or something?"

Winifred smiled. "Something like that. It mostly came from Chad, and I was able to cough up a couple grand. Off you go, Kath. Pack your bags cause you have an early morning." She extended her arms and hugged Kathleen. Winifred kissed her on the cheek.

"I'll never forget you, Winny," Kathleen said.

"You better not. I'll not forget you either."

"Winny. What about Carl? I mean—he'll come looking for you."

"I'm quite aware of that," Winifred said with a smile. "Not a problem. I know nothing. Perhaps to ease his mind, I can mention that you wanted to leave him. I won't give any indication that I helped in any way. I'm not afraid of woman beaters, Kathleen. Have you ever seen him fight another man?"

Kathleen thought for a moment. "You know—I can't say that I have."

"Classic case of masculine insecurity. He questions his own ability to protect himself and takes it out on the weaker sex. He's a bully—and needs to be called on it. By the way—I'm a brown belt in Karate." Winifred smiled from ear to ear.

"You are not," Kathleen said as she smiled back.

"You bet your ass I am. When I started in this business I simultaneously took full-time classes at night. My first encounter with an angry husband left me in exultation. He had followed me to my car as he screamed at me all of the way out of the building. He made the mistake of taking a tight grip of my hair from behind. I let out a 'h-yaaa' as I elbowed him in the stomach. As he let go of my hair, I twisted his left arm behind him to the breaking point. I didn't let up, and I bet you could have heard his broken arm snap across the parking lot. He laid on the ground and cried in pain. 'You bitch,' he yelled. I looked down at him with intense fury. I pointed my finger in his face. I told him that 'I'd watch what you say, buster, because you have one more good arm.' He looked up in terror. I smiled at him, and then I said, 'I'll call you an ambulance.' Which I did.

"No way, Winny." Kathleen was awestruck by Winifred's story.

"Yes, ma'am. Oh—the police came too because I told them over the phone that it was self defense of an attack. The police had at first asked 'if a broken arm was a suitable defense for the pulling of hair.' I told him 'absolutely.' I let the officer know that the man was much stronger than me, and that he could have harmed me much worse. Herb Ketchum, one of my co-workers, witnessed the whole thing from the doorway of the business. He had calmly concurred with my story to the officer. 'Okay—well—that's good enough for me', the officer said."

"Well I'll be, Winifred. I never knew you had it in you," said Kathleen. "Whoa," she exclaimed as she smiled large.

Winifred blew on her finger tips and wiped them on her jacket. "Oh yeah," she said smiling. "Anyway, Kath. Don't worry about me."

"I'm not," Kathleen said amused.

"You'd better go, doll. And I know I don't have to tell you, but mum's the word on this whole ticket and money thing."

"Rest assured, Winifred. I love you."

"I love you too," said Winifred. They had kissed each other on the corners of their mouths. "Bye, baby."

"Bye, honey. I'll write you."

"That's fine, Kath—but I'd wait a good while. Find some kind of job and you should be in good shape. And remember—you're not married to San Diego. If the expenses become too great, there are neighboring states to where you can flee."

Kathleen shook her head in understanding. She turned and headed for the door. She turned around once more and smiled wanly. "Bye."

"Bye, darling," Winifred said.

Kathleen quickly exited the Palmer house. She got in her beat-up old Monte Carlo and left for home. She was excited but also quite frightened about her journey.

Carl Wicham was on a road trip with his friend, Tom Bryan, to St. Louis to see their favorite regional band, *Country Savages*. They played a mixture of country with a grunge twinge. The two friends had only missed two of the band's concerts in the Missouri area in the last seven years. They had once traveled to Iowa for one of the shows, but that was several years before. Carl would not be back until late Monday afternoon or early evening. The promotions department of the band, in agreement with the venue, had offered a weekend special to see the band two nights in a row for the price of one. *Country Savages* were performing Saturday and Sunday night. The two die-hard fans could not turn it down. Both

Carl and Tom had asked for Monday off as vacation days so that they could drink the Sunday away and still be half-way sober enough to come back on Monday.

Saturday, June 9th

"It was a wonderful thing that we did, Chad," said Winifred.

"I have to admit it, Win," said Chad. "It did feel pretty good to do something out of the ordinary to help someone. That bastard of a husband of hers better not bother you."

"I'm not worried about him."

"Now—you're sure this won't be leaked to anyone."

"No one knows anything, Chad. Now—I'm taking the day off. Let's do whatever you do with the kids today. All of us."

"Fine. That's fine, Win." Chad began to stare, then he looked at Winifred. "Winifred—I—I'm sorry."

"We can talk later. I just want some semblance of a normal family day."

"She doesn't mean anything to me—you know."

"We can discuss **her** later. Okay?"

"Okay," he said. Chad realized that Winifred was being as pleasant as possible but had a definite curt undertone in her vocal demeanor.

How am I to expose Palmer's expense account to Cynthia Arnold? Karen DuPont sat at her dining room table finishing off her third cup of coffee. The phone rang. "Hello, Cameron," she said. She saw his number on the caller ID.

"Hey, baby," said Cameron.

"Cameron—for the last time, stop calling me baby. We ended years ago."

"Oh, Karen. I don't mean nothing by it. It's just a pet name."

"Well—I hate pet names. I know. I promised you breakfast and a sum of cash. You can choose the spot."

"You're so cool," he said.

"You pick me up. I don't feel like getting the car out of the garage today."

"You got it, baby—I mean, Karen. Be there in fifteen."

"Thank you. I'll be waiting." She hung the phone up without saying goodbye.

After having breakfast with Cameron, Karen handed him 100.00 for his spying. When she returned home at around 11:30, some thoughts began to encircle her mind. Her main objective was to set up and incriminate Winifred Palmer; but other possibilities, besides the extortion ploy that she created, were surfacing in her jealous and desperate mind. Karen was not a happy woman. She had little self esteem. Her prom date had stood her up in high school. She had only a few friends, and those few would make a habit of talking behind her back. They had made fun of her personal hygiene and the fact that she was too fat to find a boy friend. After graduating with honors, she had still had trouble finding gainful employment. Her lack of confidence had probably shown during many interviews. Karen had worked as a grocery store cashier for two years. At the age of twenty she had decided to go to college but was indecisive as to what discipline she would endeavor. In her sophomore year, she felt that perhaps she would find a comfortable place in the study of psychology. Psychology had been one of her favorite subjects in high school. She did do well in that discipline. In the middle of her third year at school, she had decided to switch her major to sociology, and it was in sociology that she found her calling. Karen ended up on the Dean's List four semesters, two of which were during her senior year. She had graduated with an impressive 3.7 G.P.A., and soon after landed the job at Diamond Social Services.

Karen thought up a scheme that made her smile and a little uneasy at the same time. *I am going to work today,* she thought. She had hoped that no one else was there on Saturday, and if so, not for too long. She drove her 2011 Camry to the office. There were no other vehicles in the parking lot, which made her let out a breath of relief. She parked closest to the back door as possible. To her amusement and ultimate sense of safety, the back of the building was where all employees parked and was nearly hidden from the general sight of the main traffic. When she got to the door, she took out her key and entered the building. She turned on the lights to the main office area. Karen moved quickly. There were eighteen case workers at Diamond Social Services. She randomly went to the desks of different workers. She began with Audrey Hill's desk. She looked at the three-level, metal temporary file holder which contained mail on the lower level, inter-office memorandums on the middle level, and new cases on the top. Audrey had several new cases. Karen then put on a pair of thin rubber kitchen gloves. She fingered down to the third paper from the top and grabbed it. She quickly ran to Winifred's desk and placed the paper in the middle of the new case stack. It was fortunate for Karen that no new case papers were personalized in writing to any particular worker. The cases were merely chosen by the supervisor and handed to the case worker with verbal instructions. She then went to the desk of Marilyn Straub. There were three new cases on Marilyn's desk. Karen took the top one. The next desk belonged to that of Martin Cowan. He had a few cases on his desk, and Karen took the bottom paper and proceeded back to Winifred's desk and placed the two papers on the very bottom of the stack. Karen was able to take a total of three cases from case workers and put them into Winifred's stack. After placing the second and third cases in their incriminating spot, Karen heard the back door open. She ran to her desk and quickly turned on her computer. Cynthia Arnold walked into the room.

"Hello, Karen," Cynthia said in a surprised voice. "I didn't expect to see you here today." She walked directly to Karen's cubicle.

Karen thought quickly. Her heart was beating fast. "Hi, Cynthia." She smiled and looked up at her boss. "I remembered something that I needed to do. That foster home case that I told you about? I forgot to put some essentials in my computer file for the case." Karen looked back down at the computer screen, waiting for the PC to reboot itself.

"You're sweating, dear," Cynthia said. "I take it you just got here. It is a warm day."

"Yes it is," said Karen. "How are you today, boss?" Karen asked with a feigned smile.

"I'm fine—thank you. I'm glad to see that you're taking initiative. No one else seems to have bothered coming in today. Good work, girl." Cynthia walked back to her office and closed the door.

"Whew," Karen said. She rested her head on her hands and could feel the sweat on her forehead. She then went through the motions of checking her adoption case. Karen stared at the screen and began thinking. *You've stepped into dangerous territory, Karen. Hope it doesn't backfire on you. I wonder if Cynthia will check our expense accounts soon. She usually does that around the beginning of the month for the quarter, and then checks again near the end of the quarter.* Karen wasn't sure that it hadn't yet been done for the month of June. *Cynthia has all of the access codes and goes to all the case workers' computers and checks the accounts. She rarely asks about our expenses but does on occasion. Maybe I don't have to do anything in that regard. I'll give it a few days and see what happens. But—I can't. Palmer will surely get into her petty cash account the first time that an expense comes up for her, and she'll see the change that was made.*

An epiphany came to Karen. She stood up for a moment and collected herself. She walked slowly to Cynthia's office and knocked on the door.

"Come in," said Cynthia. Karen opened the door. "Yes, Karen. What is it?"

"Ma'am. I was just wondering. Was my cash account for this last week alright?"

"Well. It's funny you should mention it. That got behind me this week. Why do you ask, Karen?"

"Oh, I just want to make sure that my expenses are approved," Karen said.

Cynthia smiled with an amused look on her face. "Well, Karen. You are something. Thank you for being so considerate. As a matter of fact, I don't have much to do here, and I'll start that as soon as I get finished. Is there anything else, dear?"

"No, Cynthia. That's all. I'll go now. See you Monday."

"See ya, honey. Have a good weekend."

"You too. Bye."

"Bye bye, Karen." Karen began to close the door. "Oh—you can leave that open, hon."

"K. Bye." Karen walked back to her desk to shut the computer down. She was elated. Her ploy worked like a charm, and she didn't have to do anything but open her mouth. She smiled. *You dog, Karen,* she thought.

"It was a pretty nice day, Winny. Thanks for joining us," Chad said.

"Well, please, Chad—don't put it like that."

Chad laughed. "I didn't mean to say it like that. I meant that it was a pleasure to have you with us today."

"That's a little better," Winifred said as she smiled.

Winifred had thought about the day's events. The family of four had attended Kira's dance practice, went to an animated movie that made

Adrian cry because the dog in the story found new human parents after getting lost from his first owners. Winifred comforted her little boy as he cried while leaving the movie theatre. "Why did the parents have to leave the puppy at the stupid neighbor's house for the day?" Adrian asked.

"Well, baby—they trusted the neighbors to watch the puppy while they were gone for the weekend. The little girl had accidentally let the dog out the front door. That kind of thing just happens sometimes." Winifred was being as elementary as she could for the six year old. "And—if you think about it—the dog was much happier with the new family. That's what the story was about."

"So—you think the doggy doesn't miss his other family?" Adrian asked.

"No. He loved his families no matter who they were. He was very young and was able to find love in the new family, even though they were not his first owners," Winifred said. Adrian's tears subsided as his mother's words helped him to understand.

After the movie, they had all went out for burgers and milk shakes, then went home. The kids were fast asleep after the long day. Winifred and Chad were also exhausted. They plopped down on the couch and turned on the television. Chad had surfed the channels, and his wife had made it clear that she didn't care what they watched. The last thing that Winifred heard before she drifted into sleep was that the Cardinals were leading the Giants by three points in the top of the 8th inning.

Sunday morning at the Palmer household was quiet and yet busy. It was Chad's idea to get the children ready to go to church. They had not gone to church for quite a while. After enjoying a breakfast of sausage and pancakes, they had set out for Sunday services at St. Mark's

Lutheran Church. While they were on their way to church, Winifred received a phone call on her cell from Cynthia Arnold.

"Hello," Winifred answered.

"Winifred. Good morning," Cynthia said.

"Oh. Morning, Cynthia. What's up? We're on our way to church"

"I'm really sorry to bother you, Winifred. I guess this can wait until tomorrow. Is it possible you can come in a little early tomorrow? There's something I'd like to discuss with you."

"Well—sure, Cynthia. What time?"

"How does 7:45 sound?"

Winifred was just a little curious. She usually didn't show up at the office until 8:30 or 8:45. "Sure, Cynthia. Is there something wrong?"

"No. I sure hope not. Like I said—I'm sorry to bother you on a Sunday morning—especially on your way to church."

"Not a problem. I'll see you at 7:45." Winifred was now more than curious but a little worried. She had detected urgency in Cynthia's demeanor.

"Fine. You have a good day, Winifred."

"You too, Cynthia. Bye"

"Goodbye."

"Hmm," Winifred said.

"What was that about?" Chad asked.

"I don't know," she said. "Cynthia wants to talk to me about something tomorrow early."

"Maybe there's nothing wrong."

"Maybe. But it's a little strange. When I asked her if something was wrong she had mentioned that she hoped there wasn't."

"That **is** strange. Well—don't worry about it. She may just need some information about a case."

"I hope that's all. Oh well." No more was said until the family had gotten to the church.

"Mommy—I have to go potty," said Kira.

"Didn't you go before you left, Kira?" Winifred asked

"Yes, but I think I drank too much grape juice."

Winifred and Chad looked at each other and smiled. Chad let out a nasally chuckle.

"There's a rest room in the church, baby," Chad said.

Winifred day dreamed in church and couldn't stay focused on what the minister talked about. All she could think of was what Cynthia wants of her at 7:45 the next morning. She also thought about Chad. It was not an easy thing to go through the motions as they had the past two days as if nothing happened. *The bastard has gone out on me,* she thought. *He won't get away with it. I don't know what I'm going to do.* Winifred was a person of principle. She had always tried her best to establish meaningful relationships with all people with whom she came into contact. Her personal life lent itself out to her friends as well as her clients. The way in which she conducted herself at home was the same as at work. *Kathleen is in California,* she had just remembered. The weekend had been so full, sending Kat away from her jerk of a husband, finding out about Chad's affair or affairs, spending the Saturday with the family, and Sunday at church. She had suddenly become faint. Sweat had built up on her forehead and she lowered her head for a moment. She reached into her small purse and took out a bottle of nerve pills, opened it and put one of the pills in her mouth and dry-swallowed it. "Chad," she had whispered. "I'll be right back. I don't feel very well."

"Are you having an episode?" he asked.

"Yes. I'll be back." She stood and began walking to the back of the church. As she walked, it felt to her as if she were spinning in a forward motion but composed herself the best that she could. She had reached the water fountain near the entrance of the church and drank. She then went to the rest room, went into a stall, sat, and urinated. Her sweating had subsided. She sat and closed her eyes and rested her head on her palms. She no longer felt faint, but it felt to her that her heart might explode. While experiencing this, she knew that it was just her anxiety disorder and that she was not dying. A sudden calmness enveloped her mind. 'Sit and think of nothing, then think of something outside of yourself to keep your thoughts away from your own body,' her doctor had told her. Winifred immediately thought of her darling children. She thought of their future and wondered how she would go about instilling positive feelings into them. A heavy stone was immediately lifted from her and she no longer felt her anxiety attack. She had thought that everything was bliss and had also decided not to discuss Chad's affair on that day unless he had brought it up first.

Monday Morning

At 7:35, Winifred pulled into the parking lot of Diamond Social Services. She saw that Cynthia's car was already there. She again had gone over the events of the weekend and wondered what Carl Wicham would do when he finds out that Kathleen had left him. *He is going to be mad as hell and will probably come to see me first.* Kathleen did tell her that she had left him a long note, detailing all that she felt was wrong with their marriage and why she was leaving. Winifred suddenly felt concerned about the consequences of her own actions. She knew at that moment that she and Chad made a huge move in regard to Kathleen's situation. Winifred's stomach turned at the thought. She parked the car and got out. As she put the key in the door of the building, she had wondered if Cynthia's reason for speaking to her had something to do with Kathleen but dismissed the notion quickly. *How could she know anything about that?* She entered.

"Hello. Winifred? Is that you?" Cynthia had said loudly from her office.

"Yes, Cynthia. Good morning."

"Good morning," Cynthia answered.

Winifred felt extremely nervous. Before she entered the main office area, she reached in her purse and took a nerve pill out of the bottle and swallowed it. She reached Cynthia's office and stood at the door. "Hi, Cynthia," she said.

"Hello, Winny. Come in and have a seat."

"Cynthia. I really need a drink of water. May I get one please?"

"What am I going to say? No?" Cynthia laughed.

Winifred returned a smile. "I'll be right back." She walked fast to the water cooler and poured a cup. Her hand shook slightly as she drank. *Calm down, Winifred. It's probably nothing.* She deliberately walked slower back to Cynthia's office to help gain her composure. Winifred placed her mind in the strongest mode that she knew—the Winifred that fights injustice, that helps people, the woman that is fearless of abusive husbands. She went in and sat down across from Cynthia.

"Coffee, honey?" Cynthia asked.

"No thank you, Cynthia. Not just yet." She smiled and Cynthia smiled back. Winifred then sensed that something **was** wrong.

"I wasn't sure how that I was going to approach this, Winifred, so I'll just tell you. It kind of has me stumped. I did my end-of-the-quarter petty cash checks on all the case workers' accounts. I found something odd in yours."

"Oh?" Winifred responded. She knew that she kept her spread sheet flawless.

"There was an expense that was noted." Cynthia stood. "Come, Winny. Let's go to your computer. I'll show you. I turned your computer on."

Winifred was silent as she followed Cynthia to her desk. There—on the screen, was her expense account page. Her eyes immediately zeroed in on the last transaction. She had felt that her heart was about to explode. As they both stood looking at the spread sheet, Winifred could sense Cynthia's eyes looking toward her. "That can't be, Cynthia. I made no such entry."

"Winifred. It's right there. How do you explain it?"

"I don't know. I didn't make it."

"Well, darling. How did it get there? Twelve hundred dollars paid out to Kathleen Wicham."

"I know. I can see it. I didn't do it. I swear I didn't."

"Perhaps if you say so, but I will have to do a physical count of your cash in order to try and confirm what you're saying. Still, there's the fact that it's right there. If your cash adds up correctly, then the only other possible reason would be sabotage. But who would do something like that and why?"

"I haven't the foggiest. Please—I have my key. Let's go count."

Cynthia had much respect for Winifred Palmer. She had sensed sincerity in her demeanor and appreciated her eagerness to open the cash safe.

Karen DuPont was on her way to work. She felt some butterflies in her stomach about what she had done and had wondered if her actions may backfire. *Even though the cash may not be physically gone from Palmer's petty cash, the fact that Kathleen Wicham was probably gone will stir suspicions when Cynthia finds out,* Karen thought. *And the cases that I took and placed on Palmer's desk should prove to be icing on the cake.* Karen was not proud of what she did. In fact, it began to make her a little sick to her stomach. *It's done though, and I can't take it back.*

"Well, Cynthia," Winifred said. "What do you think? There it is. All the money that is supposed to be there."

"Interesting, Winny. You're right. I have a question."

"Yes, boss?"

"Would you mind very much if I tried to contact Kat Wicham myself? I mean—if she is there at home and doesn't lead on that there is anything out of the ordinary to tell me, then we'll put this whole thing behind us. I don't believe that you would take cash from your account without authorization. You're smarter than that."

Winifred's stomach sank. *Cynthia could easily find out if Kathleen had left town.* Sweat formed on her forehead. "No, Cynthia," Winifred said. "Feel free to call her." Winifred swallowed without Cynthia detecting her nervousness. She had closed up the safe, and they had both walked to Cynthia's desk.

"Go ahead and dial the number, dear, and you can hand the phone to me. Have a seat." Cynthia stood.

Winifred did just that. She looked at Cynthia and noticed the time lapse of silence. She had figured that the answering machine would start. It did and she heard a beep.

"Kathleen? Hi. Cynthia Arnold calling from Diamond Social Services. If you could please call me at your earliest convenience, I would be most appreciative. Goodbye." Cynthia hung up the phone. She looked down at Winifred, who sat in her chair. "What's the matter, Winny? You look as if you've seen a ghost. Don't worry, honey. I'll get to the bottom of this computer tampering if it takes me all year."

Winifred feigned a smile. "Thanks, Cynthia. I appreciate that." *Damn it,* Winifred thought. *Why in the hell did she have to call Kathleen's house? Carl is the one that will get the message and call back. And after reading the note and throwing a fit with Cynthia, shit's gonna hit the fan.*

"Winny. Would you like the day off? You look haggard."

"No. No. I have too much to do. I have three calls to make today, plus a-a". Suddenly Winifred's face turned white and her head flew back. She had blacked out for a couple of seconds.

"Oh, darling. It's okay. I'll get you a drink of water and a cool rag." Winifred did not protest. She sat in silence.

Cynthia ran to the water cooler, poured a cup of water and rushed it to Winifred. "Here, baby. Drink up. I'll get you a damp rag."

"Thanks, Cynthia. I appreciate it." She drank the cup down and then laid her head on her desk. She could hear Cynthia's heels running toward her.

"Lift your head slowly, Winny, and put this on your forehead."

Winifred did as Cynthia said. She placed the cool rag on her forehead and rested her elbows on her desk. She felt as if she could fall asleep any moment.

"Did you take a nerve pill this morning, Winny?" Cynthia asked.

"Yes. Yes I did."

"I could tell you were a little out of sorts. Don't worry. Once you are feeling more stable, I'm driving you home."

"No—I."

"No arguments, girl. You're not fit to be here today. I'm sorry I called you in so early. Did you have a bad weekend?"

"Well—Cynthia—not exactly."

"You're over working yourself. Is everything okay at home?"

Winifred began to cry. "Chad's been having an affair," she said. She couldn't help but open up. There was much bottled up inside of her and the truth just came out.

"Oh, Winifred. Oh, darling. I'm sorry. That's what it is. You're trying to go through the motions like there's nothing wrong. And here I present you with this other crap. How are you feeling? Your color's coming back."

"Well—that's a relief." Winifred laughed in spite of herself.

"You **are** feeling better. Just give yourself a few more minutes, and then we're out the door. I'll handle any of your people that call, and I'll personally reschedule your appointments."

"Okay, Cynthia. I give. I'll be back tomorrow though."

"Don't worry about tomorrow. I want you to deal with things and come back when you're able. Just call in the morning if there's a problem. Are you ready to go or do you need more time?"

"I'm ready, Cynthia," Winifred said. She stood up feeling somewhat refreshed and relaxed.

While the two ladies were exiting the building, Karen was walking in.

"Is everything okay, Cynthia?" Karen asked.

"Yes, Karen. Winifred is feeling rather poorly this morning."

"Is there anything I can do, Winny?" Karen asked.

"No, dear. Thank you anyway."

"Hold down the fort, Karen, until the others get here."

"Yes, Ma'am. I will." A few moments later, Karen looked out the window and watched Cynthia drive Winifred away. Karen felt a little remorse but not much.

10:45 am

At the office, Martin Cowan tapped on Cynthia Arnold's office door. "Come in, Martin," Cynthia said. "What's going on?"

"Well," Martin began. "Ms. Arnold. I seem to have a case missing from my desk. Strangest thing."

"Was it just lying on your desk?"

"No, ma'am. I had it in my desk mate filer. You know--where we keep our brand new cases?"

"Okay. Let's take another look." She got up from her desk and began walking out of the office as Martin followed her. "You know—I've been thinking of doing away with that system," Cynthia said as they walked. "Those cases really should be in a locked cabinet. I realize that you all don't always have the time to enter the information into the computer right away." They arrived at Martin's cubicle. "Well—your desk is as neatly kept as ever," she said as she kindly smiled at him.

"Thank you, Ms. Arnold," he said.

"I do wish that you'd call me Cynthia. You **have** been here a year or so. What do ya say, Martin?"

Martin Cowan smiled. "Alright, Cynthia."

"Much better. Let's see. Do you still keep the new cases on the top level?"

"Yes, ma'am. I mean Cynthia."

Cynthia darted a cute look with a smile at Martin. "Thanks," she said. "And what's the name of the case?"

"Linda Cooper," he answered. Martin had never realized how attractive Cynthia was until that moment. She had black, wavy long hair, was thin, with hazel eyes, and wore a peach-colored pant suit. *And that look she just gave me. How sexy was that? Too bad I'm an employee.* He quickly looked down at his own physique and observed his slight beer belly. *She'd never go for someone like me anyway.*

She had gone through the top level of the desk mate. There were several cases to flip through. "You're right, Martin. Do you think that you may have mistakenly placed it in one of the other two sections?"

"I already checked them," he said.

Audrey Hill cleared her throat behind them. "Please excuse me, Ms. Arnold," she said.

"Yes, Audrey. What is it?"

"Well, Cynthia—I'm missing a file. A new case."

"Hhuhhh. You're not kidding me?" Cynthia replied, hoping she was, in fact, just joking.

"No, ma'am. I've gone through every level of the desk mate."

"That's just bizarre. Martin had the same thing happen to him this morning." Cynthia put her head down. She immediately spoke in a loud clear voice. "Listen up, people. If everyone would please look through their new case files and see if you have any missing. There's something strange going on here."

Karen DuPont sat silently but pretended to shuffle through her papers. *Phase two,* Karen thought to herself. She was almost sure that Winifred was approached that morning about the expense account. Her better judgment told her that was one reason why Palmer had left abruptly in such a daze.

"Right here, Cynthia," said Marilyn Straub. "I'm missing Susan Wyman's file."

Cynthia's face turned red in anger. "Well I'll be a son-of-a-bitch," she screamed. "What is going on in this place? Anybody else?" she asked. There were no answers from the other twelve case workers who were present in the office. Four others were not in the office at that time of day, including Winifred.

"Mine are all here," said Kim Stoltz from the other side of the room.

"Same here," Karen said.

"This has not been a good morning—at all," Cynthia exclaimed. "I'll get the missing files back off of my computer and reissue them to anyone who has them missing. God—what a day. Okay—I need everyone at their desks to look for Linda Cooper, Susan Wyman. And--who's case was yours, Audrey?" she asked as she looked down to the right while addressing Audrey.

"Clint Borman," Audrey said.

"And a Clint Borman. Tear your desks apart if you have to—and check your trash cans. We do have a cleaning service that could have messed things up over the weekend. I don't know." Cynthia immediately walked quickly to her office with a stern look on her face and then slammed the door. She then proceeded to pull up the missing files on her computer to print them out.

After arriving home earlier that morning, Winifred went straight to bed and slept for four hours. Her sleep was dreamless. The events of the weekend and the morning revelation of her doctored expense account put her mental faculties over the edge. She had known before lying down for her long nap that things could get very hairy at work; but in her state of mind, she decided to place all problems out of her consciousness, and that was just what she did. Sarah tended to the children.

4

The Awakening

Carl Wicham's awakening, in a different sense of the word, was not as pleasant as Winifred Palmer's. Carl was livid after reading Kathleen's note. His state of being was that of an enraged maniac. He had then listened to Cynthia's phone message. He had immediately called the agency. It was 2:45pm. "Hello, Cynthia?" he said, after she had identified herself when she answered.

"Yes. May I help you?"

"I sure hope so," said Carl in a curt tone of voice. "This is Carl Wicham—Kathleen's husband. I'm returning your call."

"Oh—hello, Mr. Wicham. I was wanting to speak with Kathleen, but what can I do for you?"

"Well—you can start by trying to explain to me where the hell my wife is?"

"Well, sir. I'm sure I don't know. Is there a problem?"

"Hell yes, there's a problem," he screamed. "She's left me."

"Please try and be civil, Mr. Wicham. I cannot continue with this conversation if you can't calm down."

"How can I be calm, Ms. Arnold? Did you hear what I said? Kathleen has left me."

"I did hear what you said, Mr. Wicham, and I'm very sorry. What happened?"

Wicham began to calm down a bit before he spoke. "It's like this. A friend and I were out of town since Friday. Makes no difference why. I just got back about fifteen minutes ago. She left me this note saying that she can no longer live a life with me and that she has gone away. Does that Winny Palmer have anything to do with this?" There was a brief silence on the phone. "Hello. Are you still there?"

"Yes. I'm here, Mr. Wicham." Cynthia took a deep breath. "It just so happens that Mrs. Palmer was taken ill today, and it's sort of a touchy situation with her and I'd rather not disturb her at home. She will most likely be in tomorrow."

"Well—that helps me a lot. Did she say anything to you about Kathleen?"

"No. She did not, Mr. Wicham. Try and remain calm. It could be a case of Kathleen wanting to get away for a day or two. Sometimes it's nothing more than that." Cynthia suddenly felt as if ice was in her stomach. She thought of the weird entry in Winifred's petty cash account.

"Well. What do I do?" Carl started to cry aloud.

"Please, Mr. Wicham. I'm so very sorry that this has happened. Would you feel better if I stopped by your house and speak to you in person?"

"Oh. Would you, Ms. Arnold?" Carl humbly asked. "I'm beside myself. I don't know what to do."

"Yes, sir. I will." She could hear the desperation in the man's voice and felt some sympathy for him. She was, however, very familiar with the Wicham case. Carl Wicham was extremely abusive to his wife. "Perhaps in the meantime you could call the police, but they will usually tell you that a person isn't missing until 24 hours after a disappearance. Don't be alarmed, Mr. Wicham. I'll be there in twenty minutes."

"Thank you, Cynthia. Thank you so much. Goodbye."

"Goodbye, Mr. Wicham." After hanging up the phone Cynthia took another deep breath. *Oh, Winifred. Winifred. Please tell me you have nothing to do with this.* She was thinking that the expense account issue was nearly too closely related to this new phenomenon to be a coincidence. "Oh, God. What a day," she said to herself.

Taking problems into her own hands was an educated forte of Cynthia Arnold. She had graduated from St. Louis University in Social Work with a G.P.A. of 4.0. She went on to receive a graduate degree in Psychology at S.L.U. with similar grades, and then pursued her doctorate in Social Psychology out of state. She had taken on a non-paid internship at a half-way house for teens and young adults. Her work at the half-way house had fine tuned her abilities as a mediator for abused and drug and alcohol abusive individuals between the housed residents and their antagonists, the latter, being either, family, friends, or the abused substance itself. She had gone to great lengths in researching select house residents' situations and what was troubling them. There was one case in particular that had established her leadership in social work. Dirk Collinsworth was a twenty three year old man that had been in and out of the facility for the better part of ten years. He had had real trouble in staying away from alcohol and had contemplated suicide more than six times. He had no interest in pursuing a relationship with a woman but was decidedly heterosexual. His love for the beauty of a woman's body was discussed at length during some of the sessions between Cynthia and Dirk. Cynthia had gone to the point of asking Dirk if he thought that she was attractive. He had said in response 'Well--hell yes.' She was simply stirring a response out of him that she felt needed sexual-preference clarification. 'Do you not feel that your attraction to alcohol has prevailed to deter you from a normal relationship with anyone?' she had asked. 'No. I mean, maybe,' he had said. In one session with Dirk, she had discussed how vulnerable some women can be and that they can depend greatly on the dependability of the man. She had gone on to inform him that no woman wants to have someone with whom she cannot depend. 'Allow me to give you a scenario,' she had said. 'Let's say that your mate becomes very ill one night and needs to be driven to the hospital. How do you believe you would be able to care for her in her time of need if you are drunk?' she had asked Dirk. 'I understand what you mean, Cynthia,' he said. He continued. 'A woman couldn't depend on me. I mean—at the rate that I am going.' Dirk had begun to sob. 'Remember, Dirk. Alcohol is a temporary fix for getting through the night or a situation. A relationship can last forever,' she had said. Cynthia had spent a period of five months counseling Dirk. Dirk had checked out of the half-way house in early winter. He had called Cynthia often for he had missed her friendship. He would fill her in on the status of his problems. He had joined Alcoholics Anonymous and had quit drinking in February of 1999. Cynthia was elated with this news. The two of them had met for lunch a few times just to talk. She had thought that the man looked ten times better. He had revealed to her that he met a lovely woman who he'd been dating for a few weeks, and that things were going well. Cynthia and Dirk had hugged after their last lunch together. One of her last comments to Dirk to boost his confidence to yet a higher level was 'If we were not acquaintances on a professional level, I'd ask you out myself, Mr. Collinsworth.' He had smiled. 'Thank you, Cynthia—for everything,' he had said. Cynthia had never heard from Dirk again. She had taken that to be a good thing and had hoped that he would never slip back to his old ways.

The Wicham Residence

"Cynthia. I know that I haven't been the best husband, but I never thought she'd leave me," said Carl.

"Carl. Before we begin, I can't help but notice that I smell alcohol coming from you," said Cynthia. "Did you drink today?"

Carl was just a little put up with the first question that Cynthia presented to him. He had thought that she had come over to console him. "Well—yeah. Just a bit. It was my vacation today. We drank a few beers before hitting the road back home." He was lying. Carl and Tom Bryan drank on the road.

"You didn't drink on the road. Did you?"

"No. We'd never take that chance with the laws nowadays."

"Okay, Carl. Let's get past that. You do know that Kathleen was very upset with the way that you drink. However, let's get back to you. How are you feeling?"

It's about time, Carl thought. "Oh—pretty crappy to tell you the truth. That note kind of sobered me right up. I don't know what to do without Kat, Cynthia."

"Carl? Let me paint you a scenario. Kathleen, like anyone else, has his or her own breaking point. It seems to me that Kathleen had reached hers. I'm not saying that she may not decide to come back to you, but you may have to give her some time to think things over. I know that it's not going to be an easy thing to wait. That's why I'm here, Carl. I am willing to speak with you as often as you'd like. You're going to experience some separation anxiety, and it won't be easy to get through. I do feel for you, Mr. Wicham. I really do. Why don't we have a seat and talk?"

"Thank you, Cynthia. That's what I need. I need to talk." They both sat. Carl was waiting for Cynthia to start talking, and Cynthia did the same.

Cynthia decided to begin. "There's a fine line between a marriage and trust," she said. "You can go through the motions of marriage as if they were the right things to do and the honest things to do, Carl. Do you know what I mean?" Cynthia waited patiently for an answer.

Carl hesitated. He was perplexed by the question although understood what Cynthia was saying. Carl was not stupid, but he was voluntarily oblivious to anything that didn't involve his own self gain.

"Yeah. Yeah. I believe so, Cynthia. You can't force love to work if you don't have trust."

"That is absolutely correct, Carl. And the more trust that a couple shares, the happier they are both going to be." Cynthia had known at that point to try and be less technical in her wording.

"Huh. Let me ask you something, Cynthia. Weren't you afraid to come over and see me today? I mean—you must have heard things about—you know—my temper."

"Winifred has filled me in on everything, Carl. It's part of her job to report everything that she finds in all of her cases. To answer your question, no, I was not scared at all. I knew that you needed to talk to someone, plus, I've been around the block and back with many cases. I did have a man try and strangle me once, but a quick knee in the groin ended that very quickly."

Carl laughed. "Good for you. No one needs to.." His eyes began to get glassy with tears. "No one has any business hitting on women. I don't mean to do it. I love Kathleen. It's just. No. I won't make excuses. Let me tell you about my pop."

"Go right ahead, Mr Wicham."

"He would come home drunk, and my momma..." Carl began to cry. "My momma was a dear thing. She could forget something like not putting a knife on the table for him to eat, and he would go off. I don't know why his behavior had to trickle down on me. I guess I knew no other way." He paused.

"It's a clear case of behavioral transference. Your childhood became a given reality for you. You even took his place as a drinker. I do hope that you are not offended, Carl, about what I am going to tell you."

"Please, Cynthia. Tell me." Carl had nothing but respect for Cynthia while speaking with her. She was being very helpful to him in his time of need.

"Okay. Alcoholism is a disease, and it can be passed down through generations. Do you believe me?"

"Yes. I do. I suppose if you say so."

"But let's not get stuck on your sickness right now. That will be something that you will have to work on in your own time. What you need now is comfort in knowing that Kathleen is okay. It's unfortunate that you have to suffer the loss of your wife at this point in time."

"What do I do? I think I've already asked you that question?" He smiled.

"Get some rest. Take a nap, or better yet, stay up for a while and go to bed early. It won't hurt you to get a long night's sleep before you go back to work tomorrow. I know it won't be an easy thing to work while thinking about Kathleen. May I share something with you?"

"Sure, Cynthia," Carl said.

"Well—back when I was nineteen years old, my brother was in a car accident late at night. We had received a call from the police at around one in the morning when my father got the news. My brother was in critical condition at the hospital. Mother and father were so frightened and worried that they may lose their only son. They had only two children—me and Robert. Mother was too hysterical to go to the hospital at the time. Father had driven there with me. I remember him praying, 'God, please don't let him die.' I was doing the same. When we arrived at the hospital room, Robert laid there on the bed semiconscious and stirring a bit. His face was black and blue. There was a bump over his left eye the size of an egg. I began to cry uncontrollably. Father had tears in his eyes but kept his emotions under control for my sake. 'Son,' he had said. 'You're going to be fine. You're going to be alright.' He placed his hand on Robert's shoulder. Robert mumbled. 'Be careful,' the doctor said. 'We don't know yet if he has any broken bones.' My father looked at the doctor with glassy eyes and shook his head in understanding agreement. 'Is he going to live, doctor?' my father asked.

'At this point, we believe he's okay,' the doctor said. He said that his pulse rate was good but he needed to do a check for internal injuries. The rest of the morning was like a bad dream. I was going to have to go work that morning or stay home. I decided to work so that I could stay busy and try to keep my mind occupied. It worked. After work, the family met at the hospital and found that Robert was fully conscious. It turned out that he was okay. There were no internal injuries and no broken bones, and he spoke intelligibly to us. My point to this story is.."

"I know, Cynthia. Go to work and go through the motions as if nothing is wrong. I'm sorry you had to go through that." He placed his hand on Cynthia's shoulder.

Cynthia had tears in her eyes. "Yes. Thank you. It was a very intense experience. Robert is still with us. Well, Carl. Are you going to settle down a bit and get that sleep we talked about?"

"Yes. I will," Carl said. "Sleep won't come easy but I think I'll manage. I appreciate you coming over—so much, you can't imagine. It was a kind gesture."

Cynthia smiled. "No charge for this one, Mr. Wicham." She held her hand out to shake his.

He shook her hand and gently pulled her hand to his mouth and kissed it. "I'll never forget your kindness."

She accepted this action earnestly. "Anytime you need to talk, don't hesitate to call." She hesitated. "It's a little strange for me to intervene in a case but I thought it was necessary." She stood and headed for the door. "You take care, Carl. Things will fall into place somehow. Now—don't expect results overnight."

"I understand," he said. They said their goodbyes and she left. As soon as she was gone, he went to the refrigerator and grabbed two beers. *I'll need these at least to get sleepy again,* he thought. He turned on a Cardinals game, sat on the couch and slipped into sleep half-way into the second beer. His last thought was what a nice lady this Cynthia was.

Cynthia had called from her cell phone to the office to let someone know that she wouldn't be returning to work that day. Marilyn Straub answered and assured her that everything would be fine. At Cynthia's inquisitiveness, Marilyn also let her know, that the missing case files were found in Winifred's desk mate. Cynthia was shocked, but due to the extent of the day's events, she was not extremely surprised. Even with what seemed to be incontrovertible evidence, she was decidedly leery that Winifred had anything to do with the missing files, as Winifred's countenance and moral ethics had always shown nothing but dependability. They had been friends since the beginning of their professional relationship, and Cynthia could not easily dismiss Winifred's implied integrity. She was thoroughly exhausted. Cynthia had returned home and viewed the rest of the Cardinals game and fell asleep during the local news.

Tuesday

The day had begun like any other at Diamond. Winifred had felt as energetic as she could after Monday's events. Her co-workers began to show up and greeted her cordially. Karen had even talked to her and asked how she was, and Winifred responded in a positive manner. At 9am, Cynthia came to her desk and asked her to join her in the office. Winifred followed her. Cynthia closed the door behind them. It was at that point that Winifred was concerned and wondered what was going on.

"Have a seat, Winifred," Cynthia said. Winifred sat, as did Cynthia. "How are you feeling, dear?"

"I'm feeling fine, Cynthia. I appreciate your concern and help yesterday. What's up?"

Cynthia showed a half smile. "Well—something very strange to be quite honest. If it wasn't enough yesterday—dealing with the weird entry in your expense account, there were a couple of occurrences that popped up after you went home."

"Oh? Whatever were they?"

"I guess I should start with some missing new case files. Three of your co-workers were each missing a file from their desk, and all that were here couldn't find them anywhere. At that point, I was confused as to where they could have disappeared. Nothing was found. Second, Carl Wicham had called and said that Kathleen had left him. She had left him a note. I personally went to the house to speak with him for he was very upset."

Winifred began to feel very curious and upset but tried not to show it. She only shook her head as if she was interested. She turned her eyebrows down as one would do while showing concern. "Really," was all that Winifred could say.

Cynthia let out a sigh. "Winny. Is there anything that you'd like to tell me?"

"Well—no. What do you need to know?"

Cynthia began to read an uneasy countenance on Winifred's face. "Well. This is not an easy thing with which to approach you. I'll just ask. Do you have anything to do with Kathleen's disappearance? I mean, aside from your counseling her?"

"No. I mean, as you say, I've told her many times that during our sessions that she needed to get away from that maniac. It's only common sense. The guy beat her maliciously."

"I know that. I know. That goes without saying. It's just—weird that her leaving him had coincided with the entry in your expense account."

"I thought that we.."

"Sorry to interrupt, Winny. I know that we checked your petty cash but Kathleen's leaving and the issue of the account is sort of uncanny." Cynthia paused and let out another breathy sigh. "It's just weird, Winifred. Let's drop that issue for a moment. As I was leaving the Wicham house, I had called work to let everyone know that I wasn't returning—that I was going home. Marilyn had mentioned that they found the missing files."

Winifred was surprised and interested. "Great. Where were they?"

"That's the thing, honey." Cynthia held the files in her hand. "Marilyn said that they found the files at your desk."

Winifred's eyes bulged. "Well—that's just crazy. That's not possible."

"That's just what I thought, Winifred." Cynthia shook her head back and forth and held her lips in a sort of a pursed manner.

"What the hell is going on, Cynthia? You know my ethics. Why the hell would I take someone else's cases. I have enough already." Winifred laughed.

Cynthia could sense that Winifred was adamant in her defense. Her next feeling was that she believed her. "Okay, Winifred. I believe you. I really do. Is there anyone who you think may be trying to frame you for some reason? I mean—first it was the expense account, and now this."

"Well—no. Why would anyone do this? I have no clue." Winifred had shown nothing but honest bewilderment.

If looks could kill, Cynthia emanated just that state of being. Her eyes slanted in a hateful way, and her mouth looked as if she were snarling. "Okay, Winny, I think it's time we both got to the bottom of this! Follow me to the lobby." They both stood, and Cynthia rushed past Winifred opening the door.

"What are we doing?" Winifred asked.

Just as Winifred's question left her lips, Cynthia stormed into the room. "Listen up," Cynthia screamed. All heads shot up. "I wanna know something and I wanna know now. Just who the freakin' hell is screwing around at Winifred's desk? She didn't take those files. I know it. Would anyone like to own up to it?" There was silence. "I'll give the guilty party one more chance to speak up or I'm taking drastic measures."

Winifred, nor had any of the other employees, ever seen Cynthia act this way. All, besides Winifred, saw her get mad the day before but not to this degree. Cynthia's face was red. "Cynthia," Winifred said quietly as she placed her hand on Cynthia's shoulder.

"Not now, Winny," Cynthia yelled as she shoved Winifred's hand away from her. "I assumed as much." She walked quickly to Kim Stoltz' desk. She picked up Kim's phone. "May I, Kim?" she asked her. Cynthia wanted to make it a point to allow everyone to hear the phone call she was about to make.

"Yes, ma'am," said Kim in a tender voice.

Cynthia dialed 9 to get out, and then dialed 911.

Emergency picked up on the other end of the line. "911 emergency. How may I help you?" a woman operator asked.

"Please, ma'am, excuse me," said Cynthia. "I didn't have the direct number to the police department in front of me. Could you please direct my call? This is Cynthia Arnold at Diamond Social Services."

"Of course, Ms. Arnold," the lady said. "One moment please."

Cynthia waited for about thirty seconds.

"Wilmington Police Department. Officer Clements speaking. How may I help you?"

"Officer Clements? Cynthia Arnold calling. Good morning."

"Morning, ma'am. What can I do for you today?"

"Officer? I manage Diamond Social Services and would very much like to set up polygraph tests for seventeen employees. Would that be a possibility today?"

"Well, ma'am, let me check with Officer Knollman. He would be the one to perform the tests, and there would be a fee. Don't believe it would cost too much. Could you hold, please?"

"Yes. Thank you, officer." Cynthia held for only fifteen seconds.

"Ms. Arnold?"

"Yes, sir."

"Officer Knollman would be glad to speak with you. Please hold while I transfer you."

"Thank you." The phone rang.

"Ted Knollman. May I help you, please?"

"Yes, Officer Knollman. Cynthia Arnold."

"Yes, Ms. Arnold. Officer Clements said you would like a series of polygraphs performed. That'll be no problem. How does around noon sound?"

"That will work perfectly," Cynthia said.

"Okay. We'll discuss the fee when you get here and, for seventeen people, shouldn't take any more than an hour. You can debrief me on the situation before I start. I won't gouge you, ma'am." Knollman laughed.

"Thank you, sir. See you at noon. Bye."

"Goodbye, Ms. Arnold."

"Alright, folks," Cynthia began. "You heard what I've just done. I am not only the manager but a joint owner of this service, so I have the authority to carry this thing out. If you have any appointments between 11:30 and 1:30, you're going to have to reschedule until after 2. If anyone refuses to take the polygraph, I'll accept your resignation papers no later than tomorrow. Understood?"

Many voices in the room were heard in agreement. Winifred smiled in admiration of Cynthia's leadership.

"I need to call a couple of people that aren't here yet," Cynthia said to Winifred. Winifred shook her head.

Far across the room, one woman sat at her desk in mild shock. Karen DuPont was undoubtedly frightened. She didn't know how she could go through with the polygraph, although knowing that was exactly what she needed to do. *I can outsmart this thing,* she thought. *I have to.* She hadn't thought that Winifred could convince Cynthia so easily that she had nothing to do with the files. Her mind raced. *And what about the expense account? They must have counted the money and found that nothing was missing.* Karen suddenly thought of something. If she gets through the lie-detector test, she would do some investigative work on the whereabouts of Kat Wicham. She thought that a call to Cameron might save her the time and trouble but had also signaled a feeling of dismay in having to contact the man again so soon.

Winifred did not stay back at the office during the polygraph tests and Cynthia requested that she be present at the police station. She had ridden in Cynthia's car. Cynthia told her that she could take the time off from the office to lessen the work load of the day. Of course, Winifred knew that she had already taken a full day off, and she would have to take up her day's contacts eventually, meaning that she would probably work late. There was a head count at the station. All Diamond employees were present.

Officer Knollman had spoken first with Cynthia. She had filled him in on the probable computer tampering and the displaced files. Knollman began to ask questions. "In your opinion, Ms. Arnold, is there any reason why any of the employees would have something in for Mrs. Palmer?"

"No. I don't see any reason why my workers would want to sabotage Winifred, unless someone is jealous."

"Jealous of what?" he asked.

"Well—Winifred is simply the best that we have. Her case load is already full, so this tells me that she had nothing to do with the files. She is also such a faithful worker and extremely honest. To get back to your question, perhaps someone is jealous of her success."

"I see." Knollman thought for a moment. "May I suggest that even the employees whose files were seemingly taken from their desks are not excluded from questions in regard to the files?"

"No. Not at all."

"Let me ask you this. Do you want Palmer to take the polygraph?"

"Whatever for? I believe Winifred is the true victim. That is why I set up this thing."

"So--you don't think that Winifred could offer any possible connection to the computer tampering."

"No—I don't. We counted her expense money. I believe she is totally in the dark about that also. I can read into people's facial expressions quite well, Officer. Winifred is totally innocent." After Cynthia had made the last comment, she thought that perhaps Winifred could be asked one question about whether she had anything thing at all to do with the disappearance of Kathleen. *No—I don't think so*, Cynthia thought. *Winny's been through enough. I would really hate to ask her to do that after she told me that she just suggested for Kat to leave Carl.*

"Ms. Arnold?" Knollman smiled. "You seem to be thinking about something."

"Oh—it's nothing, Sir. Just a thought. Never mind though."

"Okay then. Let's get started. The protocol is for me to go down the list you've provided and call them in myself one by one."

"That's fine."

Karen DuPont was going through a private hell awaiting her turn. There had already been seven to go into the room. She knew that she must prevail in order to keep her job. She was keeping emotions inside herself that would have come out in tears if she allowed them to escape. Karen was totally disgusted with herself and what she had started. *I am worthless*, she thought.

"Karen DuPont," Officer Knollman said from the doorway.

By the time she was called in, Karen had psyched herself up to try and beat the test. She had also gained as much composure as she could to accept her fate if things didn't fall her way. She knew what she had done was wrong and decided to come clean if the test showed positive results. "Hello," Karen said with a smile as she entered Knollman's office.

"Good afternoon, Ms. DuPont," he said. "Make yourself comfortable in that seat to the right of the table."

She calmly walked to the chair and sat, looking down at the electrodes that would be connected to her.

Knollman sat across from her. "Now—if you'd allow me to place these on your right index finger and right middle finger, Ms. DuPont." Karen held out her hand, palm down. "Thank you. There. I'll only be asking you a few questions, Ms. DuPont. Just relax. Take a deep breath and exhale. Fine. Now—these questions will require only yes or no answers. Understood?"

"Yes."

"Is your name Karen DuPont?"

"Yes."

"Do you work at Diamond Social Services?"

"Yes." *It's not a lie if I believe it's not a lie.*

"Is Winifred Palmer a co-worker of yours?"

"Yes."

"Did you get into the expense account on Winifred Palmer's computer and change information?"

"No." Karen made a strong effort to not look at the needles on the machine as she answered the questions. She thought that might help her relax and give believable answers.

"Did you take new cases off of the desks of three other co-workers and place them on the desk of Mrs. Palmer's?"

"No."

"Is there any reason that you would want to see Winifred Palmer released from employment at Diamond Social Services?"

"No." Karen didn't expect a question stated in that manner.

"Okay, Ms. DuPont. You're done. You may unhook the electrodes yourself. Thank you, and have a good day."

"Thank you," Karen said. "And you do the same." She smiled and he smiled back in return. She stood and left the room.

All employees were instructed to go straight to the office after their sessions were completed. Karen's test was number twelve on the list. There were only a few employees left to take their turns. As Karen left the test room, Cynthia was there sitting next to Winifred on one of the chairs that were connected in a line.

Cynthia looked up at Karen and smiled. "Thank you, Karen," she said.

"That's quite alright, Cynthia. No problem." Karen also smiled, and made sure that she made eye contact with both Cynthia and Winifred. She exited the building and took a deep breath. "God—I hope I did well," she quietly said to herself.

The time was 1:50pm when all employees were present at the agency. Cynthia made an announcement. "Thank you all for going through this thing for me. It was not my intention to leave anyone out in the process. This is why I took the polygraph myself. Winifred, as you may have guessed, was excused from the test. I do want you all to know that most everyone did well on the test, although there were some interesting results. Thanks again, and I'm sorry for any implications that I suspected anyone in particular." Cynthia walked to her office and Winifred followed as she was asked to do while being driven back to the office. The two ladies entered and Cynthia closed the door behind them. "Have a seat, dear."

Winifred sat. "What is it, Cynthia? Did you find anything out?"

"Just a little," Cynthia said. "That can wait for now. I wanted some alone time with you to ask a couple of questions." Winifred shook her head in agreement. Cynthia gently took hold of Winifred's hands from across the desk. "Winifred. Is there anything you want to tell me?"

Winifred wasn't sure she knew where this was going. "No," Winifred said. "What do you mean?"

"Winifred. Look at me in the eyes. Did you have anything to do directly with Kathleen's leaving Carl?"

"I believe I answered that question this morning, Cynthia." Winifred became alarmed.

"I know, honey, but I just have to be sure. Did you?"

Winifred hesitated a few seconds. "No. I did not." She looked directly into Cynthia's eyes.

Cynthia looked into Winifred's. "Okay. I believe you. You may go."

The ladies both made their way out the door. Winifred walked to her desk and Cynthia was seemingly following her. Winifred sat and began to make a phone call to a client. Cynthia walked by Winifred's desk, and then George Wembley's, Shirley Calliston's then stood behind Karen's. In a voice as soft as butter, Cynthia bent over and said "Karen? Could you please come to the office for a moment?"

"Sure," Karen said. She had a feeling that Cynthia was going to approach her. Karen stood and followed Cynthia to her office.

"Your test results were pretty good, Karen," Cynthia said. The two ladies sat across from each other.

"Just pretty good?" Karen replied.

61

"Well—yes. It seems that the test picked up slight jumps of the needle on the questions in regard to Winifred. The officer informed me that the jumps were very slight but still there just the same. This concerns me. Everyone else's tests were perfect."

"Well, Cynthia—I was very nervous."

"The officer and I took that into consideration. There is, however, a question of your honesty. Believe me when I tell you that this is not an easy thing for me to do. I must ask you those questions again. Look straight into my eyes, Karen." Karen did as she was told. "Karen. Did you get on Winifred's computer and enter information into her expense account?"

Karen tried to relax. "No," she said.

Cynthia was not convinced by Karen's answer. "Karen. You look as if you're staring out into space and not into my eyes. I'll ask again. Did you tamper with Winifred's expense account?"

"No," Karen answered. She tried to look as if she wasn't just staring. A tear came out of her left eye.

"Next question, dear. Did you take new case files from three employees' desks and place them on Winifred's?" Cynthia could see that Karen was upset.

"No, Ma'am. I did not," Karen said indignantly.

"You're demeanor tells me otherwise, Karen. Why do you act so upset and defensive while I question you?"

Karen exploded. "I don't know, damn it. Perhaps it's because you're treating me like a child." She began to cry.

"Karen. I do not mean to be rude, but you are acting like a child. Listen, Karen—I am willing to let this ride for now, but any strange behavior in the future will leave me with no alternative but to dismiss you. Is that understood?"

"Yes, Ma'am. I really am innocent."

"Please, Karen. Stop. Let this thing drop."

"Okay. Thank you, Cynthia."

"No problem. Now—we've all had a long day with no work getting done. Let's do some reforming."

"Yes, Ma'am." Karen began to get up from the chair when Cynthia stopped her.

An alarm had sounded in Cynthia's memory. On Saturday, she had remembered Karen asking her about her own expense account. The fact that Karen had brought the subject up had suddenly sparked an assumption in Cynthia's mind. *Karen could have been leading me on somehow*, Cynthia thought. "Wait just a moment," Cynthia said. She gave a stoic look at Karen

Karen was alarmed. "Yes?" Karen responded.

"Karen. If you recall—you had asked me about the status of your expense account on Saturday. I felt as if you were just being conscientious about your own expense affairs, but it's a bit of a coincidence that Palmer's account had recently been scrutinized. I have to be honest, Karen, that I question the integrity of your initial concern of the petty cash account. Were you by chance luring me in to see the strange entry into Winifred's spread sheet?" Cynthia gave Karen no mercy in demanding an answer to the question.

Karen's eyes became vacant and dumb struck. "No," Karen said with little inflection. She thought quickly. "Anyway. Why in the world would I want to do that to Winny? She's one of our finest workers." Karen's personal inner-strength began to surface, but to no avail.

"You're preaching to the choir, Karen. I know that Winny's work ethics are beyond reproach. The problems that I have, is the result of your test and the fact that you reminded me of the expense accounts. I'm not a stupid woman, Karen."

"I never said that you were, Cynthia. I was merely asking you about my expenses and no one else's." Karen began to gain a little confidence during the conversation.

"Perhaps if you say so, but I'm not sure if asking me was not just a ploy to discover Winifred's spread sheet." Cynthia looked closely at Karen's expressions. "I'm going to have to put you on notice, Karen. I'm not accusing you but playing my cards carefully. I hope you understand."

"Yes, Ma'am. I understand." Karen smiled, stood, and left the office. The work day had gone on like nothing had ever happened.

5

Chad had brought home, to Winifred, a bouquet of flowers. The gesture was accepted as kind by Winifred, but not without a rebuttal. It had been a long strange day for her, and she was in a deep depression. She had not gotten home until 7:00 when she relieved Sarah Morning from her sitting with the children. Winifred had reflected on the day's events and decided that she was in an extremely exhaustive state of being. She had not only thought about all that had happened at work but how disgusted she was with Chad. He had gone out on her, and she was very angry. At 7:32 Chad walked through the door with a bunch of flowers. Her eyes slanted.

"I have something for my beautiful wife," Chad said.

Winifred shook her head back and forth. "That's very nice, Chad. I appreciate the thought, but you don't seem to understand that we haven't resolved our issue." She took the flowers. "Thank you."

"Well—I thought."

"You thought wrong, my dear. You don't know how much I appreciated your helping Kathleen, but it doesn't change the fact that you've been a dog. I work hard trying to help people with their problems, and I'm exhausted, Chad. I think now's a good time to talk."

"I can't believe it," he said. "Do you realize that we've put ourselves on the line in sending Kathleen away?"

"Of course I do. I believe everything's going to be alright, though."

"Winny. I am so sorry for what I've done. You didn't deserve this."

"Okay. What I want to know is how many times you've screwed around, and don't lie."

Chad was suddenly alarmed. He didn't expect that question from his wife. He had thought that they could work through the one relationship he told her about; but if he reveals the others, he knew that crap would hit the fan. She would never forgive him for multiple affairs. He had to say something. He took a deep breath and sat down. "I'll tell you the truth, Winifred. Many. Many women—many times."

Winifred burst out in tears. "Why, Chad? You son-of-a-bitch." She rushed over to where he sat and literally got in his face. "You have no idea how this makes me feel," she screamed. "We have two wonderful children. I thought that you loved me. I thought that I was attractive to you."

Sweat poured from his forehead. His eyes bugged. "You are, sweetheart."

"Don't you dare call me sweetheart, asshole. I know that I'm not at home as much I could be, but that's my job, Chad."

Chad got brave. "Well-since you've brought it up, I felt as if I didn't know you anymore. There's been goodnight kisses that felt as if I were kissing a statue. What am I supposed to think?"

Her voiced turned shrill and louder. "What are you supposed to think? Perhaps that I'm tired. I work my tail off for this family. It isn't that I don't enjoy what I do, but my work is taxing, Chad. The least you can do is to understand that and keep your pecker in your pants until I'm ready for you."

"Here we go," he yelled. "I'm not a robot. I have feelings that I can't hide."

"You can discuss your feelings with me. Damn it, man. Speak up. I'm your wife. I can listen."

Chad's mind had begun to sway toward her reasoning, but he also was not ready to end the fight. "That's so easy for you to say. I take care of the kids. Some nights you don't get home until ten o' clock."

"All of this is so selfish of you to say, Chad. You know what I do. You never answered me about talking to me about what is on your mind. How about that? Stop changing the subject." Winifred's face was blood red, and she was getting closer to his face as she spoke.

"Get out of my face, Winny."

"Oh. What are you gonna do? Hit me? Come on. You know that I can probably kick your ass."

Chad laughed. "You're threatening me with your karate? Oh, Winifred. Don't stoop so low."

Winifred backed away from her husband, smiled, and looked up toward the ceiling. "Okay. I'm not threatening you. I was out of line. All I'm asking for is a little honesty. And about stooping? You've already topped that one, buddy boy."

Chad was giving up. He knew that his actions had been wrong. "Okay, Winifred. Okay. You win. You're right. I've been a dog. I'm so sorry, honey. I love you. I felt nothing for any of those women." He began to cry out loud.

"What's wrong, Daddy?" asked Adrian. Adrian hugged his daddy around the waist.

Winifred and Chad looked at each other in sorrow. Chad stood. "Nothing, my dear boy," he said. They had both walked to their child in unison. Chad picked up Adrian and hugged him tightly.

Winifred put her arms around both of them. "It's okay, darling. Mommy and Daddy are being bad. We're so sorry." She looked over at the doorway to the kitchen and saw Kira standing with tears in her eyes. "Come here, baby," Winifred said as she held out her arm.

Kira ran to them. "Oh, Mommy. What's wrong?" she asked.

Winifred put her arm around Kira's shoulder. "Big people can act very much like children sometime, sweetheart."

The rest of the evening grew very quiet. Together, Chad and Winifred put the children to bed. Chad had said an evening prayer for each child in their respective bedroom.

When Chad and Winifred went to bed, they had said very few words to each other. "I know that you're sorry, Chad. Goodnight."

"Goodnight, Winny." Sleep did not come easy for the couple.

6

Wednesday

Cynthia had arrived at work at 7am. At 7:10, her phone rang and she picked up. "Good morning. Diamond Social Services, Cynthia speaking. May I help you?"

"I sure hope so, Cynthia," replied Carl Wicham. "Carl Wicham."

"Hi, Carl. What's up?"

"It's been one hell of a week so far, Cynthia. I'm really worried about Kat, and not to mention that I'm lonely as hell."

"I can fully understand that, Carl. It's going to take some time, sir. Give her some time. She may decide to call you soon."

"But—it's driving me crazy. I can't sleep—and I don't think that I can handle going to work today."

"That's totally up to you, Mr. Wicham, but, as I told you before, you can't allow her absence to run your life. If you keep your mind occupied, you can get through this."

"It's not that easy, damn it," Carl said. He hesitated as he began weeping. "I need sleep. I'm sad. I."

He stopped talking. He didn't know what to say.

"I can feel for you, Carl. I really can."

"Isn't there anything you can do for me?"

Cynthia thought for a moment. "Carl. I promise that I will look into this. Why don't you file a missing person report with the police later this afternoon? It has been almost 48 hours since you had found her note."

"Yes. Yes. I will do that." He began to feel some relief from what Cynthia suggested. "I **am** calling in today, and I will do just that. In the meantime, see what you can find out on your end—if there is anything."

"I will, Carl. You get some rest and I will call you later today if I find out anything. Okay?"

"Thanks, Cynthia. You've been very nice about this."

"That's why we're here, Sir."

"Have a good day. Bye."

"You do the same, Carl. Goodbye." Cynthia felt sympathy for the man, even though the history of his abuse of Kathleen was horrendous. A thought suddenly came to her. She decided to call the Greyhound Bus service first, and if no record of Kathleen Wicham is found there, she would call the airlines. That is what she did. There was no record of a trip at Greyhound, so she proceeded to check on each airline. After being transferred from airline to airline, she had hit the mark on the fourth one at Midwest Airlines.

"Here it is, Ma'am," the agent had said. "Kathleen Wicham had departed Wilmington last Friday, June 8, at 3:48pm and arrived in San Diego at 5:05. Is there anything else that you would like to know, Ms. Arnold?" the lady asked?

"Oh. I'm sorry. What was your name, dear?" Cynthia asked.

"I'm Deidra."

"Yes Deidra. There is something. Since I am the manager and co-owner of Diamond Social Services, I need to know how much the ticket was and in whose name the flight was purchased."

"No problem, Ms. Arnold. It looks like it was paid with a Visa of a Mr. Chad Palmer for $1200.00."

Cynthia was in a mild state of shock. "Thank you, Deidra. You've been a great help."

"Anything else I can do for you, Ms. Arnold?" the agent asked.

"No thank you. That will be all."

"Have a great day, and thank you for calling Midwest Airlines. Goodbye."

"Goodbye," Cynthia said. Cynthia let out a heavy breath and cupped her face in her hands. The price of the ticket and who paid for it stunned her. $1200.00 was the exact amount on Winifred's expense account. *My God, Winny. Why? You lied to me.* Cynthia was faced with something just as difficult as dealing with Winifred. She was going to have to tell Carl Wicham something. She decided quickly that she would not tell Carl where Kathleen was but that she had left town, and would not tell him who had paid for the trip. As dishonest as the latter might be, she would plead ignorance if he would happen to ask.

As soon as Winifred walked through the door and sat at her desk at 8am, Cynthia approached her. Cynthia did not want to make a scene so she feigned a *just business* demeanor. There were a few employees already there. "Winny, dear. I'd like to speak with you about one of your new accounts."

"Sure, Cynthia," Winifred said.

As usual, Cynthia led the way into her office. She closed the door behind Winifred. "Have a seat please."

The tone of the last comment made Winifred a little uneasy. She sat as Cynthia did. "What's going on?" Winifred asked.

"I think you know, Winny. My God, I'm sorry about what is happening at home with you but we have to call a spade a spade. I know that your husband bought the ticket for Kathleen to flee the city to San Diego."

"Cynthia, I"

"Stop for just a moment. You can respond when I'm done. I called the airport and found the flight that Kat had taken. I had to ask them, Winifred, if they had a name of the purchaser of the ticket. The lady told me that a Mr. Chad Palmer had made the purchase with a Visa card." Cynthia grinned. "How fucking stupid could your husband be? If you guys wanted to help Kathleen, you should have given her cash. It's not the idea that it was done but that you lied to me, Winny. How could you?" All that Cynthia had said was spoken in a sharp but quiet manner. "Okay. Let's have it, girl."

"I didn't know that he did it, Cynthia. I'll admit that Chad and I talked about it, but I didn't know he would do it." Winifred was floored by the revelation, but kept her head. She knew that Cynthia's finding out was possible but didn't expect it. "It was the same night that I confronted him about his affair, and I believe that he bought the ticket to try and make up for his shitty action, which I found out last night were actions. He'd gone out on me many times, Cynthia, and with different women." Winifred was finished talking for the moment and awaited Cynthia's response.

"Dear Lord, Winny. I believe you again. If you had just admitted the whole thing from the beginning when I asked you, I could perhaps let this whole thing slide. You know you have me in a difficult position."

"I'm so sorry, Cynthia. I've been going through so much lately. I've a brain. You know that. I should have thought out the whole credit card thing and given her cash for the ticket. I don't know what else to say." Winifred was out of excuses and again wondered what Cynthia's decision was going to be about her employment at this agency that she worked so hard in keeping.

"Winifred. I'm a fair woman. I believe that you know that. I love you, and I hold you high on a pedestal of able personnel. Now—I'm not sure any more. I know that you have an anxiety disorder, and that you have a lot on your plate at home and with this job, but I don't think that I can keep you on. This Kathleen thing has just gotten out of hand. What you have done, involuntarily or not, can compromise the integrity of this institution. Please know that you can rely on me to give you an exemplary reference. Yes, Winny. I'm going to let you go and it kills me to do so."

"Oh, Cynthia. Please. Don't do this. We can work through it. I'll—I'll get it together." Winifred was grabbing for straws.

"I'm sorry, darling. The fact that your strange expense account entry matched exactly to the price of the plane ticket is also a clincher. The computer thing and its origin, at this point, is a moot subject. The numbers spell out the ending transaction. We'll give your day's appointments to the workers that I feel are best for the jobs. You will get paid for the remaining part of the week." Cynthia had tears in her eyes as did Winifred. Cynthia held out her hand. "Good luck, Winny, and love those children." They shook hands. Cynthia could feel that Winifred's hand was damp and limp. "Are you okay?"

"Hell no—I'm not okay," Winifred screamed.

"Please, Winifred. Consider the other workers," Cynthia said calmly.

"Fuck the other workers," Winifred said in the same volume as before. "I'm the one under fire." Winifred contemplated how she was acting and quickly fell into a docile state. The room began to spin and she fell out of her chair. She had fainted.

Cynthia shot up from her chair and around the desk, caught her to make sure that Winifred didn't hit her head and laid her down gently on the floor. Cynthia quickly called for an ambulance. She was very concerned for her former employee. Cynthia had cried in spite of the situation and made Winifred comfortable on the floor. She placed a small pillow under her head.

"Here, darling," Cynthia said. "Drink some water." She held Winifred's head up with her hand.

Winifred sipped the water out of the paper cup. She coughed after the first sip and then went for another drink. She cleared her throat. "Thank you," said Winifred.

"Honey. There's an ambulance on the way."

"Oh no—Cynthia. That's not necessary. I'll be fine."

"We'll let the paramedics determine that," Cynthia answered.

At that moment, there was a knock on Cynthia's office door. "Come in," said Cynthia.

The door opened and Shirley Calliston popped her head in. "Cynthia. Hi. How is Winifred?"

"She seems to be stable, Shirley, but she's still a little light headed." Cynthia had earlier made an announcement to the employees that Winifred had fainted in the office and that an ambulance was on the way.

"Oh—that's good news—the poor dear. Cynthia. At some point, I'd like to speak with you at your convenience."

"Yes, Shirley. After we've got Winny taken care of I'd be glad to speak with you."

"Thank you, Cynthia. I don't have an appointment until 11. I'll be at my desk."

"Fine, Shirley. See ya. Please close the door, hon."

"Yes, Ma'am."

Before Shirley closed the door, Winifred spoke. "Hi, Shirley. Thanks for your concern." She smiled, looking up at Shirley.

"No problem, sweetheart. See you later," Shirley said.

"K," said Winifred. She closed her eyes and then Shirley closed the door.

"Winny. I want you to know that nothing is personal," Cynthia said to her. "Damn. I feel like I'm quoting from the movie, *The Godfather.*"

"It's okay, Arnold. I can take it." Winifred laughed.

Cynthia smiled. She was on her knee and patted Winifred's forehead with a cool damp cloth. "Just relax, baby. I'll take care of you. Now that we're not professionally attached, I can be a friend full time." She had wondered as she spoke those words how extensive a friendship could develop after firing her most prized employee.

The paramedics had come and gone and they had given Winifred a clean bill of health. They had implied that her condition was stress related. The lady paramedic had told her that she might be well advised to see a psychologist. Winifred had finally gained enough strength and alertness to drive her self home. The conclusion that the medics had come to was something that she already knew. She had not left the office before shedding some tears and saying goodbye to her fellow employees that were still in the building. All had stood and gave her hugs after telling them that she had been let go. They couldn't believe that she was fired. Karen was not present.

At a quarter past 10, Shirley was invited into Cynthia's office. Cynthia could tell that something was preying on Shirley's mind. "What's up, Miss Shirley?" Cynthia asked.

"Well, Cynthia. This is not an easy thing to say, and I'll try and be as accurate as I can. That is, what I can recollect."

"I'm intrigued, Shirley. What is this about?" Cynthia thought to herself that the week, so far, had held one hellacious turn of events, and also wondered what information she was about to hear.

"Cynthia. I'm not sure what day this was last week, but I thought at the moment that it was quite peculiar. I had heard Winifred talking to someone on her phone, and I assumed that it was her client, Kathleen. Winny had talked about getting Kathleen away from her husband. I remember that they had talked about having lunch that day. That's not what is bothering me." Shirley stopped for a moment as she held her head down in thought.

"Yes?" Cynthia responded.

"Well—what bothers me is the conversation I heard from Karen's desk. You do realize that I don't make it a habit of eavesdropping."

"I understand, Shirley. It's close quarters out there. What did you hear?"

"Karen made a phone call and she seemed to make it a point of speaking very low—whispering, in fact. I recall her asking a person named Cameron to go to the restaurant to basically spy on Winny and Kathleen. She had described Winifred to him and mentioned to listen for a cash amount."

Cynthia was more than intrigued. Things began to fall into place. "Tell me more, Shirley."

"Well---all I remember is Karen describing Winifred and Kathleen to him. I just think that it's all a little creepy for Karen to do that. Now—a day or two later I'd heard another short conversation from Karen's desk. She was again, whispering. I heard her ask the person why they didn't stick around longer and that she was paying him for what he did. I can only assume it was that Cameron person again. That's it. Just thought I'd let you know, Cynthia."

"Thank you, Shirley. This makes sense. I still believe that Winny was innocent about the computer tampering. What you've told me has reinforced my suspicions. You know, Shirley, I had to let Winifred go for another reason that was a huge mistake on her part. It's confidential, but I will tell you that it's somehow related to Karen's sneaky activity. Thank you, dear. You've been a great help."

"Your welcome, Cynthia. I didn't want to get anyone into trouble, but, at the same time, Karen's phone calls were very weird."

"I agree. Thanks again. I've a lot to do, Shirley."

Shirley immediately darted up from her chair and showed her own way out of the room. "Have a good day, Cynthia."

"You too, honey," Cynthia said. Cynthia found this new information very interesting indeed, and a bit troubling. She suspected Karen all along since the polygraph test results, but wasn't quite positive until her conversation with Shirley. Karen was gone for the time being, but Cynthia would wait for her.

10:30am

Cynthia picked up the phone and called Carl Wicham. "Hello, Carl? Cynthia. How you doing?"

"I'm okay---as well as I can be, I guess. I haven't been to the police yet."

"Well---don't. I found Kathleen. I mean---I know she's okay."

"Oh, God, Cynthia. Thank you. Where? Where is she?"

"I did some investigative work and called the airport. She had left on a flight on Friday to another state."

Carl was amazed. "Really? Where? What state?"

"I can't reveal that information, Carl. It's against social service protocol to reveal a location, being that an abusive husband could possibly find the wife and hurt her in some way. You do understand."

"Oh, Cynthia, please. Don't tell me that now. You mean to say.."

"It is what it is, Mr. Wicham. Those are the rules. What you should consider is that she's okay."

"How the hell could she afford a trip anywhere? I bet it was that bitch—oh—excuse me. I can bet Winifred Palmer had something to do with it."

"We can't know that for sure, Carl. Winifred is an upright employee." Cynthia was lying through her teeth, especially speaking about Winifred as an employee in the present tense. She thought that if Carl finds out about Winifred's being fired, that he could come up with something.

"I'll bet she knows something, Cynthia. Her husband is filthy rich."

"With that aside, the main thing is, Carl, that Kat is gone, but she's alright. Now, listen. I know relationships. There's a very good chance that Kat might call you sometime. Now—you'll have to face up to it if she does not and get on with your life. I can feel for you, sir, but you're going to have to own up to the fact that you were abusive to her. I hate to bring that up, but search yourself for your own short comings. I suggest some professional help at some point."

Carl felt as if he'd been hit with a brick bat. He knew that Cynthia spoke the truth. "My, Cynthia. You lay it on the line, don't you?" He snickered.

"That's my job, Carl. That's what this agency is about."

"Well. Thank you, Cynthia. You've taken a load off of me. Goodbye."

"Goodbye, Mr. Wicham." They had both hung up.

On Carl's end, he thought. *I'll find out,* he thought. "I'll get to that Winifred Palmer if it's the last thing that I do," he said to himself.

Later that afternoon, Karen sat across from Cynthia. Cynthia shook her head back and forth. "As late developments have occurred, you are now under scrutiny, Karen," Cynthia said. "I have a source that has revealed to me some interesting conversations that had taken place between you and a man named Cameron. Can you tell me anything about that?"

Karen had had a long day and this interrogation was topping everything off. She didn't quite know how to respond, but gave it her best. The open-ended question had perturbed Karen but she knew that she had to answer her superior. "I had spoken with a friend who I can confide in from time to time. We had just spoken of having lunch together sometime."

"That is not what I heard, Karen. Did you or did you not ask this Cameron to spy on Winifred and Kathleen? If you want details, that's what I heard."

Karen's only recourse was to deny it. "Who in the world would have told you that?"

"That's not important. The fact is that someone did hear you talking on the phone on two separate occasions. The party said that you were trying to whisper. Now, Karen—I'll ask you again. Did you have a phone conversation with Cameron asking him or her to go to the same restaurant that Winifred and Kathleen went to in order to eavesdrop.?"

"No. I did not," Karen said.

"You are not making this easy, Karen. Please reconsider your answer. My source is reliable."

Karen pondered the situation. *Mine is the last booth on that side of the room,* she thought. *Shirley.* "Whoever heard the conversation must have misunderstood what I was saying. That's all I can tell you."

Cynthia narrowed her eyes and pursed her lips. "It was specifically reported to me that you had mentioned to your friend to listen to Winifred's conversation with Kathleen Wicham and listen for a dollar amount. The second phone call that I was told about included you telling the person that you were paying the party for what they did. How do you explain that?"

Karen knew where this was heading, but she was head strong. "It never happened. I am adamant in my answer," she said with conviction.

"Okay, Karen. If that's what you insist on telling me, I have no alternative than to terminate your employment, and I will tell you why. The results of your polygraph test were less than perfect. It showed that you were probably not telling the truth in regard to Winifred Palmer. When I had asked you about those results, you did not appear exactly innocent in your demeanor. As you recall, I was willing to let it go. It was the information that I was given about the phone conversation which included the person listening for a dollar amount that seems to link you to Winifred's expense account. It fits, Karen. You may clean out your desk, and you will be paid for the rest of the day. Please leave all of your cases at the center of the desk"

"I'll get an attorney. You can't do this." Karen was talking out of her stubborn head.

Cynthia smiled. "You do that, Karen. I doubt if you will, but go ahead if you wish. Good day, Ms. DuPont."

Karen didn't say a word. She stood, walked to the door and opened it. She began to exit.

"You can leave the door open, Karen. Good luck."

Karen said nothing. *Piss off,* she felt like saying. She walked through the lobby in a daze, went to her desk, and proceeded to clean it out. She sobbed. There was no one around to console her. Marilyn Straub was in the restroom, but no other workers were in the building.

There was a reason that Cynthia decided to only pay Karen for the remaining hours of the day and Winifred, the rest of the week. In Cynthia's mind, Karen was indifferent and a downright liar. She was also devious and calculating. Winifred, although guilty, was a victim of being too sweet and thoughtful. She admitted that what she did was wrong.

7

Winifred had relieved Sarah from the children's care when she arrived home that morning. She had fed the children lunch of chicken salad sandwiches around noon, and had laid them down for a nap. She herself had taken a nerve pill and laid down for a nap as well. She had slept for nearly an hour when the door bell had rung. After being awakened, she went to the door and looked out the peep hole. The person that stood outside was kind of a shock to her. There stood Carl Wicham with an angry look on his face. Winifred was not only in no mood for the visit but was not ready for a confrontation with this man. She felt that she had no choice and opened the door. "Yes, Carl?"

"I think you know what, Palmer," Carl said. He stood there in a jean shirt and brown khaki pants.

"No. I don't know," she said.

"Where the fuck is Kathleen?" he asked.

"Do you realize I have children in the house, Mr. Wicham? And they're sleeping."

"Then they can't hear me. Where is my wife?"

"I'm sure I don't know, Carl. I haven't heard from her for a few days."

"I don't doubt you haven't heard from her but you know where she is."

"No---I don't. If I did know, I couldn't tell you. It's"

He interrupted. "I know. Against your protocol."

"That is correct."

"Well. According to Cynthia Arnold, you no longer are employed there. I called her about a half hour ago. Doesn't that make you exempt from protocol?"

Winifred had then recalled the phone ringing while she was drifting off to sleep. She had heard Cynthia's voice on the answering machine and heard the name 'Carl Wicham,' but was too deep into slumber to think about it or care.

"Carl. I am sorry about Kathleen, but I do not know where she is. Look. It's been a bad week."

"That's funny. Bad is an understatement for my week. Now you look, Palmer. Either you tell me what I need to know or I'll call the police and have **them** question you," he had yelled. Carl tapped his boot on the porch. He had a wicked smile on his face.

"Bring em on, Carl. I'm in no mood for your crap. By the way, the children are sleeping, and I would appreciate your not yelling." At that moment, she had a strong urge to kick the crap out of this man. "You should have thought of this eventuality before you bashed her over the head with a dinner plate."

Carl grimaced at Winifred's last comment. His eyes and mouth showed remorse as he looked down in shame. He then looked up at Winifred's face. His pitiful eyes turned to a raging piercing glare. As his nostrils flared, he suddenly reached into the doorway and grabbed Winifred by the top of her tee shirt. "You tell me where she is, you bitch and I'll let this go."

Carl had crossed the line as far as Winifred was concerned. He was becoming quite violent at her own front door. She reacted in a way that she was trained to do years before. She had grabbed Carl's wrists and twisted them with a strength that Carl didn't expect, and then let go of one wrist and worked on the other one, continuing to twist his right wrist. The twisting turned into the twisting of his arm as he could not break loose from her grip. She had him in a full arm lock which turned him around. She then proceeded to hold his wrist up high behind him, leaving him helpless. "I can break your arm in a second, Carl. I'll have you knowI had a brown belt in karate."

"Let me go," Carl cried.

"Are you going to get off of this property now?"

"Yes. Yes. Let me go."

Winifred let go with a shove to send Carl stepping forward and stumbling a bit. "Now, go. I'll let you know if I hear from Kathleen. You shouldn't have grabbed me, man. I can press charges, you know. Doing that to me on my own property was stupid."

Carl looked at Winifred. He had a half grin on his face. "To answer your question, No. I never knew about your---talent." He turned and walked to his car that was parked on the street. He said nothing else. As he got in the car and drove away, he gave her a gesture that did not surprise her. He flipped her the bird.

Chad arrived home to find Winifred on the couch drinking wine from the bottle. She was crying. He knew that something was terribly wrong. He saw the two children playing a game on the computer. The day at work was trying for Chad. He had thought about his and Winifred's marriage nearly every minute. Winifred was a prize to him. He knew that her job had required undivided attention and persistence and that the long hours she worked was no fault of her own. She was only doing the best job that she could. Unlike his own job, she carried some of her work home with her, making phone calls to clients from the house after work hours. He would do the same from time to time but not to the extent that Winifred would do. All day his mind had drifted to his wrong doings which nearly made him sick to his stomach. He had had an important meeting with investors late that afternoon and more than once had to catch up by looking at his notes and asking the party to repeat what was said. He could sense that the people in the group were leery that the vice-president of the Fine Wine Emporium was giving his full attention to the matters that were being discussed.

He had apologized to them all and told them that his 'notes had fallen on the floor and were out of order as he was on his way to the meeting.' After the meeting, his boss, Roger Weatherford, asked him, 'What the hell was that all about, Chad?' Chad had told Roger everything that was going on with him and his wife. He had apologized to Roger. Roger considered the situation but told Chad that 'that sort of thing could possibly cause investors to steer away from a reputable company.' Chad assured him that nothing like that would happen again. Roger was satisfied with Chad's remorse since the meeting ended with satisfaction from the investors. "Winifred, honey. What's the matter?" he asked her.

"Oh. Nothing. I was just fired is all. Tell me, Chad. Why the hell did you have to purchase Kathleen's plane ticket with your credit card?"

Chad's stomach sank. He felt in his gut what she was saying. Her work found out about the purchase of the ticket and had traced it to his credit card. "Winifred. Oh, God. I knew it was a bad idea from the start. But, honey—that night I was beside myself and consumed in guilt. I wanted to make things right between us and thought that the gesture might help. We should have given her cash."

"Your motive is painfully obvious, Chad. I just wish you had waited and discussed it with me. You know that we would have come up with the cash solution. It's okay. It's done and over. The reason that I was let go seemed to be not so much the fact that we helped Kat, but that I had lied to Cynthia before she had found out. It was a morning from hell, Chad. I'm falling apart and my attacks are getting more frequent."

"I'm so sorry, love. I'll make it up to you."

"Oh, Chad. Don't be so stupid. How could you make this right? I'm also thinking of leaving you. You bastard. How could you even think of going out on me with so many women? Even once is bad enough."

"I've been horrible, Winny. I know that. Please. I'll make everything right again. You're my only love. I should have been more patient with your work hours."

Winifred sighed. "I don't know, Chad. Maybe I won't leave you. You have to understand that I have to think about this long and hard. I hate you for this." She slammed the wine bottle down on the coffee table. "The deception just irks me. Now. Who the hell was this last woman? That's all I want to know right now. Excuse my language in front of the children"

Chad gave a half smile. "Her name is Lisa Schavoni. You don't know her. She attended one of our wine tasting sessions back in May. It's all over, Winny. I spoke with her yesterday."

"How am I supposed to believe you, Chad? I mean—people just don't change overnight. Are you telling me that you won't have any desires to explore another world of sex?" Winifred was drunk and very adamant in getting to the crux of the matter.

"Winifred. I am telling you the truth. I have no desire to be with anyone else but you. I was caught up in the glamour of my position with the company. I was rarely seeing you at night and on the weekends, and I became disgruntled. I know that is no excuse, but it's all I can tell you."

"If that's all you have, my husband, I'll accept that. Take your shoes off and get comfortable. In fact, have some wine with me. I need the company."

During the next twenty minutes, Winifred had explained to Chad about Carl Wicham's visit. Chad was upset about Carl's visit but amused at the same time about how Winifred handled it. They had had three glasses of wine together while they talked before serving pot pies to the children.

8

To Winifred's surprise, she had received a call from Cynthia. The time was 8:55am. "Winny, how are you?" Cynthia asked.

"Oh…as well as can be expected. What's up, Cynthia?"

"I hate to bring you this news first thing in the morning. It's Carl Wicham. He's dead."

Winifred's heart skipped a few beats. "What? I mean what?"

"It seems that he went out bar hopping last night. It's been noted by the police that he reached a bar by the name of the Three Seals Tavern and that he had gotten into a riff with a man by the name of Drew Merriville. Seems to have been over a somewhat trivial matter. According to the papers, the police inferred that Merriville was said to be a neighborhood bad ass. It had started with cussing and hollering in the bar when the bartender and bouncer had told them both to leave. Carl was found with a slit throat in the alley.

There was silence on the phone.

"Winny. Are you there?"

Winifred gulped. "Yes. I'm here."

"I'm sorry, dear," Cynthia said. "Merriville had been arrested early this morning at his home."

The 'dear' was beginning to grate on Winifred's nerves since Cynthia had just fired her. "I can't believe it." Winifred could believe it. She had known that Carl was volatile and also vulnerable the day before.

"He had made a phone call here yesterday and had asked for you. I had no alternative but to tell him that you no longer worked here. Did he contact you, Winny?"

86

"Yes, he did. He came to my house." Winifred said these words before she had time to think. "He had asked about the whereabouts of Kathleen. I had told him that even though I was no longer an employee of Diamond, that I couldn't reveal anything if I did know."

"You did the right thing. Did anything else take place---I mean, is there anything unusual that happened while he was there?"

Winifred began to feel scrutiny coming through from the other end of the phone line and didn't like it much. She had reacted spontaneously. "Why in the hell would you ask that, Cynthia? Are you acting the part of the police?"

"No, no, Winifred. No." Cynthia could sense a feeling of intrusion being construed by Winifred, which she fully understood. "I only ask because you may be the last person he had spoken with before his unfortunate demise."

"I'm sorry, Cynthia. Just a little on edge is all. He did attack me at my front door."

"What?" Cynthia asked in a very curt and surprised way.

"Yes. He grabbed me by the collar---right in my house, demanding that I tell him what he wanted to know."

"Winny. Did he push your anger button?"

"You do know me very well, Cynthia. Yes. I twisted his arm until it wouldn't go any farther and told him to get off the property---which he did. That's about it."

"Winifred. You are something. Of course, I don't blame you." Cynthia smiled. "There is one slight caveat to this whole thing. The police may check his incoming and outgoing calls from his house, which may somehow implicate me in his frame of mind last night."

"I know. I know. And me too if it gets that far."

"Do you know if there were any witnesses to what happened there?"

"I have no idea. I've nothing to hide."

"Well," Cynthia hesitated, "if the police ask me about the nature of the call that he made…"

"I know---you'll have to tell them and mention me."

"Let's hope it doesn't get that far, Winifred."

Winifred's shock began to set in. "I can't believe it. Poor Kathleen. I mean---I'm sure she didn't want Carl to end up dead. I wouldn't have even wished that."

"I know, Winny. I know. One last bit of information that may sway the police's attention away from us. Carl was fired from his job yesterday."

"That's ironic. How do you know that?" Winifred asked.

"He told me. He has sort of confided in me since Kathleen's "disappearance." The man was broken, Winny. I had to try and help him help himself. You understand."

"Yes---yes I do."

"I'll keep you posted, Winny. I'm getting another call."

"Thanks, Cynthia. Bye." Winifred was in awe. The news was horrific in her mind. *Poor bastard,* she thought. She had a wine hangover and the phone call completely sobered her, but it didn't change the feeling of a splitting headache. Little did she realize that the wine that she had opened had cost around one-hundred-ten dollars.

A soft voice came from behind her as she lay on the couch. "Morning, Mommy," said Kira.

"Mornin', sweetness," Winifred answered.

Kira walked around and fell into her mother's arms. "I'm hungry, Mommy," she said as Winifred kissed her on the lips.

"We'll fix you and your brother right up."

Kira backed up a step and waved her hand across her face. "Whew, Mommy," was all that she said.

Winifred laughed hysterically which caught onto Kira. They both laughed for a few moments. "Sorry, baby," Winifred said into the air.

"Drinking wine and sleeping makes for bad breath. Let's go wake up your brother."

"I think he's awake. I heard him yawning as I passed his room."

"Well---let's just go see." Winifred smiled beautifully as sleep matter had shown in the crevice of her left eye. She had embraced what she was experiencing with her children, as she was not able to do for quite some time. In the very back of her mind she thought about the tragedy of Carl Wicham.

After rounding up Adrian for breakfast, they had had a wonderful meal of pancakes and scrambled eggs. Winifred could only stomach a few bites of eggs. While eating, she had begun to get a dizzy spell which turned into a full-blown anxiety attack. She managed to swallow a nerve pill with a sip of coffee. She began to pace back and forth.

"What's the matter, Mommy?" Kira asked. "You feelin' bad again?"

"I'll be okay, sweety. Just give me a moment." Winifred did in fact feel better but it didn't happen as soon as she had thought. In fact, she had experienced another fainting spell, followed by waking up extremely hot as sweat dripped down her forehead. She had taken off her clothes down to her underwear and then had a total blackout. She was awakened on the kitchen floor.

"Oh, Mommy. What's the matter with you?" Kira cried.

The anxiety had completely lifted off of Winifred. "I'm fine, darling. Just give me a moment." She had cleared her head and stood slowly. She looked at herself in her underwear and didn't remember taking off her jeans and tee shirt. "Let Mommy take a short nap, loves." She retrieved her clothes but decided to slip into a gown instead. She made a phone call to Sarah Morning, asking her to come over for a couple of hours to watch the children. Sarah had conceded, even on such short notice.

Winifred, even though lying down on the couch, stayed awake until Sarah arrived. "Sarah," she said, "I had a bad fainting episode and I need to sleep."

"Don't you worry, Winny. I'll make sure you're not disturbed. In fact, would you like me to take the kids to the zoo? My treat."

"Oh, darling, you don't have to."

"I will, and I don't want an argument," Sarah said.

"You're just too good for words, Sarah. Thank you."

"No. Thank you. I was going stir crazy at the house. Now--you just relax." Sarah stroked Winifred's hair.

Winifred closed her eyes. A few minutes later, she heard the door close, and then total silence. She slept soundly for three hours.

Just before the children arrived with Sarah, the telephone had awakened Winifred. The call was from someone whom she didn't expect. Much to her chagrin, it was Kathleen Wicham, one person with whom she was not ready to speak. She dreaded having to tell Kat that Carl had been murdered, but she did. As Kathleen began to greet her, Winifred's stomach turned and her hands became slimy.

"Oh, Winifred—I miss you, sweety. Your extension at Diamond did not pick up and the call was directed to Cynthia's desk. Oh, my dear—what happened? Why aren't you working there anymore?"

Winifred was groggy and it took her a few moments to answer. "It's a bit ironic, Kat," Winifred said. "First of all—how are you?"

"I'm doing well. I already found a job waiting tables at a diner. I just started yesterday but I have the day off, and then I work the rest of the week except Sunday."

"That's great, Kathleen. Full time?"

"Yes. Isn't that wonderful? I really like it so far. Yesterday, I made thirty-five dollars in tips alone."

"Oh, Kat—I'm so happy for you. Is it a nice place?"

"Yes. It's right on the edge of town in a pretty nice neighborhood. I've already had time to see some good and bad ones. So—what's new, and what happened to your job?"

Winifred wasn't sure which question to answer first but quickly decided on the latter. "I was fired, Kat. Cynthia found out that Chad and I were responsible for your leaving."

"Oh, Winny—I'm sorry. It's all my fault."

"Don't even think that, Kat. It was our decision—not yours. Anyway, it wasn't the fact that we sent you away. The boss had caught me in a lie, and that was it. Cynthia had no intention of backing down on the issue. She gave me the reason that it was her ass on the line if she didn't go through with the termination."

"Fucking rules," Kathleen exclaimed.

"Kathleen," Winifred said curtly. "I have some news. Some very bad news."

"What, Winny, what?"

"Oh, honey—I don't know how to tell you. I'll start from the beginning. Carl had stopped by the house yesterday in a rage. He found out that I was no longer at the agency and decided to come and see me."

"Did he hurt you? I hope that son-of-a-bitch didn't do anything stupid."

Winifred allowed Kathleen's words to linger for a moment.

"No. He didn't hurt me. He tried to force me to tell him where you were. I didn't sway. To answer your question, he did get a little physical with me at the front door. I guess it's in my nature to defend myself. Without going into too much detail, I physically embarrassed him by locking his arm behind his back."

"Good for you, Winny. You are my hero, you know," Kathleen said.

Winifred hesitated. "Kathleen. Carl is dead."

There was dead silence on the phone line. "No. You can't be serious, Winny."

"Why would I tell you that if I wasn't serious, Kat?" Winifred heard a semi-hysterical throaty cry that began to surface on Kathleen's end.

"Why? How?" Kathleen asked in a shaky voice.

"Oh, Kat—I'm sorry. This is what apparently happened. He was fired from his job yesterday. Now-- don't blame yourself. He's been very upset because of your leaving him. It could be why he wasn't able to concentrate on his work. I don't know why he was fired but I can surmise that it had something to do with depression." *Crying on the other end.* "He had been at a bar last night and had gotten into a heated argument with a man. They were both asked to leave the bar. Kat— Carl's throat had been cut."

"So—he was sent into an arena with the lions," Kathleen screamed.

"Basically--yes. I'm sure the bouncer didn't expect something like this to happen, although the man that killed him was known to be a mean one. He was arrested this morning."

"I-I feel like I should be there—you know—for the funeral. I never wanted Carl to end up like this, Winny." The crying had subsided.

"I know you didn't, honey. I can always wire the money if you feel that you should come. You do know, Kat, that nothing is keeping you away now. You could give it some time and see how you feel."

"I would hate to leave since I just started this job. Oh my God, I can't believe that about my husband. He was hateful, Winifred. Do you think I should come?"

"That's totally up to you, baby. Like I said, maybe you won't want to come. Perhaps some distance and independence will do you good for a while. Call me if you change your mind. Either way, I'm behind you."

"I don't know how to say goodbye. I love you."

"I love you too. You know that. Listen, darling—I've got some personal things going on that I need to deal with, and I'm going to deal with it tonight. Stay in touch. Okay?"

"Okay, Winny. I hope everything is okay with you."

"I believe that it soon will be."

"Bye, Winifred Palmer."

"Goodbye, Kathleen Wicham. I'll talk with you soon. Bye."

"Bye bye," Kat said.

Chad had come home to see his family eating dinner. He had noticed that Winifred was picking at her food. Adrian seemed to be playing with the spaghetti more than eating, and Kira was devouring her meal. All was quiet and it seemed to Chad that something was a bit askew. Things were quiet at the table except from Adrian.

"Hi, Daddy," said Adrian.

"Hey, champ," answered Chad. "How is my wonderful family?"

Winifred sighed. "Oh—we're okay, Chad." Her remark was bland.

Chad had noticed a hollow look in his wife's eyes as she glanced up at him from the table. "What's the matter, Winifred?"

"Well—I'll just say—much. I'll talk to you in a little bit. Dinner's on the stove."

Chad had gone to wash his hands. He had never seen Winifred look the way that she did that night. *She's in bad shape*, he thought. He had seen a similar look on his wife's face when she had a near- nervous breakdown years before, and he was concerned. *This is probably mostly my fault.*

Adrian was asleep at the table when Chad had come back to the dining room. He picked up his son and told Winifred he would be back after getting Adrian to brush his teeth and putting him to bed. Adrian groaned and complained while brushing his teeth but managed to get through it. He fell fast asleep after Chad had laid him down and kissed him goodnight.

At 9:30 pm, Chad and Winifred had a talk, but not just a talk. The conversation encompassed Winifred's day's events and her decision on what she had to do to get herself back on track. She had heard the terrible news about Carl Wicham, had spoken with Kathleen, having to tell her about her husband's murder, and experienced the worst anxiety attack she had ever encountered. She had reached the beginning of a turning point in her life and had decided this after the children returned home from the zoo. Sarah had suggested to her to see her therapist again, given the severity and latest frequencies of the anxiety and fainting spells. Winifred confided in Sarah, and thought of her as a friend.

"I've had it, Chad. I'm really worried that I'm falling apart."

"What makes you think that, dear?" he asked

She told him about her horrible panic attack and fainting spell that day. "I felt as though I were burning up, and then I was out like a light after I practically tore my clothes off. Carl Wicham was murdered, and as if that weren't enough, Kathleen called, and I had to tell her."

"What? Oh—that's terrible—I mean—about Carl. You poor thing. You heard that awful news, and then having to speak with Kathleen. How did Kat take the news?"

"How do you think? She was devastated. She thought that she should probably come to the funeral. I believe that she realizes that if she comes that she may not leave again, and gave me the impression that she didn't want to leave her new life right away."

"That's understandable. That poor girl. Who killed Carl?"

"It was some street tough that he had an argument with in a bar. The man cut his throat with a knife." Winifred started to cry.

"I know, darling. It's a terrible thing that happened." Chad sat, and he put his arm around his wife.

Winifred slightly shrugged and gently pulled his arm off of her. "Chad. I've done a lot of thinking. I think I want a divorce—or at least a separation."

"Darling, I.."

Winifred cut him off. "Please, Chad. Don't call me darling right now. You've been bad. I can't forgive you for what you've done. I need some time. I'm going to see Dr. Collins tomorrow. I believe she can help me to put things into perspective. And God knows my anxiety has been at an all time high."

Chad had retreated, placing his hands on his knees. He put his head down. "I can't say that I blame you for how you feel about me. And I think that Dr. Collins would be a good idea. Please don't hate me, Winifred."

She held her flattened hand straight out in front of her. "I don't hate you, Chad. I just need some time—and guidance is all. I think that you're sorry for your affairs, but please, give me some time."

"I will give you that, Winifred," Chad said.

"Thank you, Chad."

9

The Next Day

Winifred sat comfortably across from Dr. Stephanie Collins, who had a master's degree in psychology. She was a strikingly beautiful woman in her thirties with coal-black hair that was braided smartly in the back.

"What brings you back, stranger?" the doctor asked.

Winifred smiled. "Oh—you know—same old shit, different year. Panic attacks nearly every day now."

"Have you suspected that these attacks have become more frequent?"

"Well—yes. I can't really give you a number. Listen, Stephanie. I'll help save the back and forth thing and fill you in on what's going on, and then you can be more directed with your questions."

"That'd be wonderful, Winifred." Dr. Collins smiled.

"The problem is I don't know where to start." Winifred laughed. "I'll just start. Chad had affairs with other women that was first only hear say, and then turned out to be true. Of course I am devastated. That's number one. Second, I was compelled to help a client to get away from her husband, which turned out to be a disaster. My boss found out that I helped after I told her I had nothing to do with it. I was fired. Third thing.."

"Hold on, Winny. Even I need time to digest information and be able to work with what you tell me."

"Sorry." Winifred grinned.

"Okay. You have worked yourself into a frenzy. Has Chad admitted to the affairs?"

"Yes. He has."

"Do you believe him to be sorry for what he has done?"

Winifred thought briefly about that question. "Yes. I believe he is sorry, but it still doesn't make it right."

"I never meant to allude to that fact. I only want to know if you have it in you to forgive him."

"I don't think so—at least not at this point."

The doctor was shaking her head, making notes. "You said affairs. Did he have more than one?"

"Yes. I don't know how many. He just told me several, or many. I don't remember his exact words. I do know that the last one had gone on for much longer than any of the others. This, he did admit."

"What bothers you more? Is it the fact that he had one affair or many?"

"Both. I guess the last one bothers me the most. However, the fact that he had the gumption to do it with more than one woman really pisses me off."

"Do you feel that your episodes began to progress in intensity after hearing about Chad's alleged affair or affairs?"

"I guess so. My friend had told me that she had seen him with another woman about a week before the first attack had taken place. It was on that Friday that I finally asked him, and he admitted it. He did say that he was sorry and that he really loved me, but not before he laid into me about never being at home. At first, I guess I was in shock. I tried to maintain the rest of the weekend by trying to help bring us back together as a family."

"And how did you do that?"

"We went out together on Saturday, and then to church on Sunday."

Stephanie had shown a slight smile before she spoke. "Do you feel as if you were repressing your feelings by going through these motions of normalcy?"

"Perhaps I was. It was on Sunday in church when I had the first attack I'd had in months."

"Well—don't you see, Winifred? The church thing was a major act of family togetherness. It seems as though you may have brought it on yourself. What do you think?"

"As always, I believe you to be correct. I didn't even have another conversation with Chad about his unfaithfulness until later."

"Okay. Let's jump ahead a bit. You said that you had helped a client get away from her husband. How did you do this?"

"Well, she had been my client for several years. Her husband treated her horribly. He'd beaten her badly many times." Winifred took a deep breath. "So—I had told her time and time again that she needed to get away from that man. The incident that put the icing on the cake was that he hit her over the head with a dinner plate, which made a gash." Winifred began to cry. "How can someone do that to his wife? It's ludicrous."

"Stop for a moment, dear. Do you see what you're going through? This social work had pulled you in emotionally. Do you think that your job has emotionally drained you?"

"Do you think that I never thought about that? Yes. I believe that I had taken my work home with me way too much. I was the best, Stephanie, but maybe it got to me more than I'd ever anticipated. I loved my job."

"Now—what happened to your job? You said you were fired for helping out your client."

"God—that's a long story, but I'll give you the condensed version."

"Thank you," Stephanie said as she smiled.

"Well first, this girl at work was trying to sabotage me. I believe I know who it was, but that's not exactly why I was fired. One thing about it was tied in though. I'll just say that **she** had tampered with the expense account on my computer. There was an expenditure of the exact amount of money that it had cost to send Kathleen, the client whom I was responsible for helping to leave her husband, on a plane to her destination. I did not make that entry, and did not use any company funds to buy a plane ticket. The reason that I was fired was that I told my boss that I had nothing to do personally with Kathleen's disappearance from her husband. She had done some research by calling the airlines and my husband's name was given to her right over the phone. The idiot used his credit card." Winifred laughed, in spite of the situation.

"Not very smart, I agree, Winny. So—she had caught you in a lie. I hate to say it. No. Maybe I shouldn't."

"Go ahead, Stephanie. I can take it."

"Well—it's not my position to say anything and would not help the situation at all. But, to put it mildly, your boss had just cause to let you go."

"Yes. And your right. That comment didn't help." They both laughed.

"And what was the third thing that you were going to tell me a while ago when I interrupted you?"

"Okay. This is the kicker, and a big one. After finding out that I no longer worked at the agency, Carl, Kathleen's husband, shows up at my door step."

"Yuck." Stephanie smiled. "Go on."

"He tried to get me to tell him where Kathleen was, and I refused to give in. I never admitted that I knew. He began to get physical with me, grabbing me by my collar, so I put him in an arm lock. I told him to leave the premises. He did."

"Good for you, Winifred. I remember you telling me that you knew karate."

"Brown Belt." Winifred smiled, and then the smile completely disappeared. "He was murdered that night, Stephanie. Knifed by a man he had met in a bar."

"Oh, God, Winny. I'm sorry. You've been through quite a lot."

"Tell me about it."

"How do you feel right now?"

Winifred felt spry. "I feel wonderful, Stephanie. I have no anxiety whatsoever."

"That's because you've opened up and talked about your problems. You've had much on your plate. Would you like to schedule another appointment?"

"Well—that depends."

"On what, may I ask?"

"On if I have another episode like the one I had the other day when I tore my clothes off and fainted."

"You know, Winifred. As serious as that may sound, and I'm not counting the serious part out all together, extreme pressure can show its ugly head in many forms. A fainting spell is one of them. Let me be blunt. You've been shit on by your husband. You've lost your job, and you probably feel that maybe you are somewhat responsible for the death of this Carl character. I mean—putting him into a depressive state of mind that would lead him into harms way. Forget that notion, missy. The man was obviously a powder keg waiting to explode."

"That's why I love your therapy, Stephanie. You lay things on the line. Okay. I'll do as you say. I'll place all of the things you mentioned into perspective."

"Thank you, Winifred. I guess I hold the equal of your expertise in social work."

That comment made Winifred feel really good. "Thank you, Stephanie."

"There is one more thing that I would like to suggest, and listen carefully, and don't interrupt until I'm finished talking. Take a vacation. A vacation away from your problems and away from your current state of mind. God knows you need it. And when I say vacation, do it in any manner that you feel is necessary for a content Winifred Palmer. It could be a physical vacation where you actually go somewhere, or a vacation from your problems by dealing with them one by one and leaving them behind you. Only you can decide how you go about doing it, but just do it. Understand?"

"Yes, Stephanie. I do, and I will do it. I don't know how but I will." Winifred stood as did Dr. Collins. Winifred hugged her tightly. "Thank you--thank you."

"Don't mention it, my dear." They both released one another. "I'll try not to gouge you with this session," Stephanie said as she smiled. "If you need me, call again."

Winifred smiled back. "I don't think I'll mention what I thought it was worth." They both laughed. "Bye, Stephanie."

"Goodbye, Winny. I hope you don't have to call again."

Winifred shook her head in understanding, turned, and walked out the door of the doctor's office.

The Assertion

Winifred Palmer was never one to beat around the bush about anything. Before Sarah Morning had left from sitting with the children, she had asked Winifred how she was doing, and Winifred had answered "Never been better." Sarah had looked into her eyes and saw that Winifred did look very well. The afternoon after returning from Dr. Collins's office, she had read classic poetry, which was something she had longed to do again for quite some time. In between poems and verses of poems she would stop and think. Sometimes she would think of the poem she was reading. Other times she would think of the direction that she must take for her life. She knew that she must take the advice of her psychologist and run with it. Her thoughts were objective yet subjective. A turn for the better was always the aim for her newly born self improvement. Some of the possible decisions that she had contemplated were simple in nature and some extreme. In her cognitive process, she had not discounted any of the possibilities of what she may do. Winifred, for the moment, had complete solitude, for the children were down for a nap. She had allowed them an extra long nap just for that day, and felt that she was not being selfish but only assertive in regard to her mental and physical well being. Toward the end of reading *Out To Old Aunt Mary's*, which always brought tears to her eyes, she came to a final decision.

The Family Meeting

Before beginning the family meeting, Winifred had explained to them that there should be no interruptions at first.

"I would like my family to know that I have chosen to take a vacation," Winifred said to Chad, Kira, and Adrian. She had looked one by one, directly into their eyes as she spoke. She had planned and selected her words carefully so that the children could understand what she was saying. When she would address Chad directly, her wording would change accordingly. "I have decided to take this vacation based on the advice of my doctor. Since it is summertime, I've decided to go to Colorado and try and see the running of the wild Mustang horses. Adrian and Kira, I would love for you kids to go with me."

"What about Daddy, Mommy?" asked Adrian.

"Adrian—honey, Daddy won't be joining us."

"But—why?" Adrian asked.

"Adrian—your mother wants no interruptions," said Chad. As he had heard his wife's last words, his stomach sank. He thought that he knew in which direction Winifred's plans were heading.

Winifred looked at Chad. "It's okay, Chad. I'll answer his question." She looked down at Adrian and Kira. "Children—your father and I will not be seeing each other for a while. But—as your father said, please let me finish." She swallowed. "After Colorado, I will bring you back here, and then we will decide what is best for us all. I intend on going south for the fall and winter. Whether you kids go with me will be talked about at that time." Winifred began to recoup her thoughts before continuing. "I've always wanted to see the wild horses and we can decide if the trip is appropriate for you children. Everyone—Mommy has had a terrible problem in the past few weeks. It's what doctors call an emotional breakdown. It's been very difficult for me to live each day without feeling like I want to faint. I sometimes feel like I am going to die for no reason, but those feelings are not real. What I mean to say is that worries can control a person's thoughts. I need a rest. Of course, you children know that Mommy is no longer working. That is one thing that has made me feel so sad, and it hasn't helped my condition. This is the reason why Dr. Collins has recommended that I take a vacation. Are there any questions, dears?" She was directing the question to the children.

"Yes, Mommy," Kira said. "Are you leaving forever?"

Kira's question hit Winifred hard and fast. "No, darling. I don't think so. I do know that I may be gone for a long time."

"Why are you and Daddy breaking up?" asked Kira.

"That, Kira—is between your daddy and me, but it doesn't mean that we still don't care for each other. Daddy and I will talk our problem out. Don't you worry."

Chad was very tired of being the silent partner in the whole scenario that was being displayed before him, though he knew that he and Winifred would soon have words, and surely in private. The tension was killing him inside, but he knew that it was best to stay quiet. He had been a bad husband and was waiting patiently for the end of the night's final punch line.

Chad Palmer and Winifred Humphrey were the talk of the class of 1989 at Statesboro High School in Wilmington. Winifred was a confirmed 1980s alternative rock fanatic, and Chad, a classics enthusiast. He had made her several cd mixes of 60s and 70s rock and folk music. Although some of the music impressed her, she was easily bored by extensive guitar solos by those she called 'pretentious rock artists.' They both would kid with each other about their different tastes in music, although he admitted in liking some 80s rock because it sounded like old music made new. She, in turn, felt the same way. Chad introduced her to The Beatles on their fourth date, which she absolutely absorbed and loved. She liked the earlier Beatles and not so much the later releases. The earlier Beatles reminded her somewhat of bands like Tears for Fears and Crowded House, the latter, being one of her all-time favorite bands. The song that touched her most was This Boy by The Beatles, which depicts a man so much in love with a woman that he can barely go on with his life without her. Chad and Winifred was in running for the Senior Prom King and Queen, but did not assume the final designation. Chad, did however, manage to request that This Boy be played during their last dance together on prom night. She was deeply touched and very much in love with Chad Palmer.

It was around 9:30pm when Chad and Winifred had their talk. "I've got to do it, Chad. There's no other way," Winifred said in the midst of the conversation.

"So—you want to drag the children out west and leave me forever. That's just great. I've told you that I'm sorry."

"I don't mean to be an ass, Chad, but sorry doesn't cut it. You have to realize that it's much more than what you've done."

"I know. You have to find yourself. Is that fair to me?"

"Yes. I think it's very fair to you. Do you want to live with my psychological problems while we're trying to sort out our own marriage problems? This is the deal. I won't drag Adrian with me on the trip out west. I think he's too young. Kira and I will be gone for a couple of weeks—tops. I'll bring her back here, we'll say our goodbyes, and then I think I'll head south for a while. You've got to allow me some freedom, Chad. It will mean my sanity." Winifred sighed.

"I'm going to miss you, you know," Chad said. He looked into her eyes. His demeanor was that of a whipped pup. His eyes were glassy.

"Of course—I'll miss you too, Chad. Please don't blame the doctor. She didn't specify to actually physically leave, although she had left that option open for me." She walked to Chad and put her arms around him. They had embraced.

"I love you," Chad said. He cried.

"I love you too, Chad." She had shed a few tears also, but hers were more controlled.

10

In mid-July, Winifred and Kira headed off to the Sand Wash Basin in Northwest Colorado. Kira hadn't flown on an airplane since she was very young, which she didn't remember. She loved the flight. Winifred had pointed out areas that the pilot had described while flying over them, at least those that were visible from where they were seated.

They had joined a tour group on the second day of their stay in the area of the basin. The guide had given an oral synopsis of the origin of the horses that everyone waited anxiously to see, as well as information on the estimated population of the Mustangs in various areas where they could be seen. Twenty minutes into the lecture a slight rumble could be heard. "What you hear, ladies and gentlemen, are the beloved Mustangs themselves," said Oscar, the tour guide. Seconds later a herd of at least forty horses were seen running at full speed.

A collection of 'aahs' were exclaimed amongst the group. "Look, Kira, look," said Winifred. "Aren't they wonderful?"

"Yes, Mommy—they are." Kira could see from the distance of around one-hundred yards that some of the horses were very big and some were small like babies. "They're beautiful, Mommy—and the little ones are so cute."

"Aren't they though," her mother answered. Just as those words were leaving Winifred's lips, the herd changed direction, heading away from the spectators. As all could see, the awesome creatures began to disappear before their eyes into a wooded area. Hoof beats could still be heard, but turned faint with each second, and then there was total silence. Winifred guessed that the spotting lasted a period of no more than a minute.

"Don't worry, folks," Oscar said. "They'll be back. You're welcome to stay for another hour while this tour is in session today." Oscar was a gruff looking man in his late fifties who wore khaki pants and a thin long-sleeved plaid button-down shirt. "If you see them again, it's very possible that they may be more or less in number. These great creatures were approximately two million in number over one hundred years ago and have unfortunately decreased to around twenty-five thousand here in the states. The running horses can be seen in numerous states including some eastern and south-eastern states, and are visible in the states of Wyoming, the Dakotas, Utah, and Montana—to name a few. Just sit tight for a while and there's a very good chance you'll see another herd shortly."

Much discussion was going on amongst the group of people. After ten minutes another herd began to show, only smaller in number. During this sighting, a spectacular thing had happened. Two large brown mares began playful bantering. They had stood and pranced on their hind legs, tapping their front hooves against one another. Another set of sounds from the people were heard, and this time, 'wow' could be heard distinctly.

"Oh, Mommy, look," Kira said while laughing.

"I know, darling. Isn't that amazing--and so cute?"

All were mesmerized. The small herd had begun to dissipate, and then disappear soon after. There were no more sightings the rest of the tour session.

Winifred and Kira had returned for two more tours within their week's stay and had seen several more Mustang sightings. It was decided before the trip out West that one week would have been a sufficient span of time. They had flown back to Missouri on a Wednesday. When they arrived, Winifred had relieved Sarah while sitting for Adrian. Adrian was taking a nap. She had told Sarah all about the wonderful journey that her daughter and she had experienced. Sarah was awestruck when she heard about the two prancing mares.

"I'm going to miss you, Winny," Sarah Morning said.

"I'll miss you too, Sarah. It's just something that I have to do. I'll come back at some point in time. I want you to know that you have been a blessing to the family. You're the best."

Sarah smiled. "I don't do half a job. I appreciate you saying so, honey." They had hugged and kissed one another on the cheek. As the faithful sitter was walking out the door, she looked back with tears in her eyes. "Bye, Winny."

"Goodbye, Sarah darling," Winifred answered.

The fright of leaving her family began to set in on Winifred's consciousness. She was having trouble dealing with the reality of it all. She had fought through the moments that she was experiencing without the use of her nerve pills and had many long walks with her children. Chad had not been exactly talkative during her last week with the family.

Winifred had planned to leave for Gatlinburg, Tennessee the following Saturday after her return home from Colorado. She wanted the whole family to be there when she left, which she knew to be only proper.

Saturday: 6am

"I love you, darlings so much--that I could eat you up," she told the children.

"I don't want you to go, Mommy," cried Adrian.

"My precious boy—I don't want to go, but I have to," she said as she hugged him tightly and kissed the top of his head. She looked up at Chad who had tears streaming down his face.

"Mommy—take me with you," Kira said as she too cried.

"Darling—I will come back and take you back with me for a while, but right now, I need to be alone." She kissed her daughter on the lips. "I'm not leaving forever, sillies." Winifred smiled, cried quietly, and then turned toward Chad. "Chad—I know this may seem crazy, but please try and understand," she pleaded.

"I know, Winny. I've come to grips with everything, but I still can't believe this is happening," he said.

She walked over and touched her husbands cheek with the palm of her hand and wiped away some of the tears. As she began to pull her hand away, he gently grabbed it and kissed it. "I love you, Chad. Perhaps things may change."

"I sure hope so. I want you to know that I will remain faithful even while you're gone." He smiled at her.

She returned a smile. "I appreciate that, Casanova." They both laughed. The family walked outside as Winifred walked to her car. "Bye darlings." She said no more. She got in her car and took one last glance at her children who were both crying and waving. She waved back in an up and down fluttering wave. She pulled out of the driveway not looking back. After driving a couple of blocks from home, she had pulled to the side of the road and put the car in park. Winifred cried hysterically. "Oh my God," she screamed to herself. The very thought of driving away from her children sent her into a horror that she couldn't bear to think about as a possibility. She sat and cried for more than five minutes when the tears began to subside. During the time that she sat in that spot, she had to convince herself that what she was doing was right no matter how ludicrous it may have seemed at that moment. She looked in her side view mirror to check the traffic, and finding it clear, put the car in drive and continued on her trip.

Winifred arrived in Pigeon Forge, a city outside of Gatlinburg, at 5:34pm, where she checked into a nice hotel. She had immediately fallen in love with the scenery as she could see the Smoky Mountains twenty-five miles from her destination. As soon as she walked into her room, she looked out the window at the scenery and myriad of extravagant business surroundings; she went to bed and slept all night until 5:30am.

Day one in Pigeon Forge found Winifred Palmer to be a very hungry visitor. She had gone to a very quaint restaurant suggested to her by the hotel desk clerk, where she had country ham, poached eggs, and buttermilk biscuits. She had thought that she had never eaten anything so delicious in her life. Winifred was a sucker for good food and complimented the chef, and on the contrary, she was a cook's worst nightmare if the taste was not to her liking. She was notorious for sending an item back three times or more if the food was not perfect. She had once told a waiter that a certain restaurant's biscuits and gravy tasted like chewed up peanuts. This comment had really made the cook mad. At that particular restaurant she simply only drank her coffee.

11

Time had passed at a moderate pace for Winifred. She had moved into
the city of Gatlinburg in a chalet. September had rolled around and she
had joined a local church. Through a church program, she signed up for
volunteer work to assist in visiting the elderly that could no longer make
it to church. Winifred found the work to be very rewarding. Martha
Williams was one of her contacts, who, after several visits, became a
friend to Winifred. Martha was a delightful and funny lady whose
husband had died years before. At the age of eighty-eight, Martha
could no longer get around without assistance but insisted on staying
in her home. Her only child, a daughter, had moved in with her to take
care of her.

When Martha had once mentioned to Winifred that one of her
favorite desserts was chess pie, Winifred told her that she made a chess
pie that was out of this world. She had baked Martha five chess pies
during a one month period. Martha had devoured the first piece of the
first pie in less than a minute and had expressed to Winifred that it 'was
to die for.' She had giggled and said 'better not say that too loud for the
Lord may be listening.' Her tongue-in-cheek humor made Winifred
smile.

To Winifred's dismay, the church had informed Winifred that
Martha had died in her sleep on September 30th. Winifred attended the
visitation and funeral services, and at the time, thought that this work
had begun to make her melancholy. This did not, however, deter her
from continuing her work with the church's group.

After returning home on that day, Winifred called to speak with
her children. Sarah had answered and had received the call with firm

gratitude. It was the second time that Winifred had called after her departure. The conversation was wonderful. She had spoken with both her daughter and son and was pleased with what she heard from them. Kira was getting straight A's in school and Adrian liked but wasn't really crazy about first grade, although he was receiving acceptable grades in most of his classes. Both of the children had expressed that they missed their mommy very much, and, in return, Winifred told them the same. She had explained that she wasn't ready to return home but would see them very soon. As she had told them this, she wasn't exactly sure what **soon** meant. Kira had told her that 'Daddy wasn't home yet', and that Sarah was getting them ready for showers. Winifred had asked about current updates such as how their dad was getting along with his business, what the weather was like in Missouri, and anything else that was new in Wilmington. She had also reiterated on how beautiful the Smoky Mountains were, and that she had hoped that the children could join her for a week or so at winter break. The conversation had ended with tears on both ends of the phone lines.

The first snow had come in the middle of November. Seven inches had fallen. Winifred had driven many miles up the Smoky Mountains National Park on numerous occasions, but when the snow had come, she was able to see the wonderful snow caps the farther she drove. Within the four months of her stay, she had hiked to many popular sites, some very high in the mountains, and she had still not seen all there was to see. She had become an employee of the Ski Mountain resort as a tram host and loved it. Heights were something that never bothered her much, but she had at first felt a bit of queasiness on her first trips in the cable-driven tram. Each trip had begun to excite her and pumped her adrenaline, which she found exhilarating.

Winifred realized that if her children visited it would have to wait until Christmas vacation for the school. She began to wonder if that would happen or if the trip may have to wait until spring. All that she knew was that she missed the kids and was beginning to reconsider her plan of staying in the mountains for an extended period of time.

Late November had come and Winifred made a decision to not allow the children to travel to Gatlinburg. Snow had reached a peak of eighteen inches during the month and she knew that the weather was not conducive for a visit from two small children, even if Chad had driven them. She had called the household and told them that a trip would have to wait until spring.

One early Saturday evening, Winifred had gone to a reputable bar and grill in downtown Gatlinburg. It had been months since she had let down her hair and gone out for a night on the town. She wanted to get something good to eat and have a few drinks. She had chosen a table near a window where it was still light enough to see the river from the mountains rush by the establishment. There was no wait for a table that night because of the weather, so she was seated promptly.

Soon after being seated, a waiter came to the table. "Good evening, Ma'am. How are you this evening?"

"I'm very fine, Sir. And yourself?" she asked.

"Never better, Ma'am. Thank you. My name is Carlos, and I will be your server this evening. Before ordering, would you like a drink and perhaps an appetizer?"

Winifred looked up at one of the most gorgeous men she had ever seen. He was most definitely of Hispanic origin with an accent that jumped out at her. She smiled dreamily at him. "Yes, Carlos. I sure would. I'll have a dry vodka martini, please—stirred, not shaken. I haven't had the chance to look at the menu."

"That's fine, Ma'am. May I suggest our famous Crab Rangoon, or perhaps the exquisite appetizer size Crawfish Etouffee? Of course--we also have that soup dish as an entrée.

"Oh—the Etouffee sounds great. I'll have that as a meal," she said quickly with a cute smile as she tapped the table top. "No appetizer then."

"Excellent, dear," he said as he gave a slight nod of his head. "I noticed you're the opposite of James Bond." He smiled at her.

"Pardon me, Carlos?"

"James Bond. He likes his martinis shaken, not stirred. And he also likes pearl onions and not olives. How about you? Are you an olive person?"

Winifred smiled at her waiter's amusing conversation. "Olives—please."

"Okay. I'll be right back with the driest martini the bartender can muster." Carlos quickly turned and walked away.

Winifred looked down at Carlos' rear end, as most women might do in a similar situation, or of course, men, if the tables were turned. *I didn't see a ring on his finger,* she thought. *Get that out of your head, Winifred.* She gave out a single breathy laugh as her head bobbed.

After two martinis, Carlos arrived at her table with three covered silver platters on a cart that looked to Winifred to be too much according to what she ordered. "Oh my—whatever can there be under those lids?" she asked.

He carefully sat the platters down in a circular fashion, the largest one being laid closest to Winifred, then a smaller platter to the right slightly behind the large one. A very small platter was placed behind the other two. He spoke as he removed the lids. "Well, Madam—here is the main entrée." He placed each lid on the cart as he removed them. "This is a generous helping of Cajun red beans and rice, and this is your wonderful garlic bread to dunk into the Etouffee sauce. Is there anything else I may get for you? Perhaps another drink?"

"Oh, dear no. Water only please. Thank you, Carlos."

"My pleasure, Ma'am. I'll be back shortly with your water and to see if the food is to your liking."

"I don't think there'll be a problem there."

"Very good, Madam." In a professional and considerate manner, he quickly left her so that she could begin eating her dinner.

Winifred sopped up the very last bit of sauce in her plate with her bread. All that was left were small bits of onions and celery. *God—do I feel like a pig. I hope Carlos didn't see me eating.* She laughed to herself. Carlos had approached her table.

"So—was the combination satisfying, Madam?" he asked.

"Oh—yes, Carlos. It was too much though. I guess I've never heard of a doggy bag."

He only waved his hand quickly--palm down as if to tell her that she was speaking nonsense. "I don't believe that gluttony has anything to do with your appetite, my dear. Here is your check. Just let me know when you're ready." He placed the pay booklet down on the table.

"I'm ready," she said quickly. She reached into her purse and carefully removed two fifty-dollar bills. "Here—and keep the change."

Carlos only shook his head. "No, Madam. I cannot accept that much. If you would please just look at your bill. I require only fifteen percent."

"I don't have to, Carlos. You were magnificent—and so very polite and charming."

"I appreciate you saying so, Ma'am—but I can't take advantage."

"I'm not that drunk, Carlos. My husband and I have always rewarded good service in restaurants. And please—call me Winifred. It's not that I don't appreciate your etiquette. I know your name--and you may surely call me by my name because I should be back."

Carlos looked to the ceiling. "Ma'am—I mean, Winifred. I usually wouldn't get personal—but—no—I can't say." He revealed a sheepish smile.

Winifred laughed. "What is it, Carlos?"

"Well—you see—I really have no life outside of my job. You had mentioned a husband."

Winifred's mind raced. "We're separated," she said quickly. "What's on your mind?"

"Winifred? May I repay you for this outrageously large tip by taking you to dinner? Any chance?"

"There's a huge chance, Carlos. I happen to be very much in need of companionship."

"Okay then—great. I'd better not dolly around."

Winifred opened the pay booklet and took the pen in her hand, wrote down her phone number on the bill and handed it to Carlos. "Call me," she said.

"Thank you, Winifred. I will. We--appreciate your business—and—I will speak with you soon." Carlos smiled, nodded, and walked away.

What are you doing, Winifred Palmer? She asked herself.

That evening, Winifred's stomach was doing somersaults. "Oh, God—that Etouffee is about to do me in," she said aloud. "Maybe I shouldn't have eaten all the beans and rice." She laid on her back in bed after taking some stomach medicine and a needed trip to the bathroom, and hoped for the best. She began to relax after about a half an hour and the nausea subsided. Winifred was quite elated that she didn't vomit. *I'm glad the food wasn't bad. It was just a bit rich and I ate too much.* She fell fast asleep.

The next day brought with it more snow. It was a day off from work and Winifred was pleased. She had done nothing except read and watch television. She also was doing a lot of thinking. She thought of her children and about Chad. She realized that she also missed her husband. *Have I been living in a selfish dream world?* She asked herself. *No,* she quickly decided. Winifred was proud of the decision she had made and the fact that she had the same bottle of nerve pills as when she left Wilmington. The last pill she had taken was shortly after driving from the house as her children and Chad waved goodbye. She had a slight mental break down that day on the side of the road and thought that a nerve pill was what she needed, and it proved to help. Since that day she had never been in such excellent physical shape and the thought of nerve pills seemed to be a thing of the past. She had also not had one indication of any anxiety. *This vacation was needed,* she thought.

At 12:34pm the telephone rang and she picked up. "Hello," she said.

"Hello, Winifred? Carlos Guerrero speaking. How are you?"

"Oh—hi, Carlos. It's nice to hear from you."

"It's very good to hear **your** voice," he answered.

Why does this guy have to be so charming and good looking? He's a distraction—but a good distraction. "I'm glad I'm alive today, Carlos," she said as she laughed.

"What do you mean? Wait—I'll tell you what you meant."

"Okay. I'm intrigued."

"The rich dinner made you sick to your stomach. Am I right?"

"You are correct, Sir. I didn't think I was going to make it without—you know."

"Refunding into the toilet?"

"Exactly."

"I should have warned you, but it's not necessarily a waiter's job to tell a customer how much to eat." He laughed. "I did the same thing myself once, and that one time was enough to teach me a lesson for life. You probably would have been better off with the appetizer."

"My thoughts exactly, Carlos. Well—the lesson has been learned."

"Good. I'm glad you're feeling better."

"Thank you."

"Is tonight too early for a dinner on me?"

"Funny you should mention—but yes. I think I'll hibernate today and have some soup and crackers later."

"I think that's a good idea. The snow should be dissipating soon. How's tomorrow sound? I have the next two days off."

"That sounds great. I have to work until four at the ski lodge. Hey. How would you like to catch a ride on the tram with me?"

"That is something I cannot do, my dear. You see—I'm afraid of heights."

Winifred laughed. "I'm so sorry, Carlos. It just struck me as funny. I can't eat rich food and you can't ride the sky."

"Ironic—aye?" He also laughed. "How about if I pick you up at your place at six?"

"Sounds super. I live at 1331 Peak Road."

"Ah. So lucky living so close to your work."

"Isn't it though?"

"Well—it's set then. I'll see you at six 'o clock tomorrow night—and I promise to go where there is a more bland food."

Winifred laughed. "Good idea. I'm not opposed to a steak."

"I know just the place. See you tomorrow."

"Okay, Carlos. I'm looking forward. Bye."

"Goodbye, dear."

Monday Night

"You look lovely, Winifred," Carlos said as he stood at the door of her chalet.

"Thank you, Carlos. You don't look too bad yourself," she said.

"Are you ready for the best steak in town?"

"Absolutely." She closed the door and walked out into the cold night. She allowed Carlos to take her arm in his. "Now—watch yourself going down these steps. I don't even know why they would have steps outside a mountain home. Isn't that an invitation for a good slip and fall?"

"I see what you mean, but the grade of the mountain has to allow for some elevation to the entrance of some homes. I always wear proper boots." He looked down and saw that Winifred also wore boots.

After descending the short section of steps, they walked to his S.U.V. and he opened the door for her. Winifred grabbed the handle above the door and pulled herself into the seat. "Thank you," she said.

"You're quite welcome." Carlos walked around and jumped into his seat. "Buckle up. I'm gonna try something unusual."

Winifred looked over and smiled at Carlos. "Oh—you are not. You're silly."

Carlos laughed. "So—are you ready for a steak that melts in your mouth?"

"You know it. Now—you know I'm very particular about my steak."

"I thought you might be. That's why I'm taking you to The Alamo Steakhouse and Saloon. The best in the county."

"Well—that sounds fantastic. I think I trust your judgment."

"I've lived here since I was fifteen. You're in good hands."

The front of the restaurant took Winifred's breath away. At the front of the establishment there was a brown foot bridge to the rear of the parking lot that stretched over the water. The mountain river glistened and rushed below the couple as they walked the bridge. As Winifred looked to the left she saw a wagon. "How cool is that?" she said as she pointed toward the wagon.

"Very cool I'd say."

The color of the building was beautiful—with sort of a burnt red awning that caped the steps to the entrance—maybe a little more maroon. The rest of the building was an off white with spare maroon designs that lightly decorated it. The word Alamo had shown over the top in curved fashion. "It kind of **looks** like The Alamo."

"I think they were going for that," Carlos answered.

Winifred requested a seat by the front window where the river could be seen. The grilled steak that she had put in her mouth was like nothing she'd ever experienced in taste. "Oh my God," she said. "This is unreal." She had usually taken her time eating but devoured the steak in minutes, and then began on her baked potato and vegetables.

"What did I tell you, girl?" Carlos took his time eating. He ate a couple of bites of the steak, and then a couple of bites of his sides. He had tried to choose his words carefully. "Okay, Winifred. If you don't mind my asking, what are you doing in the mountains, and what has carried you so far from home? You seem to be out of your normal elements." He sipped his beer.

"I knew this was coming," she said. "Do you want the short or long version?"

He smiled. "Whatever you are most comfortable with telling to a virtual stranger."

"I appreciate your honest question and your candor." She sighed. "My husband, Chad, had been unfaithful to me. I was also experiencing some anxiety problems that disappeared when I arrived here. My psychologist suggested that I take a vacation away from my problems. I had first taken my daughter with me to the west to see the wild Mustang horses, and then I decided to come here. I had never been to the Smokies, and thought that this was the type of solitude that I needed. Enough information?"

"Do you have other children? And please—let me know if I'm getting too personal."

"No—you're not. I do have two wonderful children that I have left in order to fix my brain, although—they had nothing to do with my leaving. It's just that—well—I couldn't very well drag them away from school and their father." At that point, Winifred stopped eating, and so did Carlos.

"I understand. It was either all or nothing. I mean—you had to make a choice no matter what sacrifices you had to make."

"You're reading this so well, Carlos. Other things than my husband that sent me away—and not all—was my inability to cope with my job, being fired from my job, and the circumstances that became a trickle-down effect with my job. This is becoming a long version—isn't it?"

"No. It doesn't have to be," Carlos said. "How about if we move on to small talk? You know. Where did you go to school, Carlos? That type of thing."

"Thanks, Carlos," she said, smiling. "No. I've been through hell, man. First—my husband goes out on me, then my top problem case client...sorry--I didn't tell you I was a social worker. She flies the coop with my help and all hell breaks loose. I'm sorry. This is too much for you."

"No. It's not too much for me, but I do sympathize. You have been through quite an ordeal. Perhaps you can somehow restore what you've lost?"

"How can I do that, Carlos?"

"That is something that you'll have to figure out on your own. I could in no way suggest anything."

"Brains as well as good looks. What do you say that we call it a night, Carlos? I'm very tired and I think I'll take a hike sometime tomorrow."

"Oh? Where? I'm quite the guide in this little mountain city."

"Thank you—but I'm making this a solo thing. There's a lot that I need to mull over. We may be able to make it another day."

"Whatever you say, Winifred. I know that you have things on your mind."

The drive home was pleasant and the conversation was also. Carlos pulled up in Winifred's steep driveway, left the vehicle running, and got out. He quickly went to the passenger side and opened the door for his date. He took her hand as she stepped down out of her seat. He walked her to the door and had mentioned something about the weather. They stood in a moment of silence. He didn't want to seem too eager and decided not to try and kiss her on their first date. He had also wondered if there would be another date.

"Thank you for a wonderful dinner and evening, Carlos," Winifred said as she smiled. She took the initiative and kissed him gently on the cheek. "Good night. You're a perfect gentleman."

"Good night, Winifred," he said. He turned and walked away. As he left, he had a suspicion that he would never see Winifred again.

The day was cold and breezy on the day that Winifred hiked up to the dome. She had spent at least a half an hour atop the memorable site and had done much thinking. As she had descended the dome, an overwhelming sense of surety had struck her consciousness. After all that she had been through, and all that she had experienced in her new life in the mountains, she made up her mind what was to be done. Winifred had been running away and she knew it then. She sat in her car and before starting the engine, she got out her cell phone and dialed a number. The call did not go through. "The reception is terrible here," she said aloud. The call would be made from her home.

Winifred sat on the couch in her chalet and dialed the number again from her land-line phone. She heard ringing. On the opposite end, a familiar voice answered. The voice was pleasing to her ears. The thought of Carlos Guerrero was not even a whisper into her present state of mind.

"Wine Emporium—Chad Palmer speaking. May I help you?"

"Chad. It's me."

"Winifred. Oh, Winny. What is going on, dear?"

"Chad—I want you here. Please come."

Chad had laughed a little before speaking. "Winifred—I'd love to. I have meetings tomorrow—but—oh hell—I'll be there. I'll call home and ask Sarah if she wouldn't mind staying at the house a few nights."

"Thank you, Chad. I miss you. I miss my babies."

"I miss you too, darling." Chad broke down and quietly cried. "I thought I'd never see you again."

"Get a pen and write down this address. You can be here tomorrow?"

"Yes I can. Shoot. What's the address?" He wrote as she gave it to him. Chad was elated.

After calling Chad, she called work and informed her manager that she had made plans to return to Missouri. The manager was sorry to hear that Winifred was leaving but gave her positive feedback just the same. After hanging up, she dialed another number that she found in the phone book.

"Hello."

"Hi, Carlos. How are you?"

"Fine, Winifred. Hi. How was your walk?"

"It was very nice. Carlos—I have to tell you something."

"Okay," he said. Carlos sensed that it wasn't necessarily going to be good news.

"I'm leaving, Carlos. I've decided that I've been running, and not that I didn't need this time to figure things out. I want my children back."

"I know that you do, Winifred."

"You know, Carlos? I believe that I have you to thank for my decision."

"Oh—the talk at the restaurant. I should have kept my mouth shut." He laughed.

"No, silly. You were very helpful. I know that you probably wanted to see me again, and I found you to be a joy. If it weren't for my priorities, I would feel the same as you. I just didn't want things to go too far. You understand."

"Yes. I absolutely do." Carlos decided to cut the conversation short. "You're a beautiful woman, Winifred, and your husband is a very lucky man. You take the best of care. Okay?"

"I will, and you do the same. I can say also that who ever snatches you up will have a gem."

"Thanks, dear. Bye."

"Goodbye, Carlos." That was it.

Wednesday

At 5:05pm, Winifred heard a knock. She opened the door to see her husband standing there. She held out her arms and Chad reached in as they hugged. They had kissed passionately. "It's cold out there, Chad," she said. "Please come in."

He stepped into her magnificent abode as she closed the door. "Before we talk, I have a little surprise. Do you have a cd player?"

"Yes—but just a portable."

"That'll do."

Chad inserted the cd into the player and pressed play. Winifred burst into tears when she heard the song playing. They instantly starting dancing close to each other to the sound of The Beatles song, *This Boy*. They danced for a quite a while as the cd played other songs familiar to them.

Wilmington, Missouri: December 29th
10:30am

Winifred's return home had not been quite the adjustment that she expected. Things seemed to be everything that she had remembered. Being with her children warmed her heart in such a way that she couldn't get over the outcome. As the family sat and watched a classic episode of *I Love Lucy*, the phone rang. Winifred picked up. Chad sat beside her.

"Hello," she said.

"Hello, Winny? It's Cynthia. I heard you were back and I just wanted to call. It's so good to hear your voice."

"Hi, Cynthia. How are you?" Winifred didn't hold the same feeling of hearing Cynthia's voice. It kind of brought back bad memories.

"I'm okay. Same ol', same ol'," Cynthia responded.

"I can imagine. What's up, Cynthia?"

Cynthia had detected a slight curtness in Winifred's voice. "Well—business goes on. I'm so wrapped up in my work that work is about it. One reason I'm calling, Winifred, aside from just saying hello, is that I would very much like to have you back. We have several holes to fill, and I realized after letting you go that you were the best worker that I had the pleasure of having. Is there a chance you would consider?"

Winifred laughed out loud and couldn't hold back. "Are you kidding me? You rake me through the coals and you live by your so-called protocol to protect your own self, and you have the nerve to even suggest that I would come back to you? That is rich, Cynthia." Winifred's face turned red as a beet.

Cynthia was shocked but not so much surprised at Winifred's words. "Winifred—I never meant anything personal about what I had to do. It was a business decision that I thought was ethical at the time. You were always a faithful employee and I appreciated you."

"Save it, Arnold. I'd rather work in fast food. Plus, I have a family to take care of. Bye bye." She slammed the phone down. She looked over at Chad with a big grin on her face. They both laughed hysterically. The children even laughed although not knowing why.

"Good one, honey," Chad said.

Long Ago in Winter: The Counterpart

By

Greg J. Grotius

Around one hundred years ago, the January day began as windy and warm. There was talk in the North-Western region of America that rain was expected and that temperatures were expected to drop. Rain did begin to fall around mid-morning. In fact, the rain was extremely heavy. Although the rainfall let up at some points during the day, it would come back in hard bursts intermittently, and then non-stop. The temperature did in fact begin to drop rapidly. Rain turned to snow toward late afternoon. Very large flakes would hit the ground and melt for the ground temperature was not cold enough for the snow to stick. Given the plunging temperature, the snow did stick around early evening. The freezing wind was ferocious, which had increased the propensity for sticking snow. The year was 1910.

The Cascade Mountains stood erect above the city of Delmore Washington. Deep snow had eventually built up on the caps and adjoining ridges of the mountain. It had been three days since the blizzard had begun and snow had still blown against the slabs of the icy drifts. There were no signs of the snowfall letting up. Three days had passed and temperatures had risen at a moderate rate, which was not unusual for these types of winter storms in certain regions of the country. The snow depth reached around 38 inches in the city below, and in the mountains some drifts were 80 or more. On the fourth day, the storm began to dissipate. It was approximately noon when warmer temperatures made the lower end of a mountain drift vulnerable to the weight of the mass of snow high above.

In Delmore, many citizens heard the rumbling crash of the avalanche before it struck the railway station. They only had time to say their prayers. For three of the city's inhabitants, prayers are exactly what they said. Emily Carden, a widower who lived in a very beautiful cabin in a wooded area very much near the target of what would soon be the destruction of the tragic onslaught, said a very short and direct prayer. "Lord, please allow me to do something extraordinary after this is over."

At just about the same time, Curtis and Jamie Woodland, ten and nine years of age, respectively, said their prayer. The children stayed at the railway station's housing for railroad personnel. Their mother had died years before, and their father worked as a railroad cargo foreman. He had trusted the children to be alone, as they had become quite responsible after the death of their mother. Curtis spoke for the both of them. "Please, God. Please. Allow us to survive this-- somehow." The children had faith. Their parents were very devout in their beliefs and instilled that faith in Curtis and Jamie. Seconds after all prayers were said, snow came crashing down upon the railway and close-by residential neighborhoods. There were approximately two hundred people that were engulfed in the deep snow. No one had seemed to survive the avalanche. The portion of the city that was hit the worst had fifty-foot drifts covering it.

No one could have guessed or ever dreamed that they were in danger. The mountain was always spoken of as the most beautiful feature that Delmore and surrounding cities had as their most scenic treasure. It was never suspected that what the mountain held and eventually released on that dreadful day would be responsible for so many deaths. Much was done by the city dwellers who survived to try and save the lives of people in the aftermath of the tragedy, but to no avail. The snow would stand still over the victims for weeks to come before it melted and revealed the carnage.

1

The children could barely see four feet in front of them. It was night time. Both Curtis and Jamie were bundled up in heavy winter clothing, hooded, with scarves. "Where's Daddy?" Jamie asked in a yelling voice. The wind muffled her words but Curtis heard his sister.

"I don't know, Jamie. I'm sure he's around somewhere," answered Curtis. He spoke with little belief that their father had survived. In the distance, Curtis saw a shimmering light which resembled only a faint orange dot in the blowing snow storm. "Do you see that, sis?"

"What?" Jamie said.

"That," he hollered as he pointed. "A light of some kind."

"Yes. Yes, I do," Jamie said after a few seconds of focusing with squinted eyes. They trudged through the deep snow toward the light in their boots and woolen pants. "Do you think it might be Daddy?" she asked.

"Could be. Don't know. Daddy has a lantern," Curtis said. The light slowly became more visible to the Woodland kids. "Can't be more than 50 yards away." Jamie did not hear her brother, and she didn't bother to ask what he had said. Both of the children had enough physical work in dealing with lifting their feet out of the deep snow with each set of steps taken. Conversation was decidedly not so important at that time. Soon the orange glow was surrounded by a misty, vertical silhouette. *Must be close*, Curtis thought. Since the range of visibility was so poor, he knew that the lantern and whomever held the lantern should be approaching soon. The children saw a moving, thin extension of the figure that had to be an arm waving. The siblings waved back in near unison. They heard a faint sound that resembled only a whine in the heavy wind. It looked then as if the person approaching was moving quicker as if running. The figure fell and the light became buried in the dark. The glow soon bobbed up and down, and the figure grew again. The children's anticipation was beyond reproach.

Finally, the light became a glimmering reality before the eyes of the children, as well as the hooded figure that carried it. "He-llo," yelled the unknown person.

"Hello," Curtis hollered in return. Curtis and Jamie saw long, flowing hair hanging from the hood of the coat, and they realized that it was a woman with the lantern. The three of them met.

"Oh my. You're just children," Emily Carden said. The children rushed up to her and hugged her tightly, as she did them. "Are you alone, my darlings?"

"We're looking for our daddy," said Jamie.

"Well—don't you worry. I'll do my best to help you find him, babies," Emily said. "I have a wonderful cabin that we can stay in tonight—and tomorrow we will search for your father. Come. Please trust me. My name is Emily."

Curtis spoke first. "Thank you, Ma'am. I'm Curtis—and this is my little sister, Jamie."

"Little," said Jamie. "You're only a year older than me, Curt." This comment made the lady smile.

"Alright, then," said Emily. "We can discuss your ages later. Right now—let's get out of this storm."

"Good idea, Emily. Let's go. And thank you so much," said Curtis.

"Thanks are not necessary. This is more than what anyone expected. Come. Let's go," said Emily. Emily, holding the lantern in her left hand, took the hand of Curtis; and Jamie, her brother's hand. The kids were eager to be led by this wonderful lady who appeared from practically nowhere.

Emily's large cabin was a sight for sore eyes. The door opened with some trouble since about two feet of snow was wedged against it. Emily immediately turned on the lights. The kids were in awe at the beauty of the well-kept, spacious home. It was a two-story cabin with a stairway going up the center. There were paintings of all sorts, two large curios with ornate nick knacks, a large kitchen to the back left, and a huge living area with comfortable-looking, decorative couches. "Have a seat, kids," Emily said. The children plopped down immediately. They both exclaimed explicitly over the comfort of the one couch in which they sat. "First, I think you need to sleep, darlings. Then—we can talk and maybe have some fun." The children nodded in agreement and laid down on the same couch. They were fast asleep, or something like sleep.

The kids arose to the sound of tinkering in the kitchen. "Children," Emily said. "It's time for a game." The children rubbed their eyes and stood. Emily appeared before them. Curtis noticed that Emily was a beautiful woman. She had long, brown curly hair and wore a lovely blue flowered house dress. The fire was roaring in the fireplace and everyone was comfortable. They played a quite extensive card game of Rummy. All had felt amazingly vital. At the break of dawn, they had all set out on a journey into the winter weather. They walked until they felt tired. They rested in the midst of trees and then continued. There was something that was missing in their daily routine that Curtis and Jamie hadn't figured out. It did not matter. They followed Emily in the search for their father. Curtis knew to some extent that the search was useless, but he allowed himself to be led regardless of his underlying suspicion.

"Where are we going"? asked Jamie.

"To find your father," said Emily.

"Shouldn't we have found him by now, Emily?" Curtis asked.

"It was a terrible storm, loves. We will find what we are looking for," said Emily. The walk through the snow seemed to last forever for the trio. Day turned to night, and rest turned to more walking. The lantern continued to light their way through the continuous search.

2

February, 1924

Daniel Dorwitz sat on the porch of his rural home at dusk. Friends and neighbors called him Cornwitz because of his past-time hobby. He was enjoying sips of his homemade corn liquor, especially during the *dark days* as he would call them, in reference to the alcohol prohibition that had started years before. He absorbed the radiance of the passing sunset, looking west from his country residence. A distant light appeared that seemed to burn bright orange in the darkened field. It was a tiny light from the point where Daniel observed. He guessed that the distance of the light was around a quarter mile away. It was a clear, early evening, cold but not freezing. He then distinctly saw figures walking. He took another sip. "By God—that's strange," he said quietly. He had no intention of seeking out the strangers. He only watched and scratched his balding gray-haired head. Daniel's wife had died 14 years prior along with his two children in the avalanche while he was on the road selling tractor parts that he had proficiently made in his work shop. He had no one with whom to share the strange vision that he saw that evening. Soon after, the figures were gone. The nearest neighbor was a third of a mile away. "Sure is peculiar," he said under his breath. "Wait'll the boys at the hardware hear about **this**."

"I think that liquor has gone to your brain, Cornwitz," said Gary Bovine. "What in the world would someone be doing with a lantern so early in the evening? And—in the middle of nowhere?"

"Hell if I know," Daniel said. "But the fact is—I really saw it. You can believe what you want, guys. Plus—I wasn't even drunk yet."

"Well—those corn squeezins of yours have a way of creepin' right up on ya," Ed Bowers said. "I know. I've drank enough of it." The five men surrounding all laughed.

"I second that," said Bill Tiekens. "The first batch you made of that stuff put me down after the first glass." A few snickers from the guys followed. Daniel grinned and let out a one-breath laugh.

"Oh well. I figured you guys might give me a hard time," Daniel said. The guys were all around the same age as Daniel. They never really knew Dorwitz to be a liar; but perhaps at the age of fifty, and the fact that he was virtually a lonely man, led some of them to believe he was trying to get attention. They were all still sad over the fact that he had lost his wife and children. Bill Tiekens himself lost his oldest son who worked at the Delmore Railroad. He was a victim of the heavy snow cover on that terrible day. "The fact is guys--I saw it. I saw it," he said as he shook his head up and down.

"Well—perhaps if you say you did, Daniel, you did," Bill said.

"Thank you, Bill," Daniel said with a smile. "Listen. I'll talk to you men later." They all said their good-byes and parted ways from the front of the hardware store.

The Beer Garden of 1936

Every summer since the end of the prohibition, Delmore had thrown a festive beer garden to raise money for the city's trust fund. The Great Depression had taken a toll on the region's farming and economy as a whole. Tens of thousands of men had lost their jobs throughout the state of Washington. As the state began to get back on its feet, there was much in the way of fund raising to help the economy. The Delmore Beer Garden was a favorite event even among numerous neighboring cities. People would travel many miles to attend. The event was always held on the second Saturday in September.

Elmer Gould had spun the money wheel in hopes of winning the jackpot. The cost of spinning the wheel was a dime, and there was twenty-three dollars in the pot. "Number three," yelled Richard, the barker. Elmer had won the pot. That was his fifth time spinning.

"Thank you, God," Elmer screamed. "I've won."

"Congratulations to Mr. Gould for a fine winning," remarked the barker. "There you go, Sir." He handed Elmer the bag of dimes and quarters.

"Thank you, Rich," said Elmer. He walked away smiling, getting many pats on the back. He held his winnings in one hand and a large cup of beer in the other.

"Well. There's the man of the night," hollered Chris Johnson from behind.

Elmer turned around. "Hey, Chris. How are ya?" Elmer asked, smiling. They gave each other buddy hugs. They had known one another for the better part of thirty-four years, going to the same grade school and high school.

"Good. Good," Chris said. "I just heard you won the big money."

"Oh, yeah. This is gonna feed the family well this week." The two men stood at the foot of the drive where the exit from the beer garden began. "Are ya leavin' already?"

"No. No. I've just gotten started." Chris took a huge swig of beer.

"Well—I guess I can stick around a little while longer. Just hold on a minute--will ya? Let me stick the winnings in my car."

"I'm not moving."

Elmer saw something out of the corner of his eye that looked like a shadow moving through the parking lot. "Did you see that?"

"See what?" Chris asked

"There. Down by the lower row of cars. There it is again. Some people walking."

Chris squinted his eyes and looked, but he saw nothing. "I don't see anyone. Maybe some folks are just arriving, but I don't see em, Elmer."

"Hmmm," said Elmer. "Oh well. I'll be right back."

"I'll be here," said Chris.

Elmer walked down to the second row of cars nearest the pavilion where he had parked. He was approaching his automobile when he saw a woman with two young children walking toward him. "Hello," he said. She was holding a lantern. The woman looked directly into his eyes.

"Hello, Sir," she said. "Do you have any idea where the railroad is from here?"

He stood right in front of her and the two children. He examined all three of them closely before he spoke. She was pale and so were the children. She wore a hooded coat as did the children. "I--I believe you're a little too far west, Ma'am. The railroad is about a mile east of here."

The children looked up with faint smiles. Their demeanor, as well as the woman's, was tired. "Thank you, Sir. You've been a great help." She turned and walked away, and the children followed.

Elmer stared at what seemed to be more than a strange apparition. He watched until the three of them were about twenty paces away. His attention to the strangers was interrupted by a yell.

"Hey. Elmer. What are you doing?" Chris yelled. Elmer craned his head back to look toward Chris.

He didn't say anything back. He turned around again to see only a light dissipating and then disappearing into nothingness. Black was all that he could see. Elmer was shaken inside. Sweat streamed down his cheeks. He shook his head as if to wake himself up. He collected his thoughts and thought of his direction and proceeded to throw the money bag on the floorboard of his car. After taking a deep breath, he turned and headed back to the pavilion but began to feel light headed. *It's okay, Elmer,* he told himself. *Were they---were they real?* He kept on his direction toward Chris and the beer garden. He reached Chris. "Let's have a drink, Chris."

Chris observed Elmer's face, which looked pale. "What's wrong, Elmer?"

"Nothing. Nothing at all. Let's get drunk." Elmer feigned a smile.

"Alright. Okay. Let's," said Chris. Chris was still concerned with Elmer's demeanor but decided to let it go for the time being.

Chris didn't see a thing. He looked where I told him to look but I'm the only one to see it. And I saw them up close--and she—the woman, talked to me, and I spoke with her. Elmer was bending his mind in thought. He believed what he had seen but didn't believe it in reality. As the two friends sat at a long table, Chris couldn't help notice that Elmer was virtually speechless. He would comment with a 'yeah' or a 'no' from time to time when he asked Elmer something. After drinking a few beers, Elmer spoke. "Did you see them, Chris?" Elmer looked into Chris' eyes.

"See who, Elmer?"

"The woman. The children. Couldn't you see them?"

"No. Is this about the shadows? The people walking?"

"Yes."

"I told you at first, Elmer. I didn't see anyone."

"Well. I thought that you may have seen me talking to the woman."

"No. I didn't, my friend. Are you okay, Elmer?"

"No. I'm not. I'm not okay at all. I think we need something stronger than beer." Elmer half grinned.

Chris looked at Elmer seriously. "Elmer. I think I need to get you home."

"Yeah. Please. Get me out of here," Elmer said with no objection.

"Alright then. We need to grab your money out of the car. You can come and get your car tomorrow. Elmer had forgotten all about the money. He had forgotten about everything that happened that night. All that he could remember was that lady and those kids.

'Those ghosts'? Elmer asked himself.

Weeks had gone by. Elmer hadn't told anyone else except Chris about what happened at the beer garden. The night of the beer garden he had very troubling sleep. He had dreamed of the woman. It was a dream that was vivid. The woman spoke to him. 'We're looking for their father,' she had said. 'I do believe we're getting close to finding out about him. I have a feeling he's not alive.' The children were not in the dream. Only the woman. He had tried to speak to her in the dream but his words only came out garbled. He thought that he was trying to tell her that everything would work out. He did notice that her face was not pale but green. He had awakened in cold sweats and was terrified. It was around 5:00 a.m., and he decided not to go back to bed.

On week seven after the incident, Elmer broke down and decided to tell his wife, Claudia, what he experienced. She was very attentive as he spoke to her. After explaining what had happened, his beautiful blonde-haired, blue-eyed wife said "I believe you, Elmer. There are things that happen in this world that can't be explained." Elmer sobbed and hugged her tightly.

"Thank you, darling. Thank you," he said.

Months had passed and Elmer had regained his composure. To Elmer, the night of the ghostly visit became somehow immaterial and useless. For the sake of his sanity, this was a good thing. He had even blocked out the incident almost entirely from his mind; but every once in a while, a dream would remind him. As he had pushed the incident away as immaterial to his life, the notion that it was useless was, in reality, far from the truth.

Many years had passed and Elmer Gould had died of a heart attack in his sleep at the age of 58. He had left behind his wife and three grown children in the year 1954. His wife, Claudia, was talking with their children after the funeral. Jane, age 32, Brandon, 29, who were both married, and Kyle, 25, who was not yet married, had stayed with their mother on that night. In the course of the evening, many memories were shared amongst the Gould family about the husband and father whom they all had dearly loved. The spouses of Jane and Brandon had also joined in on the reminiscing of the man that had left this world so unexpectedly. They had all drank several libations to help soothe the suffering of that day. At the peak of the evening, Claudia Gould told the story that her husband was so reluctant to talk about throughout his life. She told them about the beer garden and Elmer's most unusual experience. All present were mesmerized by what they heard. Questions and inquiries were directed at Mrs. Gould, of which she could only speculate in order to provide answers. The night had ended in deep slumber.

3

"We're getting close, children. I know we are," said Emily Carden. The three of them were still walking through snow.

"How long have we been walking, Miss Emily?" asked Curtis Woodland.

"I'm not sure anymore, kids. I do know that there'll be an answer just around the corner."

"What do you mean, Emily?" asked Jamie, who walked forthright behind her brother and Miss Carden. "I'm tired."

"I know you are, my darling--and so am I. I believe that just before the avalanche, God had assured me that all things would be taken care of. I prayed to him."

"You too?" asked Curtis.

"What, Curtis?" asked Emily.

"We—I also prayed when I heard the thunder from the mountains. We prayed to survive whatever was happening to us."

Things began to fall into place for Emily. *We were meant to be together,* Emily thought. *Whatever spiritual force is guiding us is because of our prayers before the snow covered Delmore. But when does this end?*

"That man was nice. The man that gave us directions to the railroad?" said Jamie.

"Yes. Yes he was," said Emily.

"But why did he look at us so scared, Emily?" asked Curtis.

Emily's mental faculties froze at that question. She did not know how to answer. She had also noticed the man to be somewhat incoherent in their meeting. She felt that she must answer quickly. Something was distant in the man's demeanor. "He—he must have had to think about the direction for a moment. I think he had been drinking." That was the best that she could come up with to pacify the children. Emily had also sensed that her answer could very well be true.

"Oh. I guess so," said Curtis. The three walked on.

A flash came into Emily's mind. The flash was sort of a picture. The picture was a cement wall in front of them. *What is this wall?* Emily asked herself. Aside from the unsure journey in which they embarked upon, she felt that there was an answer in the near future.

4

November, 1977

Kyle Gould had just turned 48 years of age. He had gotten off of work from the saw mill on a quite frigid day in late November. He and his friend and co-worker, James Browning, had gone to the usual tavern that they had frequented on most Fridays in Delmore to partake in a few beers. Both of the men had families, so they didn't try to get drunk but just a little numb from the day's hard work. It was around 5:45 p.m. when Kyle had mentioned that they had better get home.

"Yep. The wife'll have a cow if I stumble in at 7:00," said James. They stood and proceeded out the door, saying their goodbyes to the bartender and some of the towns' folk. The night darkness was already upon them as they reached their cars that sat side by side in the parking lot. "Well—see you Monday, Kyle."

"Do I really have to?" asked Kyle. They both laughed.

"Yes. You really have to. Unless you want to live in poverty this Christmas," James said.

"Heh. See ya Monday. Be careful driving home, you drunk," said Kyle.

"Look who's talking," said James. They both got in their cars and turned the key.

Kyle's car, a beautiful, classic shiny green '69 GT Torino, had some trouble turning over but finally did. He rolled down his driver-side window as James rolled down his passenger side. "Gotta get that carb fixed."

"Tell me about it. What? It's been like that for about a year?"

144

"I know—I know," Kyle said. "I'll see ya."

"See ya, buddy." Kyle backed out first and put the car in drive. A few seconds later, James did the same.

Kyle turned right from the parking lot onto Mill Road. James had followed. They would go in the same direction until the road forked where Kyle would stay to the right and James, left. Kyle was looking momentarily down into the valley to his left as he heard James' car skid behind him, then looked ahead. "What the..?" Kyle exclaimed as he slammed on his breaks. Kyle shook his head back and forth. "No. This can't be," he said aloud. He stared at the three people crossing the street and didn't take his eyes off of them. He saw that it was a lady and two children who were wearing heavy winter clothing. The lady held a lantern. They seemed to be unaware of the car that nearly ran over them, as they were only around twenty feet in front of Kyle's vehicle. The woman and children walked down into the valley off the left side of the road and soon disappeared down the hill from Kyle's field of vision. He could still see a glow from the lantern for a short time. He put the Ford in park, jumped out of the car, and ran to the edge of the hill. "Hello," he yelled. He could still see the glow of the lantern but could barely make out the figures that walked. "Are you trying to get yourselves killed?" There was no response from the people walking. Kyle's mind flashed back to the story that his mother told him and his siblings. "This just can't be," Kyle said. "That was forty-something damn years ago."

"What the hell is going on?" yelled James. Kyle turned around.

"I--I don't know. Those people. They walked right in front of me."

"I know that," James said. "I think I saw them before you did. What the hell were you looking at besides the road."

"Well—I just looked down to the left quickly—and--I--don't know. They just appeared all of a sudden." Kyle thought for a moment. "You? You saw them too?"

"Yes, I saw them. But it's like you said. They just sort of appeared from nowhere," James answered.

"James. Pull back in," Kyle said.

"What?" James asked.

"Pull back into the lot. I have to tell you something."

"Okay." James got in his car as did Kyle. Both men entered the lot, parked, and shut off their engines. Kyle got out first, then James. They both leaned against the cars and faced each other.

"James. This is gonna sound crazy," Kyle said.

James raised his right eyebrow and made the corner of his mouth crooked. "Well—what in the world did we see, Kyle?"

Kyle took a deep breath. "Okay. Okay. Those people we saw. I think..." He hesitated. "Back in the fifties—after my dad died—we stayed at Mom's house the night after the funeral. Before we all hit the sack, she told us this story. You see?... I don't believe this!" Kyle grinned and shook his head again.

"What, Kyle? What?" James asked insistently.

"Dad was at the annual beer garden in '36. He was walking to his car. He had seen some shadows before he went to the car. His friend was waiting for him at the pavilion. Before he got to his car—there they were. The woman and children. The woman held a lantern. And.."

"Are you saying the same woman and children?"

"Yes. I think so. Just let me finish." James threw up his hands. "Okay. So anyway—the woman talked to him. She asked him where the railroad was, and he told her. Something tells me, James, that this is the same woman—and children that we saw. I feel it in my gut. She carried the lantern tonight. The whole story gels. I mean—it doesn't make a lick of sense that she's still around, but something in my heart tells me they are the same visitors. You see—Dad's friend didn't see a thing. Only Dad. This led me and my family to believe that they were ghosts."

"I don't believe this is coming out of my mouth, but yes. Yes I do. Ya see, Kyle. I found out a long time ago as a child that strange things happen in this world that are not of this world anymore. Our house was haunted."

"Really?" said Kyle. "Oh, thank you. That's great." He smiled. "Not that your house was haunted but that you believe me. What happened in your house?"

"Well—we never really saw anything, except that the bathroom light would turn on and off by itself. The light switch moved too. There was banging on the wall, something seemed to walk up and down the stairs…, and one night it sounded like someone hit the house so hard that it could have made a hole in the bricks. We got tired of the occurrences, and my dad sold the house. Yep. I believe you. Creepy shit about that woman."

"I've got to tell my sister and brother when I get the chance—but how do I go about it? It'll freak them out."

"You'll get up the courage—and you'll have to choose the right words to describe it. Hell—just tell 'em what happened."

"I guess so. I wish that Mom was still around, bless her soul. But this news might have been too much of a shock to an old lady. We gotta get. Please—keep this under your hat for now. You can tell your wife if you want, but make sure she doesn't spread the word."

"If I do tell her, she'll keep her mouth shut—or else." James laughed.

"You nut. You'd never touch her," Kyle said.

"I'm more afraid of her than she is of me." Both men smiled, shook hands, said their goodbyes, and left for home.

Kyle Gould was filled with adrenalin. He couldn't wait to tell his wife, for she had already known about the incident that happened forty-one years before. As it turns out, she was totally supportive of all Kyle had to tell her.

4

Present Day Delmore

Lorelei McNeill, a lovely dark-haired woman with an olive complexion who looked more Native American than her Irish ancestry had lent itself, sat at her desk at the Delmore Daily Press. It was 4:30 in the afternoon, and she was tired. She yawned big and wide. "Oh, my," she said quietly. *Do I love my job or not?*. Lorelei was lead journalist at the newspaper and had been for the past ten years. She was a very good writer, but she thought that she was still not working at her full potential. *Am I a dreamer in this Podunk little burg called Delmore?* she asked herself. She had worked very hard at her job, but she always wanted more of a challenge in her life. Ms. McNeill graduated with honors at the second top of her class from USC. Aside from her expertise in journalism, Lorelei was an historian. She had considered making her choice of college majors either in history or anthropology but believed that those disciplines would turn out to be non-lucrative in regard to finding work. Her personal love was past civilizations, but she was very intrigued by major events that changed societies. She was not interested so much in the vein of wars that made differences in the growth of nations but more in natural events that sculpted a given territory's civil persona. The ancient Egyptian civilization mesmerized her. The construction of the pyramids was still a mystery to her, yet she went through pain-staking research to try and figure out how the Great Pyramid was built. She had almost written an essay for her World Civilizations class on the aforementioned study but had come up with a hand full of nothing to back up her speculations. Easter Island, the island of the huge concrete heads that is famous for its undetermined explanation of not only how the heads were built but, more importantly, how they were transported, also interested her to no end, which also led her to a dead end in her studies.

Will I always be a Miss or Ms.? Lorelei asked herself on this early December day. *32 years old and no prospects of marriage.* She knew that her current job was killing her social life. She had had many dates but all turned out to be disasters. She stood up from her desk and went to retrieve her coat to leave for the day. There was a winter storm watch in effect which depressed her even more. It was Friday and she welcomed the weekend, being that she usually didn't work weekends. She did, however, take her work home with her by always looking for information on the region's current events. Lorelei began to despise current events. When she had left the building, cold wind blew her long, dark hair around to the point of virtually stunting her sight on the way to her car. As she drove home, the blowing tree branches suddenly struck her as ominous, and not only in the sense of an impending storm. The weather had triggered a deep interest in the back of her mind that lent itself to a memory, but she couldn't put a finger on it. She quickly dismissed the thought for the fact that all she wanted to do was to go home to her dog and cat, snuggle up on the couch, and perhaps watch a movie if she could stay awake.

Lorelei watched *Sleepless in Seattle,* her favorite movie that she had seen countless times until her eyelids got heavy. It was 7:00. A feeling stirred in her subconscious which didn't clarify itself to her until early the following morning. Her eyes opened at 6 a.m. on Saturday. She thought about what she couldn't remember the day before. *Sleepless in Seattle,* she thought. *Washington. The Rain State.* She smiled dreamily. She often slept on the couch, especially on Friday evenings after a week of *hell work* as she referred to it. Her eyes popped open wide. The memory struck her intensely. *Winter in Washington,* she thought. *Why did I never think of this before? I live in the city of the most devastating avalanche in the known history of America.* She sat up. She quickly got up and fixed her strong morning coffee, then went to the computer and got on the internet. She typed in her search: **Delmore Avalanche**. The number of sites that contained information were numerous; but being the great researcher that she was, she sought out the most official site available. She had clicked on the link named "washingtonavalanche. com." As she perused the information, she had seen that over 200 people had lost their lives, and that the brunt of the snow cover had hit the railroad first. Lorelei left the computer to get her coffee, then returned.

On that same website, there was a press release from the very newspaper where she worked dated January 15, 1910, as follows:

"DELMORE DAILY PRESS

HORRIFIC AVALANCHE DEVASTATES CITY OF DELMORE

By Richard Brahams

In the midst of what had been considered just an unusually warm day in January, the Delmore residents came to realize within several days that tragedy had befallen their quiet small town in North Central Washington. It is suspected that over two-hundred souls are still buried in the snow stretching from Delmore's Railways to a quarter of a mile outside the worst hit area. If there is any upside to this terrible unforeseen avalanche is the fact that over 9, 000 citizens were unscathed by the natural phenomenon.

On January 5, reports of rain and falling temperatures were expected, which seemed to be, according to Chief Weather expert, Jeremy Spain, as "somewhat normal seasonal conditions given the mid-winter processes in this part of the country." How far down the temperatures were expected to fall in such a short time frame was, however, not known, and neither was the fact that precipitation was expected to continue for so long after the start of the first drops of rain. It had been reported a day before the 14th of January that railway cargo cars were stuck in snow. The engineer and all workers had to walk back to the station. On that ominous day, warmer temperatures began to give some hope to the railroad employees and citizens of Delmore even though snow had continued to fall.

"It was the most terrible thing for me to realize that when I heard this roar just outside while I was at work that my 10-year-old daughter was probably out playing in the snow, and that my wife and child could be in danger," said Brian Cole, an employee at Delmore Mills. "I had never been near anything as horrible as an avalanche, so I didn't know what one sounded like, but I knew something awful was happening. It sounded like the crashing of a thousand trains. I remember covering up my ears. But I thank God that my family is still alive," Cole had said as tears streamed down his face.

The forecast for our area remains favorable for clearing conditions in the aftermath of the avalanche. What remains is the desolate venture in finding and counting the victims that have left this world in such an untimely manner. We should pray for those who are gone, and most importantly, for those who were left behind to suffer the loss of their loved ones.

For the hope and sake of Delmore, I am sure that this type of unprecedented event should cast out notions that we will be in danger in this magnitude for decades or perhaps centuries to come. Of course, we should all realize that our future destiny is in the hands of God, with whom this country is depended upon to protect us at His will.

Rescue missions will begin as soon as lighter weather conditions prevail. I am sure that this will be in the next day or two. There are already some farmers and excavation businesses that have begun to plow through the deep snow in order to penetrate the most affected areas. Further information will be provided daily on the progress of the city's integrated mission. Words cannot describe an explanation for this unforeseen tragedy so I will leave the citizens with this thought. If God sees fit to provide solace to this heartbroken community, we all ask that He makes the mending as painless as possible."

Lorelei sat with her right hand pushed upward against her cheek. A tear ran down the same cheek. "Hmm. Not bad writing for that time period," she said. *It's been a little over a century since it happened,* she thought. *What angle can I use besides rehashing the event of the great state of Washington? Is there anyone still alive from 1910? I kind of doubt it, but people do tend to surprise us now and again.* Lorelei began to get ready to go to the library. She had still loved to go through traditional channels to do her research. Computer navigation sometimes irritated her to no end. She quickly had planned to go through the Delmore Archives at the North Branch Library. *They should have most of the information I need to get started.* She had still pondered on the angle that she would use for her article. A light turned on in her mind. *I will write a direct inquiry asking those citizens who may be past the age of 100 or younger to come forward so that she can interview them. Even though they may not remember the tragedy, perhaps they will recall stories from their families or acquaintances.*

She had put her plan for the library on hold to write the inquiry. Lorelei typed:

"INQUIRY FOR THE SENIOR CITIZENS OF DELMORE

By Lorelei McNeill

The intention behind this inquiry is based upon a future article that I intend on writing within a couple of weeks. It would be my honor to speak with any elderly citizens of Delmore who have lived in this community their entire lives. The subject that I wish to discuss with all who are willing to participate is of a somewhat poignant matter in the history of this city.

If any of you are anywhere near the age of 105, you would be my most sought after interviewee. However, if you have lived a long life and are between the ages of 75 and 100, I would most graciously love to interview you as well. The aforementioned subject matter concerns the Great Avalanche of 1910. The avalanche, being a decidedly dark event in the history of Delmore, I would understand anyone's apprehension in discussing your memories with me. Rest assured that any information you can provide to me will be kept in strict confidence until you decide what you are willing to share with the community. My purpose is to help our community understand and appreciate how safe they are in these modern times, and to also personally commemorate those who had lost their lives and devote sincere thoughts for surviving family members and friends of the victims.

Thank you in advance for your consideration of the possibility of allowing me to interview you. You may contact me by writing to:

Senior Journalist
Delmore Daily Press
1410 Squire Drive
Delmore, Washington 98045"

Lorelei printed out her inquiry and headed directly to the office. She had first thought of forwarding it to her office email but decided to try and get it finalized, authorized, and printed in the Sunday release. *The library would have to wait,* she thought.

5

The 83 year old man picked the Sunday paper up off the front porch, went in to the living room and sat. He sipped his hot coffee and set the cup back down on a side table. "Let's see here," he said to himself. The headline about the cost of living convinced him to look farther down the front page. "Things haven't changed much in the high cost of living. Doesn't interest me in the least." He then read a short article about an accident on Route 3. No one was severely injured in a two-car collision. He turned the page and zipped through the editorials. *Don't know why I get the paper anymore,* he thought. *Delmore's as boring as ever.* He glanced at the obituaries and saw that he didn't know any of the deceased. The man put his glasses on because his eyes began to hurt and the words began to blur. After shuffling forward to the sports section and seeing that the *Supersonics* lost another one, he backtracked to the editorials. He read the headline of a very small article entitled *INQUIRY FOR THE SENIOR CITIZENS OF DELMORE*. He raised his eyebrows and read the article. "Hmm," the old man said. He looked at the clock. It was 8:05am. "Doubtful Lorelei is at the paper this early, and on a Sunday," he said. His assumption was correct.

Monday Morning

The old man called the paper at around 8:00. "Delmore Daily, Josh Spangler speaking. May I help you?"

"Yes. May I speak with Lorelei McNeill, please?"

154

"One moment, sir. I believe that she is in." Josh transferred the call.

"Lorelei McNeill. How may I help you?"

"Ms. McNeill? Good morning. I had read your inquiry yesterday."

"Yes, sir."

"I believe that I'd like to talk to you, Ma'am."

"Oh—that would be wonderful, sir. May I have your name, please?"

"Well—first I'd like to mention that I don't know much about the avalanche except what I'd heard from my father and in literature I'd read at the library."

"Well—that's okay. That is why I had placed such a span of age groups in the article. When would you like to come in and talk?"

"At your earliest convenience, Ms. McNeill. I really don't have much to do."

"Okay then…Let's see. How does 10:00 sound?"

"10 is fine."

"Alright, then. I'm very glad that you called, Mr…." She laughed lightly.

"I'm sorry. Gould is the name. Kyle Gould."

"Thank you, Mr. Gould. See you at 10 then."

"Thank you, Ms. McNeill. Bye." Kyle Gould hung up the phone. At that time, Kyle had no idea how he would conduct his side of the interview. He was sure that Ms. McNeill would ask the appropriate questions to help. Kyle's wife had died of cancer two years prior. He had two children, a boy and a girl, who were both in their fifties. They lived in Seattle. His friend, James Browning, was still alive. He couldn't wait to tell him about the interview. Kyle was lonely. He wanted to tell his story about the ghosts. He wasn't sure how he would work in that information. All of those years, ever since he heard that his dad had seen the ghosts, the story reminded him of winter. Since the ghosts were wearing winter clothing, it somehow triggered a notion that the ghosts had something to do with the avalanche. He didn't know why. Then, on that eerie night that **he** saw the vision, he was convinced that these were somehow people that died during the winter.

THE INTERVIEW OF KYLE GOULD

"Good morning, Mr. Gould. How are you?" asked Lorelei.

"I'm fine, Ms. Gould. And yourself?" Kyle responded.

"Please. Call me Lorelei, Kyle."

"Of course. Thank you Ms.---I mean—Lorelei," Kyle said. He smiled and so did Lorelei. Kyle was kind of nervous.

"Just relax, Kyle. This should be just as casual as talking to a neighbor. Where were you born, Kyle?"

"Here. Right here in Delmore in 1930," said Kyle.

"I see. So—twenty years after the avalanche."

"Yes, ma'am."

"Did you, by any chance, Kyle, know anyone who perished in the avalanche?"

"As a matter of fact I did. They were on my mother's side. My uncle—he worked at the railroad, and my nephew and niece."

"I'm sorry. What were their names?"

"David Woodland was my uncle. The children were Curtis and Jamie. I don't remember the ages when they died."

"That's fine, Kyle. You've helped me already—and more than you know. Do you know anything about your aunt, Mrs. Woodland?"

"I believe that she had died when the children were young. That's what my mom told me."

"I see. Were the children left alone at home?"

"I guess so. I believe that they stayed in what was called railroad housing—for the families of some of the workers. I guess that since the, well—my aunt was gone, Uncle David had no choice."

Lorelei was writing in her notebook as Kyle spoke to her. She looked up at Kyle. "Is there anything else, Kyle, that you can tell me about the avalanche—or your family that you feel that I may need to know?"

Kyle hesitated. "I don't think so, Ms.—I mean Lorelei. That sure is a pretty name. You're pretty too."

"Thank you, Kyle. Well—if there's nothing else..." Kyle interrupted her.

"Well actually—there is something else that I'd like to share with you. I'm not sure that it has anything to do with the avalanche or not, but—it's quite a story—and a bit creepy."

"My. That sounds intriguing. What is it, Kyle?" She looked at Kyle's face closely. He looked as though he was in some kind of deep—emotional strain. "Are you okay, Mr. Gould?" she asked.

Kyle left his little trance behind. "Yes. Oh, yes. I'm fine, Lorelei. It's just that..." He broke down in a brief cry.

"There, there," Lorelei said as she stood and gently patted Kyle's back. "What in the world is it?"

He quickly answered as he looked up at her. "I don't know," he said. His expression was that of desperation. "You see, Lorelei, it had started with my father." He had told Lorelei the whole story of the visitors that had seemed to walk the earth forever. As he spoke, he didn't miss a beat. He remembered everything so clearly as if it were yesterday. He told her of **his** experience many years later. "..and so anyway—that's my story."

Lorelei did not quit writing the entire time that Kyle spoke. She was a professional, so she was able to look at him in the eyes while she wrote from time to time. "That is definitely a strange story, Kyle." She smiled.

Kyle let out relieved laughter. "You can say that again."

"Interesting, Mr. Gould. Very interesting indeed. Is there anything else you'd like to tell me?"

"As a matter of fact, there is. The way that the visitors were dressed— somehow leads me to believe that they may have been victims of the avalanche. I don't know. That may be reaching the matter a bit."

"Not at all. You could be very well correct. I must say that I have always based my research on facts. I never considered supernatural occurrences as note-worthy information in my studies…"

"So, you think my story is useless?"

"I wouldn't say that, Kyle. It is definitely food for thought. I can say in pure honesty that I believe everything that you have told me. I have a feeling about you. I've always had a gift of intuition. The supernatural has always interested me, but I never had time to research it. I am going to dabble in it now. Thank you for your time, sir."

Kyle knew that she was done interviewing him. He stood. "Thank you, Lorelei. It has been a pleasure meeting you."

She held out her hand to shake his. "The pleasure has been mine, Kyle." He had felt the softness of her skin and had felt smitten. "Let's keep in touch, Mr Gould. Okay?"

"Okay," he said. The old gray-haired man walked out the door. "Goodbye."

"Bye, Kyle. I'll talk to you soon," she said.

"Alright."

Lorelei closed the door to her office. "Well I'll be," she said aloud. "Good first interview." Her next task that she had planned was to head to the library to try and find a list of the deceased from the avalanche. She got on her coat, and with a small briefcase in hand, left the building into the gray and cold day. The sky was spitting snow as she got into her red VW Jetta. She turned the radio on and had caught the middle of a weather forecast.

"Again. The National Weather Service has issued a severe winter storm warning for some areas of Northern Washington. Seattle, Delmore, Mt. Vernon, Mt. Rainier, and Bellingham are all possible areas that are subject to this storm front. There is a strong storm front ranging from Northern Montana to the southwest regions of Alaska. The front is moving in a westward fashion that is sure to hit the state of Washington no later than midnight tonight. The forecast calls for at least 6-8 inches of snow with blizzard-like conditions since the wind is expected to reach around 50 to 60 miles per hour at its peak. Stay tuned to KSAR for further updates."

Lorelei turned the radio off. "Great," she said. "I like snow—but not that much." She drove through the windy day with new cares. The interview with Kyle Gould proved to be very good. She headed to the library to retrieve data on the deceased of the 1910 avalanche. She knew that the concrete wall that was erected at the railroad in commemoration of the avalanche victims had the information she needed, but she wanted to be able to print out the information from the microfiche scanner. She still did not have the exact approach that she wanted to use for her article. Originality was a must for Lorelei.

Lorelei was able to obtain the information that she needed from the library. She not only accessed the list of deceased, but she was able to do some extensive research by reading old newspaper articles that were published weeks and months after the 1910 disaster. This information would help her to culminate a good background reference in order to intelligibly put together a fine piece of work. She had never settled for mediocre writing. She put on her maroon-colored coat, and with briefcase in hand, headed for the door. Lorelei was looking very striking and smart when a man had entered who had made her heart flutter. It was Jason Bellamy. She had not seen this man for many years. He was the high school heart throb according to the young ladies. At times, Lorelei felt timid about talking to people that she was glad to see because she was always highly critical of her appearance. She knew that she was a pretty woman but that wasn't good enough for her. Her stance on meeting a possible suitor was that she must prepare for such an occasion. In reality, Lorelei had nothing to worry about because she looked very beautiful on that day.

"Lorelei? Is that you?" Jason asked.

"Oh—hello, Jason. Great to see you." *You're being too anxious, Lorelei,* she told herself. "Yes. It's me. How are you?" *That must have sounded stupid. Yes it's me. Gawd!*

"Doing well. Thanks. How about yourself? I read your articles whenever I get the chance. You look beautiful."

"Well--thank you, Jason. That's so sweet. What are you doing here?" *Another stupid comment.*

"Well—I do read." He laughed.

"I know that you must read." She grinned. *Lorelei—this conversation's one for the books.* She saw that he was holding a couple of books.

"Just returning a couple of things that took me forever to finish. I'm on the road quite a bit, and when I finally retire for the night, I begin to read then fall asleep."

"Believe me. I know that scenario. What kind of work do you do on the road?" she asked.

"I'm an engineer. We distribute car parts and other parts of machinery. I actually design the machines that make them."

"That sounds great."

"It pays well. I also get the hard part of traveling and introducing the operation of the machines in other parts of the country and abroad. It never ends. Have you had lunch?"

Lorelei immediately looked at Jason's ring finger and he was wearing one. "You married?" *Good one. Why don't I just beat around the bush?*

He looked at his ring, then looked at Lorelei and smiled. "Technically—yes. We're separated. About three months now."

"Oh—I'm sorry. I didn't mean to get personal."

"No. You're fine. I looked at your finger too. One of those automatic eye reflexes," he said as he smiled.

Lorelei smiled back at him. "To answer your question—no. I have not had lunch." They walked out together as he talked about the winter storm that was supposed to be coming.

"May I pick the spot?" he asked.

"Pick away," she said.

"How about Middleton's?"

"Oh—I love their food. My favorite is the escargot."

"I love escargot—especially Middleton's," Jason said. "Let's follow each other, Lorelei. I have the day off, but I need to pick up some things for my trip to Detroit tomorrow."

"That's fine, Jason."

"Okay. See you in a bit. Whoever gets their car going first is the one to lead."

"Alriight then." She was the one that ended up following, as she intended on doing.

"The scenery here is gorgeous," said Lorelei. "I just love the mountain view and the trellises all along the street with the English Ivy."

"Yes. It is beautiful," said Jason. "Since I'm a guy, I'm not aloud to use the word gorgeous unless I'm referring to a woman." He laughed, and Lorelei followed with a laugh.

"You're silly," she said. "Well. Does the escargot still tantalize the taste buds?"

"Oh yeah," Jason said. "The way that they use the bread crumbs, parmesan and garlic butter makes it."

"Oh, yes. It tastes as wonderful as always." Lorelei paused for a moment. "Jason. I'm currently working on writing a story about the 1910 avalanche."

"Ahhh! Very Delmore like. And I'm not being facetious. That's a wonderful idea. What approach will you be taking?"

She cutely grinned from one side of her mouth and bobbed her head once. "That's the golden question, **Mr.** Bellamy. I did quite a bit of reading at the library taken from many different perspectives. I do want to sort of focus on the families **DASH** ancestors of the deceased, but in order to help give the article impact, I must be original."

Jason sat, mesmerized by Lorelei's beauty and intelligence. His knuckles rested under his chin, his eyes slanted as he nodded. "I can see that, Lorelei. You want to make this one of your best articles you've ever written. Am I right?"

"You are right. Right on target. I've been getting…well.."

"Depressed with your job?" Jason asked.

"Well, damn, Jason. Right again. Are you psychic?"

"Not hardly," he answered. "I just know that people get bored with jobs that they love from time to time. I do as well."

"It's not so much depression as a temporary writer's block," she said. "I had an interesting interview this morning that I must tell you about. It was the first of my interviews in regard to the avalanche. A man named Gould. He had lost an uncle and cousins, which was unfortunate, of course. But the bizarre part of his story may have had nothing to do with the avalanche."

"Okay," Jason said.

"He told me about a vision that his father had back in the 30s. He was at The Annual Delmore Beer Garden where he saw something that scared him half to death, so to speak. He saw a woman and two children in the parking lot. The woman was.."

"Holding a lantern?" Jason asked.

Goose bumps covered Lorelei's entire body, then she smacked Jason's arm from across the table. "What the shit?" she said. "Are you serious? How in the hell did you know that? You're really freaking me out, Jason."

"Calm down, Lorelei. I didn't mean to scare you. You see—I had a great grandfather who had heard a similar story from a local townsman who was thought to be a drunk. I will fill you in in a minute. You go on."

"Well I'll be damned," Lorelei said, eyes wide open, and shaking her head in amazed bewilderment. "I definitely want to hear about that. Anyway—Mr. Gould said that he and a friend saw the same woman and children some forty odd years later. He said that he definitely believes that these were ghosts. Oh—and also—let me backtrack. His father's friend did not see the three people. Only he did. The woman spoke to him. She asked him where the railroad was and he told her. His son had said that his father mentioned to his wife that the woman looked pale, and so did the two children with her. The woman and children vanished after he looked away and looked back. Now, when Kyle Gould saw the vision, it was after he and his friend left a bar, and..." She stopped. "What?"

Jason sat with a smug smile on his face. "Oh—I was just thinking. It strikes me as kind of odd--or--a bit of a coincidence, rather, that these men, as well as my great grandfather's friend had all been drinking before seeing the vision. I am not saying that I believe that they didn't see it. I just think—well. I'll come right out and say it. I don't really believe in ghosts. It's not that I've never questioned the possibility, but...I don't know. It's hard to say. Go on, dear."

"It's funny you should mention that. I never was a supernatural-type person myself—but---the fact that this son of a well-respected citizen of Delmore saw the same thing, and now—especially with your story, is almost too much of a coincidence. And--your take on the drinking thing is almost funny, but not substantial in the repetition of these incidents. Let me hear about your story."

"Well. There's not much to tell except that a man who lost his wife and kids in the winter storm of 1910 saw a taller person with a lantern amongst two other silhouettes, from the front porch of his home while drinking his home made liquor. Like you—I believe the coincidence is uncanny. Very weird. I suppose you want names. My great grandfather's name was Gary Bovine—on my mother's side. The man who saw the people walking was a man named Daniel Dorwitz, I believe."

"When did the incident take place?"

"I'm not positive about the exact year, but I know that it was the early 20s. Hey. Maybe you can work these visions into your story," Jason said, darting a pointed finger at Lorelei. He sipped some coffee, then looked at Lorelei.

The look on Lorelei's face was that of someone who had just encountered an epiphany. She smiled and twitched her eyebrows up and down, while pressing her tongue against her upper teeth. "I believe you have something there, Jason Bellamy."

"You're serious? I was half kidding."

"Why not? It would definitely be original—even though you thought of it first. I had the thought in the back of my mind but didn't know how I'd go about working it in. That's it. That would be the main subject of the article. Kyle Gould said that he sensed that the ghostly visits had something to do with the tragedy. I'll rehash some of the horrific details of the storm and avalanche, then work in the visits as something that Kyle and I surmise to be connected. It's not like his story is the only one. There's yours."

"You **are** serious. And I suppose you'll include my name as secondary evidence. Brilliant. I think it could work." Jason was that much more attracted to Lorelei for the way that she thought.

"I just wish that I had more to go on, but I will give it a shot. Thank you, sir." She held her hand out to shake Jason's. He took her hand and lightly shook it, then brought her hand to his lips and kissed it.

"It's my pleasure to help out, Lorelei."

Lorelei blushed. "You **are** full of charm, Mr. Bellamy."

"You—are gorgeous, Lorelei McNeill."

"Thank you, Jason," she said, blushing again. She looked at his dreamy brown eyes. "Well—I really should get back to the office. I've been gone for hours."

"Yes. Me too. Gotta run. I'll call you when I get back from Detroit. Oh. May I have your number?"

She quickly got a pen and paper pad from her purse and wrote it down. "Sure. Give me a call."

Jason paid the check, then, they both got up from their chairs. He held his right hand on the small of her back as they walked out the door. Lorelei felt butterflies. "Well. This is it until next time," said Jason. "I'll be back on Thursday." They stood at the driver's side of Lorelei's car.

"Okay, Jason. Thank you for a lovely lunch."

"Lovely is another word a guy can't say." They laughed.

"You're a nut," Lorelei said. "Bye." *Too early for a kiss, Jason. Don't do it.* He didn't.

"Bye Lorelei." Jason Bellamy turned and headed for his truck. Lorelei got into hers. Jason waved while he drove away. Lorelei returned a finger fluttering wave.

As Lorelei drove, she thought briefly of Jason, and then starting focusing on her story. *How am I going to go about working on this,?* she asked herself. "I wish that I had more to go on," she said aloud. She would find much more than she thought very soon but didn't know it.

6

"Isn't she a beauty?" Kyle asked James.

"I can't believe you still have this thing," James Browning said. "It sure is nice."

"69 GT Torino—newly restored body---freshly painted with a new engine. Back to its original specs."

"I know what it is, Kyle. I always loved that hood scoop with the turn signals on the back of it. Sharp car, my friend. And the engine?"

"351 Cleveland, not a Windsor." Kyle smiled. "And you know what? It's not leaving the garage except on special occasions. Gotta keep that engine going so I'll rev it up every other day."

"You're probably one of a few people in this area who still has a car with a carburetor."

"Hey. I love carbs. They can be a pain now and then but you can at least rev the engine to your heart's content. These newer fuel injected engines. Pfff."

"Well. What did you want to tell me about, Kyle?"

"I spoke to that beautiful journalist today. Lorelei McNeill. Told her about our experience back in the 70s. Remember?"

"No. Not the freak-out incident," James said.

"That's the one."

"Oh, Kyle. Why bring that creepy thing back in the open."

"Well—you know, James—I've lived with that secret for years, and I guess I was ready to talk. See? She wrote this short article in the paper yesterday morning."

"I know. I read it. I don't know why she wants to delve into that depressing time of this town's history. Everyone knows it happened. Why not leave it behind?"

"She's a journalist."

"I realize that. But what does your story have to do with the avalanche?"

"Good question, friend. I think—or rather feel—in my heart--that those ghosts were victims."

"Of the avalanche. Come on, Kyle. What are the chances?"

"Pretty good, I'd say. They were wrapped up in winter clothing. When Dad saw them it wasn't even winter. In fact, it was in summer. I remember when **we** saw them it was November, but I recall it being cold. Maybe she can use the information and maybe not."

"Well, Kyle. Thanks for making me remember that event that gave me the willies for months." James laughed.

"No problem. What are friends for?"

The day's wind became colder and colder. Lorelei left the office at 5:30. She went home and immediately made herself a cosmopolitan. She sat and watched the local news at 6. What started out as a forecast of 6-8 inches of snow on the way increased to 10-12. "Oh—that's just what I wanted to hear," she said. One cosmo led to a second. She ate a quick dinner of a ham salad sandwich. She had stayed up until she fell asleep while watching *Frasier*. Her female cat, Simone, laid in the secure narrow separation of her legs as she slept on her back.

Lorelei was walking through a snow storm in her dream. She was unusually warm during her walk through frigid wind. She wasn't even wearing a coat, but her nightgown. Jason Bellamy accompanied her. He seemed somewhat aloof in conversation during the walk. "Do you like the snow?" he asked.

"No. I really don't," she answered. "I mean—this is too much." She looked over at Jason who wore khaki pants and a dark long-sleeved shirt.

"I don't like the snow either. It prevents me from doing my job," he said.

"What are we doing out here?" she asked There was no answer. Lorelei realized that Jason was no longer present. This didn't seem unusual to her in the least. *This must be a dream.*

"A dream? Yes. But not far from being real", a woman's voice said gently from behind her. Lorelei turned around to see that a woman with a hooded coat stood before her. She was holding a lantern that illuminated two smaller vague figures standing behind her.

"Lorelei," the woman said. "Lorelei. It may be happening again."

"What?" Lorelei asked. "What is happening again?" Lorelei began to feel the cold.

"Something bad. People may die." Lorelei tried to focus on the woman's face, but she could not see her face. Only the shape of one. The light from the lantern was nearly blinding.

"Tell me. Tell me please," Lorelei pleaded.

"The snow. Please—warn the railroad. They must evacuate," the woman said.

"Are you? Are you the woman who people have been seeing?" Lorelei could finally see some of the woman's face but it was a blur. She could also see the children's faces with the same blurred look. All of the faces were completely white. The woman did not answer Lorelei's last question.

"Is there a wall?" the woman asked.

"Wall? What wall?" Lorelei asked.

"A concrete wall. Where is it?"

Lorelei's mind was finally able to think. "There is a wall, ma'am. There's a wall at the railroad. It has names on it. Names of those who had died in the avalanche." Lorelei knew in her dream state that for some reason, this was the wall for which the woman was searching.

"Thank you. We've been searching for so long. Remember. Warn them. The snow may kill them if they don't leave." The woman and children turned and walked away.

A small light was all that Lorelei could see, and then it disappeared. "Wait. Wait. I need to talk to you," she cried. The wind filled her ears, and then she woke up.

Lorelei sat up quickly from her lying position. "My God," she said. "My God. What did that woman tell me? And why did she want to know about the wall?" It suddenly occurred to her that the woman and children may have wanted to see for themselves that they were dead. Lorelei had extreme cold chills from the dream. She looked at the clock above the fireplace of her old beautiful cabin. It was 3:05. She got up quickly and ran to the window. The snow was falling heavily. She got a pen and piece of paper and sat down at the table. She began writing all that she could remember from the dream. *Jason. Jason was the first person I saw,* she thought. All that she could remember him saying was that snow may keep him from working. *Something like that.* She then directed her thoughts on everything the woman had said. *This is too freaky. Why did she choose me to visit?*

Lorelei had fallen back to sleep in her bed at around 6:30am. Her alarm clock had awakened her at 8. She went to the living room and turned on the television. The weatherman was saying that 6 inches of snow had already fallen and that 6-8 more will easily follow. *Jason didn't tell me what time his flight was. I wonder if he's in the phone book.* Just then, the telephone rang and she answered it. "Hello."

"Lorelei?"

"Yes."

"It's Jason. Sorry for calling you so early."

"This is too weird. I was getting ready to look for your phone number, Jason."

"Well. Surprise," he said.

"What's up, doc?"

"I just wanted to see how you were getting along with the storm. My flight for 11 has been cancelled. You see.."

Lorelei got a cold chill. "Wait, Jason. This is triple weird. I had this dream and you were in it."

"Already dreaming of me?" he asked. "I'm flattered," he said. "Heh heh."

"It was not a good dream, Jason. We were walking in a snow storm. You didn't have much to say but you said something about the snow keeping you from working."

Jason raised his eyebrows. "That **is** strange," he said. "It looks like your dream came true."

"I interrupted you. You were saying your flight was cancelled and…"

Jason thought. "Oh. All I was going to say was that the airport is not snowed in yet, but will probably be later this morning. I tried to get a flight out of Seattle but it's the same story there. I get the feeling there's more you want to tell me about your dream."

"Yes. There is more but I think I'd like to tell you in person."

"Well—my schedule's wide open today. I actually called to see if you needed anything. I don't recommend that you get out in that Volkswagon."

"I couldn't get out if I wanted to. That thing sits so low I'd have trouble leaving the driveway. Thank God for the garage."

"Do you need to go to work?"

"No. I'm going to call and let them know that I'll do my work from home."

"It must be nice to have a job like yours. Showing up when you want."

"It has its amenities. Would you like to come over for breakfast or brunch? I fix a mean lobster omelet."

"Whoa. Sounds delicious. For starters, I need to go by my wife's house and blow off her driveway. She called and whined about not being able to get out."

Lorelei's stomach sank. "Jason. I hope I'm not being too personal. But—do you still have feelings for her?"

"That's kind of a loaded question, Lorelei. I don't mind it though. We were married for seven years but realized that we just can't tolerate each other. However, you never lose your entire feelings. At least not this soon. To answer your question more directly, I love her but I am no longer **in** love with her. You've heard that a million times, I'm sure."

"Sure. I have, and I understand. Never mind about that. What time can you make it?"

"I would say around 10:30 or so, give or take a half hour."

"Great. I'll get out the lobster and get that cooked. Then we'll make the omelets together."

"Wonderful. I'll see you then."

"Jason?"

"Yes."

"Would you like to know where I live?"

"That would be good." He laughed. "Just give me your address and I'll put it in my GPS."

"You ready?"

"Shoot."

"It's 11228 Cherry Hill Lane."

Jason spoke under his breath as he wrote. "Cherry Hill Lane. Got it. Do you need anything else from the store?"

"Some red wine might be nice."

"I'll tell you. Drinking in the morning."

"Jason."

"Just kidding. Red wine sounds great. I'll pick out some good stuff. Good enough. See ya then?"

"Okay. Looking forward to it. Jason?"

"Yes?"

"Very nice of you to call."

"No problem, Lor. See ya soon.

"Okay. Bye."

"Goodbye."

Lor. That was kind of cute, she thought. She went to the freezer and grabbed the whole lobster to thaw in the sink. She knew it didn't have to thaw completely in order to steam it. She also knew that the more that it thawed the less steaming would make the lobster more tender and not tough. She showered and dressed smartly casual for this unexpected date. After getting ready, Lorelei woke up from her dream world with an urgent thought. *The dream. The lady warned me to let someone know that something bad was going to happen. She had mentioned evacuation.*

Lorelei picked up the phone and dialed information.

"What city, please?" the operator asked.

"Delmore."

"Yes. Go ahead."

"Delmore Railroad."

"One moment."

A recorded voice came on over the phone. "The number is area code 206-389-4509. Repeat--206-389-4509. Please make a note of it." FAST BUSY LIKE SIGNAL.

Lorelei dialed. "Delmore Railways information, Leslie speaking. May I help you?"

"Yes, Leslie. Would it be possible to speak with the manager?"

"And who may I ask is calling?"

"Yes, ma'am. Lorelei McNeill."

"Oh—hello, Ms. McNeill. How are you?" The switchboard operator acted as if she knew her, but Lorelei knew that it was just because of her name in the paper that residents are forced to see on a daily basis.

"I'm fine, Leslie. And yourself?" Lorelei was a little irritated by the small talk.

"Fine, Ms. McNeill. The weather is awful though. Hold please."

Lorelei sat and listened to minutes of music as she waited for an answer.

"Stuart Clemens speaking. May I help you?"

"I hope so, Mr. Clemens. This may sound kind of odd. This is Lorelei McNeill."

"Oh—hello, Ms. McNeill. How are you?" Lorelei rolled her eyes. *Talk about sickening repetition,* she thought. "I'm fine, Mr. Clemens. Listen, sir. I'm concerned about the weather."

"As we all are, Ms. McNeill. What can I do for you?"

Lorelei fudged the truth. "Well, sir. It has been brought to my attention that we are going to get one heck of a snow. I guess you already know that."

"Yes, ma'am."

"Like I said, this may sound kind of odd. At what point does an operation like yours evacuate people?" She knew this may have sounded stupid.

Clemens laughed. "Well, Ms. McNeill. I do admit that was a very odd question."

"I'm sorry. But being a journalist, I have to know." *Good thinking, Lorelei.*

"I understand, ma'am. To answer your question, it would have to be under circumstances much more serious than a winter storm."

"I assumed as much, sir. I will cut to the chase. In 1910, the railroad was the first to get hit by the avalanche."

"Yes, ma'am," Clemens said in a solemn voice. "I hope another one of those is not a factor, ma'am. But--I don't think you have to worry. The chance of those conditions is probably a million to one. Now—I will say, that if we encounter feet of snow as was the case in 1910, necessary precautions will be taken. Have I answered your question?" Silence on Lorelei's end. "Ms. McNeill?"

"Yes. Yes—of course. You have, Mr Clemens. Thank you, and be careful out there."

"And you do the same, Ms. McNeill. Have a good day."

"You too. Goodbye."

"Goodbye." Lorelei was satisfied at that point in time. She remembered that the avalanche did not take place until days after the onslaught of the snow. *Still—I have to keep track of the weather.*

"I have never tasted such a wonderful omelet," Jason said.

Lorelei smiled. "And I have never seen anyone eat one so slow."

"Well. This was worth the slow eating."

"I owe it all to the range free hens. There's nothing like farm-fresh eggs. I'll never touch another store bought. They taste like water in comparison."

"I'll have to say. I'm going to have to switch. Where do you get them?"

"Carmichael's Country Store. They're four dollars a dozen but well worth it. Not to mention that the chickens aren't tortured."

"I know. I know. I've heard the stories. I don't want to think about it on a full stomach." They both laughed. Wind gusts were sounding like Lorelei's cabin windows could implode any moment. "Wow. Listen to that wind. We must have at least ten inches on the ground already."

"I hate to think of it," Lorelei replied.

"Do you realize that your house is an archival monument?" Jason asked.

"Of course I do," she said. "It's one hundred twenty-five years old to be exact. I bought it from a couple back in the mid-90s. The Schaffers."

"Being an historian, have you ever traced the owners back to when the home was built?"

"No—I haven't. Thanks, Jason. I did get a brief history from the Schaffers. I believe the previous owners before them were the Grendeers."

"Hmm. Perhaps it would be a good idea to investigate. You know that this place was very near the snow cover from the avalanche that you're researching."

"Oh my God," Lorelei exclaimed.

"What?"

"You're right." She got a cold chill. "Jason. I have to tell you the rest of my dream."

"Oh. Right. But why did you say 'Oh my God'?"

"Well—the fact that this cabin was most undoubtedly covered in the snow sparks another possibility in my mind. And the dream I had seems to fit somehow."

"I'm all ears," he said.

Lorelei grinned. "Oh—you're not that goofy looking." They looked at each other and laughed hysterically.

"And you called me a nut? Oh my."

Once the laughter subsided, Lorelei began to explain. "Well--you see—in the dream—I saw the woman and children, and I spoke with the woman."

"Okay. Interesting. Go on."

"They were dressed in winter clothing just like Kyle Gould had described them. I couldn't see the faces very well, but I knew who they were. I mean—I knew I dreamed it because of Kyle's story. He said that he believed that they may have possibly been victims of the avalanche. I think he was correct in that assumption. It all seems to fit. Especially the part that I'm about to tell you. It's what the lady asked me and what

I told her." Lorelei jumped up and grabbed her notes off of her desk. She ran back to the table and sat, and began to read. "The woman asked me if there was a concrete wall. I told her that there was a concrete wall at the railroad with names on it, and that the names were those who died in the avalanche. She thanked me and said that they had been searching for so long."

"Now **I'm** getting goose bumps. Go on."

"That's about it, but they disappeared right in front of me. Oh—she also told me to warn people that something may happen again. The key words are 'may happen.' She had also mentioned evacuation. To tell the people at the railroad to evacuate. Do you think, Jason? Do you think that this storm is going to cause another avalanche?"

"That's a bit far fetched but you never know."

"I've got to get on the computer right now."

"Now?"

"Yes. I've got to try and find out who lived here during the avalanche. This is creeping me out. Why did the woman appear to me? Aside from my subconscious retaining Kyle's story, there may be a link to me somewhere." Lorelei's vivaciousness poured out to Jason.

"You are something, girl." He smiled at her. "Go for it woman," he hollered at her.

Lorelei got up and went to Jason and quickly kissed him on the cheek. She then ran to the computer desk and sat down. On the internet search bar, she typed 11228 Cherry Hill Lane. There were numerous sites that came up. She looked closely at the sites on the first page. Within one description on the third site down, it read 'Delmore, Washington cabin attains landmark status 2008.' She clicked on it. There it was. A colored picture of her cabin. Below the picture the site read;

BEAUTIFUL RED OAK CABIN ATTAINS LANDMARK STATUS

In the midst of one of the worst avalanches recorded in American history, there sits a large red oak cabin built in the late 1870s in Delmore Washington. It had been built by a carpenter named Rupert V. Hamlin. Hamlin had taken residence there and was very proud of his work. He lived with his wife, Maria, in the cabin until the year 1902. Mrs. Hamlin had died of influenza in 1901, and the cabin, being such a vivid memory of his devoted wife, Rupert decided to sell the property and leave the state. He had moved back to Montana to live with his only son and his wife. The cabin and surrounding one acre of property was sold to Mr. and Mrs. Gene Carden. The Cardens lived in the residence for several years. Gene Carden had died in a timbering accident in the year 1908. He had left behind his wife, Emily, to live in the big cabin alone. Emily Carden was said to have been very heartbroken over the loss of her husband. The couple had never had children for Emily was barren. Then, in the year 1910, Emily had met her fate on the darkest day in Washington's history. She had perished in the avalanche that had fallen from the Great Cascade Mountains.

The cabin had sat dormant for years until a man by the name of Paul Grendeer, a bachelor, bought the property from the city of Delmore for a meager amount due to the moisture damage that the cabin incurred during the lengthy snow cover. He had refurbished the wood, inside and out, of the cabin, and brought back the home's luster. Grendeer had inhabited the residence for many years. He took a wife, Cynthia, at the age of 28. The Grendeers lived in the house, while early on, raising three children. After the children grew and left the residence for college and marriage, Paul Grendeer passed away at the age of 68. His wife died two years later. One of their children, Micah, moved into the cabin with his wife, Sheila, in 1959. Micah was forced to leave his family home behind because of his work. He had to transfer across the states to Maryland. The cabin was sold to the Emmett Schaffer family in the year 1973 until the sale of the house in 1996 to a post-grad college student by the name of Lorelei McNeill. Ms. McNeill became a well respected journalist in the city of Delmore and still resides in the landmark cabin to this day.

The three features of the cabin that most citizens and visitors of Delmore appreciate is its lustrous pure red oak, the articulately sculpted columns that support the front porch awning, and last but not least, the size. If one were to enter the cabin they would see a ceiling that reaches about seventy feet in chalet fashion. A wide wooden stairway that leads to a large open loft with railings, and a stone fireplace that sets off the beauty of the entire huge lower room. The cabin had been granted Landmark Status by the city of Delmore in 2001. Why someone waited so long to do so is beyond understanding. If anyone who has never had the pleasure of seeing this beautiful home and property, they would be awestruck. The 120 years plus landmark is surely a sight to behold.

"Wow," Lorelei said. "I don't think I have to look any further for information."

Jason had read along with her. "You got your name in there too."

"Did something strike you as ominous?"

"What. Am I dumb? Of course. Emily.."

"Carden lived here." She had finished Jason's sentence. "Jason?"

"Yes, Lor."

"I think that explains the link to me. What I'd like to find out is if the woman in the sightings and in my dream is Mrs. Carden. But, I may never know for sure." She saved the article from the site to her desktop. She typed in another search; Emily Carden.

7

Lorelei McNeill wasn't able to find a photograph of Emily Carden in her computer search or on microfiche at the library where Jason had driven her. Two days had gone by after Lorelei and Jason's brunch. Snow was still falling at a steady pace. There was 28 inches of snow on the ground. Lorelei had decided to speak with the mayor and state governor. The mayor was somewhat passé on the subject of evacuation of the railroad and the close surrounding residential areas. Lorelei hung up on him in mid sentence when he was saying, "Ms. McNeill. I don't think that you realize that an evacuation would mean extreme effort for a substantial but non-threatening snowfall. I think that you are.." CLICK.

Lorelei was furious. She was adamant in reaching an effective source that would shut down the city of Delmore in complete affirmation of the circumstances that prevailed. The governor's line had been accepting only phone-mail messages. Lorelei left her message. "Governor Knight. This is Lorelei McNeill with the Delmore Daily Press. I believe that a state of emergency should be issued for the city of Delmore and any surrounding cities that border the Cascade Mountains. Due to my intense studies in regard to current weather conditions, I feel that evacuation is a factor of major urgency to relieve the affected areas of this unprecedented progress of the snow that we are incurring. Time is a major factor. Please call me at 206-879-4760, extension 413. Thank you. Have a safe day."

A thought came to Lorelei. *Why not call the railroad back again?* She did call. "Yes. Mr. Clemens, please." She again had to identify herself before the call was transferred. There was no small talk this time around.

"One moment, Ms. McNeill," the operator said. There was music again while waiting, only this time for a shorter period of time.

"Stuart Clemens speaking. How may I be of assistance?"

"Mr. Clemens. Hi. This is Lorelei McNeill again. I'm so sorry to bother you."

"Not a problem, Ms. McNeill. We **are** very busy at the moment trying to get a train car moved. We've got a snowplow working on it. What can I do for you today?"

"Well, Mr. Clemens—it's basicly the same thing. You see—I"

"Stop right there, if you please, ma'am. I can understand your concern. Why **you** of all people in the city—I'm not sure. That sounded arrogant, ma'am. I'm sorry."

"I know what you mean, sir. No offense taken. I have just had a sense of some kind is all."

"Good. We are experiencing some problems as I said before, but nothing that some plowing can't handle. This is however—heh--some healthy snow we're having. They said up to only about a foot, and we're now up to almost two and a half. I'll tell you what, Ms. McNeill, if it will relieve your mind at all; if the snow--reaches three feet or more, I will take action with our employees and their families who live in our housing communities, and contact all of our receiving ports to postpone delivery. Does that help, ma'am?"

"Oh—yes. Yes. It sure does, sir. And I won't bother you again. Thank you."

"Okay, Ms. McNeill," Clemens said in a laughing voice. "You take care."

"And you too, sir," Lorelei said. Clemens hung up the phone without saying goodbye, which didn't bother her at all. She knew about business. Lorelei was quite relieved with what Clemens had told her. "Don't you worry, Emily Carden," she said aloud in the privacy of her home. "I believe things are going to be okay. Find that wall, baby. Find that wall." The semi-isolation and stress was beginning to get to her emotionally, and she began to tear up. She had been able to get to work in Jason's truck the day before and write quick editorials to cover her work for three days of releases. Jason's trip had been postponed indefinitely but he had gone to the plant to work on routine inspections and supervision.

On Friday, Lorelei turned on the 6:00 news. "This is Ray Stiles with KASL Channel 5 News. My co-anchor, Connie Freeman, has the night off. Delmore mayor, Syler Franks, has declared a state of emergency for the city of Delmore."

"Well—hallelujah," Lorelei screamed.

"the accumulation of snow has reached a near record of 35 inches in Delmore and surrounding cities. The last time that snow had reached this depth was just before the great avalanche of 1910. Mayor Franks insists that 'people stay in doors and only proceed outdoors unless you own appropriate vehicles such as trucks or S.U.V.s, and even then', he said, 'proceed with extreme caution.' There have been a total of twenty-one road accidents this week. Fortunately—none have been fatal. "Chief Meteorologist, Donald Dierling, has more on the late breaking weather news."

Lorelei got up from her chair. *I have to call Jason,* she thought. She didn't want to admit it before but she was getting scared. In the background, Donald Dierling spoke. "current temperatures in Delmore are holding in the lower to mid 30s. In the year of the avalanche, snow had reached 38 to 39 inches when the tragedy occurred. Mountain drifts had been 80 to 100 inches in depth. There is already, as of today, mountain drifts of 70 inches or more. If the temperatures increase gradually—this is the scenario that we all should hope for. This was not the case in 1910. The immediate increase in temperature was the catalyst for the avalanche, according to expert studies. When a weak base, due to temperature change, is unable to.." Lorelei turned the TV off. She had become familiar with the scenario of which Dierling spoke. The telephone rang, and she picked up.

"Hello. Jason?"

"Hello there, Lorelei. You doing okay?"

"No. I really am not. Could you please spend the night?"

"Well—I just got home, and I need to shower. Sure. What's wrong?"

"It's just that I'm getting stir crazy is all. Plus—I need your company if you don't mind. I don't want to move things too fast"

"Stop right there, Lor. You don't have to explain. These are unusual circumstances, and you don't need to be alone. I could use some company myself. See you in about an hour?"

"Thank you, Jason. You're a good friend."

"Thanks, Lor. So are you. I'll see ya."

"K."

"Bye."

"Bye bye."

Jason had arrived in less than an hour. That morning, Lorelei had to go to the garage for a snow shovel because her front door wouldn't open. It had taken her more than a half hour to clear the snow away enough so that the door would open.

"Come in, Prince Charming," Lorelei said as she opened the door for Jason. *Oh, my. That must have sounded cheesy and cliché.*

"Don't mind if I do," Jason said. He walked in and tracked snow onto the wood floor. "Sorry about that."

"If you had wings, I'd accept your apology," she said.

"You never run out of clever comments, do you?"

"Well—living in this bright little Washington city tends to bring out the worst or the best in people."

"Do you like Chinese food?"

"God, I love it. What do ya have?"

"Hong Shu Harr."

"Oh—fried shrimp with vegetables. One of my favorites."

"I figured you might be ready for a hot meal."

"Am I ever. Have a seat, Jason. I need to wash my hands."

"Me too," Jason said. "Handling cash usually makes me want to sterilize myself."

Dinner had come to an end and each had finished their 2nd martini. "Have you noticed that martinis seem to slam you all at once? I was in mid-sentence about the weather report and lost my train of thought."

Jason laughed. "Tell me about it. I was talking to my ex on the phone just after our break up. I was into my third double and realized I was a zombie." Lorelei laughed hysterically. "Really. I was talking about something pretty important, I thought—then I kissed a star without knowing it." Lorelei had doubled up in laughter while sitting at her chair.

"Stop it. Stop it. You're killing me," she gasped. "Ohhh!! That's good stuff, Jase."

"What. Do you think that just because I call you Lor once in a while that you can call me Jase?" They both were in stitches, when suddenly, they stopped. The mood changed abruptly to seriousness. They stared at each other like they were in a trance. She had looked more beautiful to him than ever before. Her flushed face brought out the richness in her olive complexion that made him want to spill out what he thought of her. And he did. "My God—you are so beautiful, Lorelei."

Lorelei gritted her teeth. "And you. You are so damned handsome." She jumped up and sat on his lap with her long legs draped on both sides of his thigh. She shook back her long hair which drove him even wilder. They kissed. They had nearly devoured each other in that first kiss. "Let's go to the loft, darling," she said in his ear. The fireplace continued to burn, and the love making that ensued may have put the flaming logs that remained to shame.

Eventually, the president of Delmore Railways closed the operation down. All residents that lived in the vicinity were sent to shelters and hotels. Employees were notified by phone that the present weather situation was crucial enough to take immediate action to take the necessary time off from work until conditions were more favorable. Not only were railroad employees and residents evacuated but also the surrounding residential neighborhoods. The snow had reached its peak of 37 inches on Saturday evening as the snowfall began to diminish. Lorelei's phone call to the governor had made somewhat of an impact. One of Governor Knight's ancestors had died in the avalanche a century before. He had sensed the urgency in McNeill's message enough to take the situation seriously, and had stayed abreast of the weather.

THE OUTCOME, THE COUNTERPART

The temperatures in Delmore remained stable for the following two weeks. Because of this weather outcome, chances of a disaster had become unlikely but evacuated residents were still in their safe havens. Snow had begun to melt at a normal rate and it seemed as though citizens were safe. Two days prior to Christmas Jason had stayed over at Lorelei's. At around 8am they were having breakfast when a sudden rumble was heard. The noise lasted only a few seconds. Jason and

Lorelei looked at each other. There was a knock at the door. Lorelei was visited by a National Guardsman that told her that she must evacuate. After the guardsman had left another massive rumble came which lasted longer.

"What was that?" Lorelei asked.

"Get dressed, honey," Jason said. "Fast." They had both moved quickly. There was another burst from the hills before they had reached the door. Jason opened it and Lorelei followed. "Come on, Lor," Jason said.

Lorelei froze. Standing there in front of her was the woman and children. "Are you really there?" asked Lorelei.

"We're here," the woman said quietly. "Thank you for everything you've done."

"Lorelei," Jason yelled. "Who are you talking to?"

"One moment, Jason," she said. Lorelei knew then that Jason could not see what she saw.

"You're going to be safe," the woman said.

"That's good to know. Ma'am. Who are you?"

"I'm Emily. Emily Carden. This is Curtis and Jamie." The two children looked at Lorelei and smiled. Lorelei smiled back.

"You have no idea.."

"I believe that I do," Emily said. "You know—I once lived here."

Lorelei began to cry. "I believe that you'll find what you're looking for, Emily." Emily smiled and then all three slowly disappeared. Lorelei covered her mouth and cried harder.

"Darling—we have to go. You saw them. Didn't you?"

"Yes. I did." Lorelei snapped out of her trance. "Come on, Jason." They ran to Jason's truck and got in. Suddenly, the roar turned to thunderous crashing. As Jason pulled out of the driveway all that they could see was white ahead of them. "Be careful, love."

"We'll be fine. I can still see snow covered cars." Jason was very careful, and when they had reached the intersection, he turned swiftly as the vehicle began to broad slide. He straightened the truck and headed toward the freeway. The vision ahead became clearer, although the white behind them was thick. "It's another one. Another damned avalanche." The roaring had stopped.

"I don't believe it's as bad as before," Lorelei said. "Look. You can still see houses."

"I hope to God you're right." She was correct. The avalanche had barely touched the residential neighborhoods that surrounded the railroad.

"I'm so glad that they extended the evacuation." Jason just looked at her frantically and kept driving. They were out of harms' way and most of the city was fairly safe. The avalanche was over.

8

Emily, Curtis, and Jamie stood before the wall in the darkness. There was blowing snow. There was always snow for the threesome. Conditions had never changed for them for they existed only in their own wandering state-of-being. Time was of no consequence and was never an issue for them to realize. Even through the years when seen by the people during summer, fall, or winter, Emily, Curtis, and Jamie saw only the weather in which they had perished. Emily held her lantern up high against the wall to begin reading the engraved names. She had seen her own name first since Carden was toward the front of the alphabet. She was not shocked, and she remembered her prayer before she died that she pleaded with God to allow her to do something extraordinary after the avalanche. She smiled. "Children—God does work in the most unexpected ways," she said in a sweet voice. "Move to your right, darlings." They did as they were told. She moved the lantern toward the end of the list of names. "There. There you all are, loves." Before the children's eyes they saw Curtis Woodland, David Woodland, and Jamie Woodland. It had just occurred to Curtis what had been missing since that very first day of their search. They had never slept nor eaten.

The first thing that Curtis and Jamie did was to look at each other and smile. The children remembered their own prayer and knew that survival was what happened but not in the way that they had hoped. "I love you, Jamie," Curtis said.

"I love you, brother," she said. They embraced.

"We've found your father," said Emily.

"Yes. Yes we have," said Curtis. Both children hugged Emily tightly. The lantern began to drift upward. The three stood hugging while their images turned dark as silhouettes, and then to an opaque image. They had dissolved into a misty glow that mingled with the also dissolving light of the lantern. They had risen until there was nothing but blackness.

THE LEGEND OF ROAMING SURVIVORS

By Lorelei McNeill

All anyone can really say is that it had happened again. Whether the snow conditions that had prevailed gave precedence to a second avalanche, it is hard to say. There were thankfully, no fatalities. Over a century ago the outcome of the event was not as kind as the snow cover that took place only weeks ago. Many Delmore citizens know of the devastation of the 1910 disaster. It is clear that it was something that one would just assume to forget. Nature, however, does not always allow us to do so. It is not my intention to recap the event that occurred on the more recent morning just before the holidays or on that terrible mid-day avalanche many years ago. I do, however, would like to share a series of events that has convinced me that what I am about to tell you is tied in directly to the Delmore avalanche of 1910.

During an early February evening in 1924, Delmore, Daniel Dorwitz was enjoying a product of which he was proud. Daniel was a citizen that protested the alcohol prohibition by making his own corn liquor. He had sat on the front porch of his house watching a breathtaking sunset. The night was cold but not unbearable. In the distance, Daniel had seen an apparition, a vision of three individuals walking. The tallest of the three was carrying a light source, what Daniel thought to be perhaps, a lantern. In his most vivid memory, he had shared the vision with friends, some of whom did not believe him. Dorwitz had lost his wife and children in the avalanche fourteen years before. This was only one occurrence that sets this story into motion.

Years later, in 1936, a man by the name of Elmer Gould, had just won some money at the 2nd Annual Delmore Summer Beer Garden. Delmore, as well as every community in the country, were trying to survive the Great Depression. Gould was ecstatic over his winnings, for he had a family to support. He had met up with a friend from school that shared his joy. As Elmer Gould walked to his car to put his money away, he had also seen a vision. On this particular occasion, the woman spoke to him. She was holding a lantern, and she was accompanied by two children. He had described the trio as being very pale in facial color. Faces were all that he could see of the three people for they were wearing thick winter clothing. She had asked Elmer where the railroad was located. He had simply told her in which direction that they needed to go. She thanked him and the children and she walked away from him. He was distracted for a moment as his friend yelled to him from the beer garden pavilion. When he looked back for the three that were walking, they were gone. He had returned to the pavilion very shaken, and also to find out that his friend saw no one. The two strange occurrences that I have mentioned have been backed up by descendents and friends of the witnesses. The sightings did not stop there.

In 1954, Kyle Gould, Elmer Gould's youngest son, had also seen the apparition on the way home from work one early evening. On this occasion, his co-worker had also seen the three people walking. The story was the same. It was a woman with a lantern and two small children. Kyle Gould is still a resident of Delmore, with whom I had the honor of interviewing. It is with Kyle Gould that I had first learned of the visions. He had believed that the roaming people were victims of the avalanche of 1910. In accordance with that assumption, the visions did not all occur during the winter months, yet, the clothing that the visitors wore every time was that of full winter garb. Kyle Gould had lost an uncle, nephew, and niece in the snow cover.

I had first learned of the case of Daniel Dorwitz, the first witness in the series of events, by a current Delmore resident, whose name I choose to keep confidential, but I will say that his great-great grandfather was one of Daniel's friends. The story that Daniel had told had been passed on through generations. Before anyone judges the credibility of the story that I have shared, I must place myself in with the witnesses.

The night after my interview with Kyle Gould, I had a dream. I dreamed of the roaming visitors. I could not make out the faces in the dream. A woman with a lantern and two children stood before me. She had asked me about a wall. In my dream state, I thought immediately that she had meant the wall with the engraved names of the deceased from the avalanche that stands at Delmore Railways. I told her it was at the railroad. She had also pleaded with me to try and warn people to evacuate, and that a disaster may happen again. Some may call it coincidence, but to me, it was uncanny that the snowfall had begun that very night. The snowfall—that proved to be the catalyst for the recent avalanche in Delmore is more than just a coincidence. It is with this hypothesis, on my part, to provide some insight to those who may consider a supernatural explanation to be in an issue in regard to what I have laid down in this editorial.

As for skeptics, with whom I can most certainly empathize, for I too had been subject to doubtful predispositions on the possibility of ghostly inhabitants in our universe, that is, until I encountered the recollections of real people and actual strange visions in the local community of Delmore, Washington.

Matthew Gant, president of the Delmore Daily Press, sat disgruntled at his desk and eyed Todd Richland, the senior editor down. "So, Todd. You approved this piece of—gibberish?" asked Gant.

"Yes," Richland said. "I thought it was very original."

"Original is not the issue, Richland," said Gant. He smacked the paper containing the article with the back of his hand. "McNeill is a general interest journalist—not a horror writer. If I wanted something supernatural, I would hire someone from some paranormal society."

"Sir—if I may interject.."

"I am not finished, Todd. You see—we have a reputation to uphold. Lorelei McNeill is, in fact, our finest writer. She is an historian, and she writes articles of interest that hold true to our region and country. We have already received two calls that made fun of the piece. Go ahead."

"Well, sir. Those types of calls are to be expected. What I wanted to tell you is that Lorelei came to me—emotionally if I may say, and said that she wanted to write this piece to stir the thoughts of the town's people. She also said that it could be her best work ever. She then let me review it."

"And you just said okay."

"Not at first, Matthew. I had warned her that this type of diversion could have some negative consequences. I explained that the article was highly unusual and that positive feedback is our second most important asset, our advertisers, being the first. She then convinced me that a stir is what advertisers want to see, and that unusual publicity often takes a positive turn. She's just so damn smart, Matthew. I couldn't say no."

Matthew Gant half grinned and bobbed his head. "Yeah—she **is** at that. Alright. I will let this thing go for now, but if we get advertisers to pull their spots, there will be consequences. Got it, Todd?" He gave Richland a stoic look.

"Got it, sir. Thanks for your understanding."

"Not a problem. And—would you please tell Lorelei to get her ass back on track? So to speak."

Richland smiled. "Yes. Yes I will, sir."

One Week Later

Lorelei and Jason sat on her couch watching her favorite movie, *Sleepless in Seattle*. Jason had made fun at first, but he quickly conceded. "You know, Jason. I could have been fired," said Lorelei.

"It was a wonderful article, baby. It's good to throw a stick in the spokes now and then." He grinned.

"Where did that saying come from?"

"My dad. He always thought that it was good to do something unexpected from time to time—that it made people think."

"That was my idea. You know, Jason. I wonder if Emily and the kids are still roaming around. I have a feeling they're not."

"I think you might be right, Lor. You do know that your last vision totally freaked me out. I didn't see a thing, but the funny thing is—I didn't doubt you for a moment. And I still don't."

Lorelei looked at Jason with dreamy eyes. "Thank you, darling," she said.

"I was wondering why you didn't tell about that last vision in your article."

"Well—Jason. I'm thorough but not a complete idiot. Everyone **would** think I was nutso if I added that, and second, I probably would have been fired." They laughed.

"Something else. Now listen carefully." Lorelei looked at him thoughtfully. "Emily Carden was on a quest. We agree on that. Right?"

"Right."

"And obviously, so were the children. Do you realize that **you** became their counterpart in their mission? I mean—they may have never gotten the answers they needed if it were not for you. It's like— you were meant to take up residence in Emily's home."

"I thank you for your keen observation, *Sherlock*," she said. "But you know, Jason—not to be conceded—I already thought that." They smiled at each other in mutual understanding.

"There's something I have to tell you, Lorelei—that's very important." He looked into her beautiful brown eyes. "I love you."

"Oh, Jason. I know that this is fairly sudden. I love you too." She started to cry and they kissed.

No one had lost their lives in the recent avalanche. It is apparent that Emily Carden's and the Woodland children's prayers are what saved the city of Delmore. When aspiring to look for answers in regard to the universe and nature, they are not always cut and dry issues. In the case of Emily, Curtis, and Jamie, there was something definitely spiritual guiding them, and the fact that they reached their destiny is a miracle in itself.

The Catalysts

By

Greg J. Grotius

There are many circumstances that leave people wondering if they are, in some way, mentally ill. This was the case in the life of Jeremy Oldman. He was, for the most part, a quite witty individual. In assuming a half-hazard approach to his early education, he had day dreamed much while most of his classmates were paying attention to the lessons that were being presented by the teachers. Jeremy was, in fact, a brilliant person. He had strong points that others could have not claimed. He was the story teller in class, which was not a big surprise to the teachers and classmates. He had excelled in English and was a fairly good artist. His main adversity to his self growth was that he became a follower in some aspects of his life. Bullies took advantage of his easy-going nature. Jeremy did however, have a vicious temper. After being pushed so far, he could lash out and throw a swing so hard it could break a jaw, which he had once done. The class room bully, Tim Conners, had him in a headlock. Tim jumped up and down while he did it. Jeremy was in excruciating pain and began to punch wildly at whatever part of Tim's body he could reach. He had managed to hit Tim in the testicles. As Jeremy was let go from Tim's grip, he stared Tim down in red fury. He then turned and took a full swing with his right fist. The contact of the fist to Tim's face sent Tim flying back on the asphalt playground. Tim began to cry and scream threats to Jeremy. Jeremy knew at that moment that he was no longer afraid of Tim. In High School, Jeremy had contact with marijuana. This was due in some part to some of the company that he kept. He never blamed anyone for eventually trying harder drugs. The story that you are about to hear will explain about his experiences and how adolescent events changed his final direction in life. The year was 1968.

1

Deep secrets are things that are often never revealed. Jeremy Oldman had many and had revealed only a few. He had an extreme habit of lying. This was his way of putting himself upon a pedestal. Whether the prop was good or bad, Jeremy didn't care. It drew attention to himself. The day after watching the movie *Bonnie and Clyde* at the drive-in theatre, he told a 3rd grade class mate that he saw a man with a gun walking on top of the school garage. His class mate immediately told the teacher, which resulted in Jeremy being questioned by Sister Rosemary. He had just told her that he was kidding. The nun saw this as a desperate need for attention, but also as a possible problem. She had called his home that evening and spoke to his father, James. James Oldman had assured her that this behavior would not happen again. He'd also mentioned to her that the family had just seen a movie the night before that surely prompted his imaginative story. Being a parochial instructor, she had questioned Mr. Oldman if that type of movie was the best thing for a seven-year old child to see. This questioning angered Jeremy's father to no end, but he didn't allow his feelings to be detected by Sister Rosemary. He had just agreed with her and told her that Jeremy's home entertainment would be more closely monitored. James was a railroad man whose pay did not sustain his prosperity.

"Who do ya think you are, Warren Beatty?" James Oldman hollered as he smacked Jeremy with the back of his hand. Jeremy cried in terror. "I didn't raise no liar."

"I'm sorry, Daddy. I didn't mean anything by it," Jeremy said as he rubbed his reddened cheek.

"Don't you ever pull any stunts like that again. You want me to be a laughin' stock of Sacred Rosary Church?" James Oldman asked. At that time, James looked down at his son. Jeremy was crying uncontrollably. James cried at the sight of Jeremy's tears. He took Jeremy in his arms and hugged him tightly. "I'm sorry, Jeremy. I just can't have liars in my family. Our reputation is at stake, boy."

"I'm sorry, Daddy. It won't happen again," Jeremy responded. James loved his boy, but he had a bit of an anger problem. His father had the same problem. When James was twelve years of age his father beat him with a strap for saying the word *fart* at the dinner table. James had experienced some unsavory events at the Oldman house. The domineering character of his father had, unfortunately, trickled down to him.

Jeremy had an older sister, Doreen, and a younger brother, Frank. Doreen was usually the sibling that received most of the attention from the parents. His mother, Lana, spoiled Doreen with most of what she wanted. She had bought her fine dainty clothes since the age of four with no expense a problem. Doreen was sent to dancing school, was financed a trip to England with her sophomore class, and sent to the most elite signature school during her junior year in high school through a grant. Jeremy, on the other hand, had difficulty getting extra money for candy sales on Fridays at school. Younger brother, Frank was only 5 years old and attended kindergarten. Jeremy didn't go to kindergarten. He remembers his mother saying that he was just fine staying home and practicing his math and reading, which he did. He did or else he would get less for lunch and dinner than his siblings. Jeremy was deprived. He was deprived of attention and fairness. He just went with the flow, and he took what he could get in regard to love and respect from his parents.

Jeremy was not what one would identify as an attractive boy. He was very skinny with a face that was too long, buck teeth, with unusually misshaped facial features. At first glance, one would notice a forehead so large that it seemed out of proportion to his body. He received many insults from classmates and children from his neighborhood. He became so self-aware of his looks that he would stand in front of a mirror and tried to make his long lustrous brown hair as attractive as possible and use his bangs to cover some of his forehead. He made sure to wash his hair every night.

Years at school went by at a moderate pace for Jeremy while most other classmates experienced a more rapid time lapse. One day after getting off the bus from school he ran home and immediately went to his back yard to feed his pet rabbits. They were not in the cage. He was quite bewildered and ran inside to ask his mother about it. Lana Oldman said, "I'm really sorry to tell you this, Jeremy. Well—it was your father's idea. He said that it has been a long time since he'd eaten rabbit. I…"

"What?" Jeremy screamed. He cried as if he'd been hit with a crow bar. "How you could you have done that, mom?"

"I was trying to explain, young man. I told your father that you would be upset, but he insisted on.."

"Those were my pets. Upset? Upset. I get upset if I get a B in English. That bastard had no right." His mother slapped his face.

"Now you have something to cry about, smart mouth," responded Mrs. Oldman.

"I hate you. I hate him. How could you?" Jeremy ran out the front door and down the street as fast as he could. He cried and cried until he reached the creek that ran aside one of the adjoining streets of where he lived. He sat at the edge and threw pebbles in the running water. He sat there for about five minutes when Mr. Sawyer hollered out his front door.

"Hey, Jeremy. Get off of that bank. I work hard to keep those rocks where they belong," said Mr. Sawyer. Mr. Sawyer had noticed that

Jeremy had streams of tears that had streaked his face. The man began to walk toward the creek and Jeremy.

"I'm sorry, Mr. Sawyer. I won't do it again. I-I, just-just."

"What's the matter, boy?" Mr. Sawyer asked when he finally approached Jeremy.

"Aww. Nothin'" Jeremy said in a broken voice.

"Jeremy. I know there's something wrong. What is it?" Mr. Sawyer stood with his dark eyes glaring down at Jeremy.

"He cooked my rabbits," Jeremy said.

"What's that, boy?"

"My pets. My dad, or my mom. I don't know. They cooked my rabbits." He began to cry again.

Mr. Sawyer stood in disbelief, his mouth opened. "You don't mean to say."

"Yes. Yes. It's true. I came home from school to feed my rabbits—and they were gone. When I asked my mom, she told me that Dad hadn't eaten rabbit for a good while." He looked up at Mr. Sawyer in shock. "Can you believe it, Mr. Sawyer? Can ya?"

Sawyer knew Jeremy to be a stretcher of truth from time to time, but he knew that what the boy said was all true. He could see it in the boy's demeanor. This boy was petrified. "Oh. Oh. I'm so sorry, Jeremy. That's terrible. That just ain't right."

"I don't have to go back there, do I, Mr Sawyer? I mean. How can I go back?"

"Well, son. You do. But just sit here a bit." Jeremy suddenly vomited. He went to help Jeremy to his feet. "Come on, son. I'll get you a glass of water. He walked Jeremy into the house. Mrs. Jan Sawyer stood at the kitchen doorway.

"What? What's wrong?" she asked. Brian Sawyer scratched his bald head and looked seriously into his wife's eyes.

"Have a seat, Jeremy. I'll be right back with some water." He walked with his wife into the kitchen as the swinging door closed behind them. Jeremy sat and listened to Mr. Sawyer talking, almost whispering. He heard the word 'rabbits.'

"What? What?" Mrs. Sawyer screamed. "That son-of-a-bitch. That man's insane." She began to cry. "Oh, that poor boy. I've got a mind to call the police on him. That son-of a-bitch," she repeated. Jeremy heard more whispering, then water running from the faucet.

The couple came back into the room. Mrs. Sawyer ran to Jeremy, got on her knees, and took Jeremy in her arms. Jeremy began to cry again.

"I know. I know, honey," she said to him.

Although it sounded to Jeremy that Mrs. Sawyer was as disgusted and mad as he was, Jeremy gently pushed her arms away. "Thanks, Mrs. Sawyer. But you don't... You don't know," Jeremy said. "You're very kind. And I'm glad you think of my asshole of a dad in the same way that I do. But what can I do? What do I do?"

She stood. "I don't know, darling," Mrs. Sawyer answered. "Perhaps we can talk to him for you."

"It won't do any good, Jan," Mr. Sawyer said. "Here you go, Jeremy," he said as he handed the glass of water to the boy. He looked at Jeremy. "Son, you go home and face up to this. It sounds like your mother is just as much to blame. If you have any problems tonight, our home is open to you. And that is anytime." Jeremy knew what he had to do. He had to go home and do exactly as Mr. Sawyer said.

Jeremy took a few sips of water. "I won't forget your kindness, Mr. and Mrs. Sawyer." He managed a smile, and received smiles in return. Jeremy stood.

"Stick in there, boy," Mr. Sawyer said. "We'll be here for you."

"Thank you, sir. Bye, Mrs. Sawyer." Jeremy walked out the door.

"Bye, Jeremy," hollered Mrs. Sawyer. "Come back anytime." It never occurred to any of them that Jeremy would indeed return. He had found friends in this kindly couple.

"I know what you called me, Jeremy. Your mother told me. You won't get a whoopin' this time 'cause I know what those rabbits meant to you. But you have to understand, son. I'm on a fixed income. We sometimes have to sacrifice things in order to have food on the table." James Oldman said these words to his son as Jeremy only stared back at him hollow eyed.

"Yes, sir," Jeremy said with no emotion whatsoever.

"If you'd like a sandwich, there's bologna in the fridge."

"Thanks, Dad." Mr Oldman closed the door to Jeremy's room. Jeremy delved into his geography book. He was to have a test the next day. There was nothing as devastating as what happened that day for quite some time. Jeremy was, however, plagued weekly by verbal and occasional physical abuse. His mother would remind him from time to time that she'd wish that he was more of a math scholar like his sister. She seldom acknowledged Jeremy's personal strengths in reading and writing. She would merely only express to him that he read an awful lot.

2

At the age of 10, Jeremy was gathering his books to take home from his 5th grade class. "Now, class. Remember that tomorrow we'll be covering what is important in the development of volcanic eruptions," Mr. Sims said. The bell rang. Jeremy went to the rest room. Kids ran to their lockers and grabbed their jackets. After using the rest room, Jeremy went and got his jacket from his locker. It was mid-October. Instead of heading to the front of the school where the busses would soon pick children up for home, Jeremy stepped into the library, went to the fiction section and picked out a book to read. He grabbed a hard-back copy of *Mary Shelley's Frankenstein*. He didn't turn on the lights to the library because he didn't want to attract attention. He found a spot near a window that was out of sight from the hallway. As he sat at a table, he could hear teachers talking and walking down the hall. It was very lucky for him that no one decided to look into the library. He began reading. He read, and he read. Jeremy was a very fast reader. There was no more noise anywhere in the building. Jeremy had never felt so much peace in his life. He looked out the window at one point and saw that dusk was about to fall. It was then that he got up and turned on the lights. He chose another seat, sat, and began reading again. He continued to read for another hour. Jeremy could not believe how wonderful this book was that he had chosen. He'd never known how sad the story of *Frankenstein* really was. He suddenly heard footsteps at the far end of the hallway. He thought for sure that it was too late to turn the lights off in order to keep himself from being discovered. He was right. The footsteps were heavy and he knew to whom they belonged. Mr. Sheller, the custodian. "Hello. Who's in the library?" Jeremy quickly marked his page, ran to the book shelf and placed the book exactly where he had gotten it. Just as he shoved the great book into place, Mr. Sheller stepped in and said, "Kid. What the hell are you doing in here?"

"Just reading, Mr. Sheller," Jeremy answered.

Mr. Sheller laughed. "Well. This is the place to read alright. But why in God's name are you here this late? Are you the Oldman boy?"

"Yes, sir. I am."

"You know--your mother's worried sick. Called the nun's convent about a half hour ago. Sister asked me to search the school. And blazes, here you are. Better come with me, boy. We'll call your mom." As they walked through the school, Jeremy's mind wandered.

I was dismissed from class. The last class. Why didn't I go to the front of the school to catch the bus? I wanted to escape. Escape from what? For some reason I lost the time of day. I didn't care about the time of day. I did escape. It was wonderful. Frankenstein. I want to be with that monster. I can relate to that monster. He was created in an unfriendly world. That's what I am—an experiment. I was created by evil people to satisfy their own sick pleasure. Home? Was I supposed to go home? I guess I was.

Jeremy didn't want to go home. His reason for going home didn't feel to him as a need. He wanted to stay away from home forever. As he walked toward the nun's house, he became terrified. He was terrified of his father picking him up from school. He began to feel sick. He threw up in the parking lot.

"You all right, son?" Mr. Sheller asked. He put his hand on Jeremy's back.

"Yes, Mr. Sheller," Jeremy said. "I'm okay. Maybe I need to eat is all." Thinking of eating made Jeremy feel even more ill. *Food wasn't the problem. Home was the problem*, he thought.

"Yeah. I'm sure that's it," Mr. Sheller answered. As they walked up the steps to the nun's house, Jeremy looked up to see Sister Katherine standing at the doorway. She opened the door. She had called Jeremy's house when she saw them walking through the parking lot.

"What are you doing here, Jeremy?" Sister asked. Jeremy looked straight into her eyes.

"I don't know, Sister," Jeremy said. The nun saw that Jeremy's eyes were vacant. This boy knew nothing that was going on.

"Well, dear boy," Sister said sweetly. "You must have had some idea why you stayed in the school while all of your classmates had gone home. Didn't you want to go home?" Jeremy was silent.

"Answer the Sister, Jeremy," Mr. Sheller said as they all stood inside the door of the home.

"I don't think that I wanted to be home, Sister Katherine," Jeremy responded.

She shook her head in misunderstanding and slanted her eyebrows downward. "But—why didn't you want to be home, Jeremy?"

"I just didn't," he said, and began to cry. Sister Katherine looked at Mr. Sheller and waved her head for him to leave them alone together.

"Have a good night, Jeremy," Mr. Sheller said.

"Thank you, Mr. Sheller," Jeremy said. Jeremy knew that he probably was not going to have a good night. Mr. Sheller opened the door and left.

Sister Katherine looked at Jeremy. "Jeremy. What is wrong?"

"It's my dad. Things are weird at home. My mom too. I feel like I am a nobody, Sister."

"But you're not, Jeremy. You are most definitely not. I wish that I had your imagination."

"But—my parents don't see it. I don't think that they like me," he said.

"Who couldn't like you, Jeremy? You're funny. You have excellent grades in English. You do lack some math skills, and you can work on your science a bit, but you are a very delightful boy." Jeremy smiled.

"Thank you, Sister. I kind of think that too. I do what I can to keep my English grades up. I know that my math has kind of fallen, but I can do better. I know I can." Just then, a car horn honked. Jeremy's stomach filled with ice. "That's him. I better go."

"Just remember, Mr. Oldman. You're a special boy. Don't allow anyone to influence your talents to go to waste." Sister smiled at him earnestly. "We love you, Jeremy. Remember that."

"Thanks, Sister," Jeremy said. He smiled with one corner of his mouth, opened the door and walked out. The ride home was strange. Mr. Oldman didn't say a word during the entire ride. *This is even scarier than if he laid into me*, Jeremy thought. He could see that his dad was upset in the way that James Oldman worked his jaw muscles constantly.

They had pulled into the driveway. "Jeremy," his dad said as he looked at the boy.

"Yes?" Jeremy asked. A quick slap sent Jeremy's head against the glass of the passenger window. Instant tears shot out of Jeremy's eyes. His upper lip quivered in disgust and hatred. He opened the car door and James Oldman did the same.

"Get inside and do your homework. Get a bite to eat before bed," his dad said sternly.

"Yes, Dad." Jeremy saw no need in trying to explain. He did as he was told.

As he sat studying his spelling words, his dad spoke. "Your mother is at her bridge club. She made some chicken salad before she left." James Oldman went up to his bedroom and shut the door. Doreen walked over to Jeremy.

She caressed Jeremy's hair. "What's the matter, baby?" she asked. Doreen was a pretty girl with streaked blonde hair.

"Nothing, Doreen," Jeremy said.

"You sure? You had us worried."

"Just lost track of time is all. Got to reading a good book and just forgot about the bus," he said.

Doreen smiled at him and Jeremy smiled back. "Can I get you some supper?" his sister asked. She saw a red mark on his face where he'd been slapped.

"No thanks, sis. I'll get it."

"Okay, dear. Just hang in there. Okay?"

"Okay." Jeremy continued studying as his sister went to her room.

3

Jeremy had awakened to something very strange. He had heard a few bumps against the wall. He thought to himself. Is that laughing I hear? It **was** laughing of some kind. He knew by listening that it was a woman that he heard.

"No. Don't do that. You naughty man." More laughing was heard, then screamed words. "Stop that." Jeremy's mind raced. What is going on? He was suddenly mystified. Can it be? he asked himself. Daddy and Mom? What is he doing to her? He silently ran to his window and looked out. *Mom's car isn't out there yet.* Jeremy heard footsteps. He quickly ran and jumped into bed and got under the covers. His bedroom door had opened. He could hear only breathing. The door shut. *No-no-no*, he thought. *This can't be happening.* He had heard whispering in the hallway and definitely a woman's voice. He had heard the descent of footsteps. *It's not Mom.* Jeremy knew this for a fact. The front door closed. *Is it someone who lives close to us? There was no car*, he thought. Jeremy stared at the ceiling. He stared until his eyes burned from unrest. He heard a car pull up, and he was somewhat relieved. That was the only sound that he had heard until his alarm clock awoke him at 6 am.

Jeremy showered and dressed quickly. He went to the kitchen. Doreen sat and drank coffee. Her eyes looked tired. His mom was serving cold cereal. Frank doodled with his cereal and ate a couple of oat rings out of his bowl with his fingers from time to time. "You'd better eat, Doreen," Lana Oldman said. "You've got a big day taking your assessment tests at the college."

"I'll eat some fruit and stuff before the test," Doreen said. "There's a nice lounge at the college dining center." Doreen's voice was monotone.

No expression revealed her normally vivacious self. Jeremy sat, poured himself a bowl of cereal with milk, and began eating.

"What in the world did you do last night?" his mother asked him. "Dad said you spaced out and didn't catch the bus home."

"Oh—why don't you leave him alone, Mother," Doreen said. "He's a good boy. He just wanted to catch up on reading."

"Catch up?" Lana asked. "I'd say he's passed that avenue years ago."

"Mother. Jeremy is special. I don't see anyone else in this house reading," Doreen responded.

"You watch what you say, young lady. You or that boy don't have the right to question your parents. Remember who made it possible for you to go to college."

Doreen felt that it was time to clam up. She wasn't stupid. She had been spoiled growing up, but she knew what her parents were really like. She had recently learned very much about her parents and one of them in particular. Jeremy's day at school was great. He had immediately gone to the library and checked out *Mary Shelley's Frankenstein*. He read until his first class, read in-between his classes, and during lunch. His fifth period class was Study Hall, and he finished the book. He sat, amazed at the story. The bell rang for sixth period. He walked in a comfortable daze to science class. He suddenly wondered if he had forgotten something. *Damn*, he thought. *Volcanoes*. He forgot to study about volcanic eruptions. *Maybe Mr. Sims won't call on me to answer any questions.* Jeremy knew that this notion was highly unlikely. He immediately pulled out his science book and found the chapter the class was on and read quickly before reaching the class room. *Saved*, he thought. Jeremy smiled.

That evening Jeremy studied for all of his classes. He worked the hardest at understanding math. He started at the beginning of the book. He worked out division problems, the area where he suffered most. He finally got it. Jeremy worked on multiplication and figured out a short cut on multiplying large numbers in his head. He was quite a happy boy that night, and he couldn't wait for school the next day. Jeremy showered and went to bed. He was very surprised that his mother came in and kissed him goodnight. "Good night, Mom," he said. Jeremy felt as if he were somebody. Before falling asleep he thought about his dad seeing another woman. It nearly made him sick but there was so much bad stuff in his family life he decided to not let his new knowledge bother him. He slept peacefully.

4

Jeremy did well at school the following day. He had impressed his math teacher by answering all the questions that he could. Sister Jane congratulated him on completing his in–class work without asking any questions. She could tell that he had begun to apply himself. His classmates seemed to treat him differently than before. Friends came out of the wood work, so to speak, and they wanted to play with him on the playground. He had a couple of good friends: Stan Richter and Charlie Matthews. Now he had five good friends. Jeremy was quite elated.

It was Friday, and he had saved up some money for the end-of-week bake sale. He devoured the chocolate donuts that he bought after lunch. Jeremy had bright thoughts of his life on that day, and he took a turn in a more positive direction. After returning home from school, he asked his mother if he could go to Roster's Field down the block to play baseball. She had agreed but told him to make sure that he came home before dinner. He hopped on his bike and rode like the wind.

Mr. Sawyer was at the field. He acted as sort of a coach for the boys who played ball. Jeremy had hit a home run in the fifth inning of the game. His team won 7-3. Mr. Sawyer asked Jeremy if he'd like to come by to see his boy's train set.

"I sure would like to, Mr. Sawyer, but I need to get home," he said. "Thank you. How about tomorrow, Sir?"

"That would be fine, Jeremy," Mr. Sawyer said. "Hey. How are things going? I mean—at home."

"Oh--I guess they could be worse," he answered. Jeremy laughed.

Brian Sawyer smiled. "That's good, son. I'll see you tomorrow then- say--around noon?"

"That'll be fine. That is unless my chores aren't finished."

"Well—just make it when you can. We aren't going anywhere."

"Okay, Mr. Sawyer. Thanks again. I'll see ya."

"You're quite welcome, Jeremy. Bye."

When Jeremy arrived at the house, there was a strange car parked in the driveway. He put his bike away and walked in the front door. His mother was sitting on the couch crying. A man Jeremy had never seen before, Trainman Archie Borman, was sitting next to her patting her on the shoulder. "It was all that we could do to try and keep him from falling, Mrs. Oldman. He was hanging on the rung of the moving train car when his foot slipped off the bottom rung of the ladder." Jeremy stood in shock.

"Well. Why the hell was the train moving?" Lana Oldman frantically asked. "Isn't that a regulation that the train must be stopped?"

"Yes it is, Ma'am. But Jim Carter was the only one with a radio, and he wasn't near that train car. By the time he ran toward where we were, in order to tell us, James had slipped off and fell. I tried to grab him, like I said, from inside the loading car, and Gary Smith tried to get under him but lost his footing and fell to his knees. The engine had jerked the cars, and that's when James began to slip. He held on with one hand for about thirty feet or so before..."

"I don't want to hear anymore," Lana said. "That place is gonna pay for this." She looked at Jeremy in horror. "Jeremy," she cried. "Your daddy's dead." Jeremy ran to his mother and hugged her tightly.

"No, Mother. No," he cried.

"Yes, son. He broke his neck falling from the train ladder." They both embraced one another and cried. Archie Borman sat with tears in his eyes and stared.

"I know it wasn't your fault, Archie," Lana said. "You did what you could. I told him that job was a deathtrap. When he told me what he did, it frightened me to no end."

Jeremy wiped the tears from his face. "Mom. Where's Doreen and Frank?" he asked.

"Doreen took your brother to get a haircut. Oh, God. It'll be horrible having to tell them when they get here." This made both of them cry even more. Jeremy never realized before that he actually loved his dad. He didn't like him but he never wanted him dead.

"Well, Mrs. Oldman. I better go. I phoned my wife from the station after it happened. She'll be anxious to see me." He stood. Lana Oldman stood also and hugged Mr. Borman.

"Thank you, Archie—for trying to help and coming here to tell me in person," she said.

"I told the boss that I didn't want you to hear about it over the phone. That I would come over instead."

"Thanks again, Archie," she said. "That is much appreciated." They said their goodbyes, and Mr. Borman left.

Jeremy's life was in turmoil again. He thought suddenly how he could continue to live without a father. Deep in the back of his mind he knew that he would. He also briefly thought that he'd been given a break by God. *No more beatings*, he thought. He had felt guilty about even thinking that thought, however true it might be. Another thought occurred to him. *Mr. Sawyer had just asked me to come over to play with the train set. Weird.*

The train company did pay for James Oldman's death. Funeral expenses plus a settlement out of court in the amount of $100, 000 was paid to Lana. She had laughed at the amount but was willing to settle anyway. She knew that she could have sued for millions. The company should have never operated without every single employee who worked the cars to have a radio with them. The Oldmans, of course, also got paid from James' pension. Life went on for the Oldmans. Doreen eventually transferred to an Ivy League college. Frank became as bright a student as Jeremy and Doreen. Lana Oldman lived life in a delirium and didn't work. She had also taken to drinking heavily.

5

Years went by and Jeremy started smoking marijuana at the age of 16. He attended a public high school where he met new friends that smoked. Even though Jeremy was quite a good student, his grades began to fall by the wayside. The pot caused him to drop much of his previous ambitions. All he wanted to do was to get high. He began drinking alcohol as well. He had taken barbiturates one night while drinking beer and was rushed to the hospital, as he had overdosed.

"I knew that you'd never amount to anything," his mother told him as he lied in the hospital bed. This hurt Jeremy. For a while, he and his mother got along okay. His father's death helped them to bond a little better than in previous years. She had even began to show interest in Jeremy's welfare, which wasn't the case when he was a child. Things began to fall apart when she started drinking and she became her old self again. She would talk to Jeremy like he was dirt under her feet. Doreen was still a princess to Lana, and Jeremy, to his mother, was a worthless bum. She loved Frank because he was her baby. There was just some strange chemistry in the Oldman household that Jeremy could never figure out.

Jeremy came to a conclusion. *My father was, and mother is insane,* he thought. *Just not right.* Coming to grips with his feelings about his parents began to make dealing with his dilemma a little easier. But still, Jeremy was one who starved for acceptance. He knew his sister and brother loved him, but that wasn't enough. He was still bound by his *Frankenstein* complex, which he created in his own mind. His lying became an issue again, and his actions cried for attention.

One day while riding the bus from school, a pretty girl sat next to Jeremy named Shirley Law. Although she was attractive, her hairdo was big and old fashioned. "Where'd you get your hair from, Shirley?" he asked. "Some ancient actress?"

"Ha ha," she said. "Thanks a lot, buddy."

"Just jokin'," he said. "Well—no I'm not." He laughed. She smacked his shoulder. He loved the attention from this buxom brunette. Shirley was holding this strange looking wooden piece of art. It looked like a wooden swing with plastic balls attached to strings that were glued to the top. He looked at it. "What the hell is that thing?"

"It's art. I know it's stupid looking. Got a B for it though." She raised an eyebrow and shook her head like she was special.

"You got a B for that? Huh. That teacher should go back to school."

"I'm just gonna pitch it," she said. "You want it?"

"Sure," Jeremy said. "I'll put it with all my other junk."

"You're so mean, Jeremy. I mean it. You can have it."

"Serious?"

"Yes."

"Okay. I'll take it." She handed it to him. "Thanks, Shirley. Wow." The bus was getting ready to approach the overpass. Jeremy slid down the window.

"What are you doing?" she asked.

"This," he said. He threw the art piece out the window while the bus was on the bridge. He had managed to pitch it off the overpass.

"Oh my God," she said. "Are you crazy?"

"Yes, I am," he answered. He laughed, but not for long. Much to Jeremy's chagrin, Mr. Allman, the bus driver, was looking directly at him in the rear-view mirror. Mr. Allman turned on the red flashing lights of the bus and extended the STOP sign.

In the meantime, the piece of art had just struck the windshield of a passing semi truck below the overpass. The truck driver was startled, but he luckily kept his attention on the road and kept going. The piece of wood was smashed to pieces. Another car was hit by a piece of it, but the old lady driving paid no attention to the tap.

The bus stopped. Mr. Allman got up and walked toward Jeremy and looked as if he could kill him for that stunt. "Jeremy," he screamed. "Are you out of your mind, boy?" Allman darted a quick look at the traffic down below. It looked to him that traffic was still flowing. "You're lucky that didn't cause an accident, boy. You know—I don't have to tell you that you are in deep trouble, my little joker." Allman turned quickly, went back to the driver's seat, shut off the lights, and began driving again.

"We have no alternative, Mrs. Oldman, than to turn this matter over to the Commons Detention Center. If the action would have been a mere practical joke that had no potential to harm anyone, I can see limiting it to your own jurisdiction." Principle Harding was very soft spoken, but firm.

"Oh, please, Mr. Harding. I'll do anything. He's never done anything like this before," replied Lana Oldman. "He's a good boy. He just needs a little more discipline is all."

"On the contrary, Mrs. Oldman." The principle hesitated and let out a sigh. "I have checked with his grade school. Umm—Sacred Rosary. The principle seemed to think, Mrs. Oldman, that Jeremy—well, he may have been physically abused at home. Sorry to have to mention this. Is that true?"

Mrs. Oldman had a shocked look on her face like someone who had been hit with a reality stick. She became furious. "No! That's a lie. I don't know how they came up with that nonsense. Jeremy had a normal, kind upbringing." She knew at that moment that she was lying 'through her teeth.' "Anyway. What does some old crow of a virgin nun know about family anyway?"

Principle Harding was astounded by what he just heard. *This isn't the talk of a woman trying to save her son by showing that she cares*, he thought. He saw the problem at once. *This woman is unstable.* "I'll tell you what, ma'am. How about if you and your son meet me here at the school for counseling? We like Jeremy a lot. He has just seemed to fall short on his grades lately. We can meet after school every day for say—an hour or so for three weeks." Mr. Harding knew that this proposal was not an easy thing for the Oldmans, but counseling is exactly what was needed. *It'll sure beat the detention center*, he thought.

Lana had a droll look on her face, knowing that it would cut into her personal time. *It'll cut into my drinking time really*, she thought. In the far reaches of her mind as a mother, she knew that she did care about Jeremy. She shook her head. "Yes. Anything, Principle Harding. Anything." The principle had let Jeremy off easy.

"Okay then. Can we meet Monday starting next week at 3pm?"

"Yes. Yes. Whatever it takes," she said. "Thank you so much, Mr. Harding. You have no idea what relief you have taken off of our family."

"That's very fine, Mrs. Oldman. Thank you for coming and trying to straighten out this problem."

"You're most welcome, sir. Goodbye until next Monday."

"Goodnight, Mrs. Oldman." She walked out the door of his office. She was relieved, bewildered, and furious all at the same time.

I have to save my boy—the little shit, she thought. *That'll be the last time he pulls a stunt like that.* She was right.

Counseling

Days of counseling were grueling for both Jeremy and his mother. Principle Harding was able to tap into his field of study. He received his Masters of Education in Psychology. The first day proved to be quite interesting. Harding's line of questioning was typical in trying to find out things about the Oldmans. "Good to see that you're willing to show up, Jeremy. Mrs. Oldman."

"Anything to clear up this mess," Lana Oldman said.

"And I hope that we do, Mrs. Oldman," Harding said. "Please, if you will, Mrs. Oldman, allow me to begin asking Jeremy a few questions."

"By all means," she said. She held her knuckles to her chin with her elbow rested on the principles desk.

"Fine. Well let's begin. Jeremy. How are you today?" Harding asked.

"Good," Jeremy responded. Jeremy was not good. He had had nothing but silence from his mother since her meeting with the principle except her warning of 'you'd better tell him what he wants to hear if you know what's good for you.'

"Good. Good. Jeremy, at an early age, were you ever abused, either physically or verbally? Now. Take your time. Just think."

Jeremy didn't have to think, but he had no intention of telling Mr. Harding anything unsavory for the moment. "Well—no. Not that I can remember," Mr. Harding.

"Okay. Okay. Are there any events that you may remember that upset you as a child? Were you on the level with your teachers in school?"

"Sure. Sure I was." Jeremy's good nature forced him to comment. "I stretched the truth now and then about some things. But I never said anything that would hurt anyone."

"So. Do you think it was just a child's imagination that overcame your senses, so to speak?"

"Well. Yes, Mr. Harding. I do." Jeremy began to analyze himself while being asked questions. *I was alienated as a child by my parents*, he thought. *I was jealous of my siblings as a child.* "I was always a story teller. I loved fantasy and reading."

"Well, you know. I think that I know about that, Jeremy. Your grade school teachers said that you were very creative. And that's a good thing. Let's jump ahead a little. You began early in school making, I might say, by making poor attempts toward receiving good grades, but—things had changed. You applied yourself and began making exceptional grades in all of your subjects. What do you think caused you to find your true potential?"

Jeremy didn't know how to answer this question. "Well," he said. "I guess I just woke up. I came home one night and felt like I had to prove that I wasn't stupid."

"But you're not stupid, Jeremy. Was there anyone that made you feel like you couldn't learn? Were your parents supportive in helping you understand your lessons?"

"They helped. Dad helped me with math when he had time." Jeremy was never helped with his studies by either of his parents. Jeremy knew that he did it all on his own. He was telling the principle 'what he wants to hear.' Jeremy realized that the warning by his mother really meant what **she** wants the principle to hear.

"It's good to hear that your dad tried to help you. Now. Allow me to direct some questions toward you, Mrs. Oldman," he said as he looked at her. What Mr. Harding saw in Mrs. Oldman's eyes was a careless stare. Blank dreamy nothingness.

"Okay, Mrs. Oldman?"

"Sure, Principle. Sure," she said.

"Did you help Jeremy with his studies in grade school, Ma'am?"

"Of course I did," she answered. She lied. Lana knew that she didn't give Jeremy the attention that he needed; school related or personally. "He was a bright student who didn't ask for help that often."

"But what I was told was that Jeremy lacked ambition in math, science, geography." He left his comment open for Mrs. Oldman to respond.

"Like I said, Principle Harding, Jeremy never asked for help in many areas of his studies, but I did help when he did ask," she said.

The principle accepted her answer for what it was worth. "Did he confide in you about any life issues that he was experiencing that may have needed attention?" Harding asked.

She assumed that she knew where he was going with this line of questioning. *He's trying to prove that I'm an unfit mother*, she thought. "I-I always did what I could to accommodate Jeremy in his life experiences. We went to St. Louis and rode the elevator to the top of the Arch. We.." Harding interrupted.

"I'm not talking about sight-seeing, Mrs. Oldman. I'm talking about personal attention to Jeremy's problems," Harding said. "Did Jeremy ever come to you with personal problems, Ma'am?" There was a momentary staring game. Lana looked at her son with a blank expression. Jeremy looked back at her with a *don't look at me for an answer* type of facial expression.

"I raised all of my children with equal attention, Mr. Harding," Lana said. "Jeremy was slow. That's all." Jeremy held back his true feelings during this usual passiveness from his mother. He wanted to lash out. He wanted to tell the principle what an unfair bitch his mother really was.

"So. You say that he was slow. Did you or Mr. Oldman try to remedy this slowness with any type of corrective measures?" Harding asked. Jeremy was beginning to enjoy this critical analysis.

"Yes," Mrs. Oldman said, almost robotically. She virtually froze, not knowing what to say next. She improvised, and she chose her words carefully, as to sound less than novice in delivering a sensible answer. "We gave Jeremy special attention when it came to his special needs. We made it clear to him that he was as good as any boy of his age, and he had the potential to gain anything in life that he desired. It is a little hazy at this point, Mr. Harding. I'm sure that you understand that it has been quite a while since his childhood, but I assure you, Jeremy was well attended to in his early years." It astounded Jeremy that his mother was quite the impromptu speaker. She sounded every bit the story teller that he was, and she did this with a prudent sort of general explanation.

"Very well, Mrs. Oldman." Harding had moved into a different direction with his examination. He picked up a small stack of papers. "Jeremy. What I am about to give you is the Rorschach Test. Otherwise known as an ink-blot test." Jeremy rolled his eyes, for he knew about this type of test. Harding observed Jeremy's reaction. "Are you bored, Mr. Oldman?" Harding asked indignantly.

Jeremy straightened up and cleared his throat. "No, sir," Jeremy said. "I'm sorry about that."

"Thank you," Harding said. "I have a feeling from your reaction that you know what I'm about to explain. Bear with me. I'm going to show you a series of pictures. You give me your first reaction about what you see." He held up the first one. It looked like two blue inverted pyramids intersecting one another with red, blue, and purple oblong shapes covering the entire picture.

"A storm in Egypt," Jeremy said. This comment brought an amused smile to Harding's face. Harding put that one face-down on the table and held up the next one. It looked similar to a multi-colored Picasso painting, detailed with perhaps green trees and black animal shapes throughout. "A nightmare during the day." The third contained green, pink, and mauve splotches. "Traces of what you might see looking—through a tree at the sun." The fourth had shades of black and gray, barren of detail at all except yellow spots encircling the outer edge. "Lying in bed just after turning out the lights." The fifth and final picture contained white shiny small spots on top of a background of pure royal blue. "Glimmers of light beams on a bright blue ocean," Jeremy said. Principal Harding was pleased that Jeremy gave his reactions immediately for each picture.

"You have a very keen sense of observation, Jeremy," Harding said. "Your reactions were very interesting. Very interesting. The 'nightmare during the day' comment was odd. What made you say that?" He held the picture up again.

"Well—look at it," Jeremy said. "It looks like a forest in the day with scary looking demons standing around." Jeremy smiled.

"Hmm. I thought they just looked like dogs or something," Harding answered. "Well, that's okay. You saw what you saw. Other than that one, your answers seemed fairly normal—and creative." Lana Oldman felt jealousy toward her son. She knew that she contained no such imagination. "Okay, folks. That's it for today. We're running quite shy of an hour. Let's stop. I think we broke ground enough for our first session. See you tomorrow at 3." He stood, then the Oldmans stood. Harding held out his hand to Jeremy's. Jeremy shook it.

"Whoa. Firm grip there, sir," Jeremy said. He smiled.

Harding smiled too. "Mrs. Oldman." She held out her hand as a lady should do first. Mr. Harding shook her hand with much less strength. "I was careful with your hand, Ma'am."

Lana smiled. "Thank you, Mr. Harding, for your time," she said.

Each day was somewhat different at the principle's office. On the Friday of week one, Harding had increased the personal nature of his questioning. "Mrs Oldman," he began. "Did you and your husband have what you would call—a good relationship?" Lana Oldman was taken back by the intrusiveness of the question.

"Mr. Harding," she said. "James and I had a wonderful relationship. We had our differences at times." She paused and thought. Lana was off in her own world for a good 10 seconds as she stared at the bookcase in the office. *We had only made love a few times a year,* she thought. *It became less toward the end.*

"What type of differences? If I may ask. Just give an example."

She had to think. "Well---we were both brought up in middle-class families. You could say that my family bordered on being poor. My father was a teacher at a catholic school. There were sometimes fights between my parents that kind of—gave me a complex."

"What type of complex, Lana? May I call you Lana?"

"Yes. Yes. Of course." The principle's use of her first name made her feel important. "Well, like I wasn't as good as other people. The fighting was usually over financial problems. You see, my mother didn't work, and women usually didn't back in the 50s. So, I felt out of sorts many times. As far as James and me, we kind of had the same situation. I didn't work either. You know. I tried to spend time with my children."

"That's a laugh," Jeremy interjected. He looked straight at his mother.

"You zip your lip, boy. I'll smack the crap out of you," she said with a sardonic look on her face. She suddenly froze in terror. She looked at Mr. Harding as if she'd been caught in a lie. She **was** caught in a lie, and that was the lie of treating Jeremy with respect.

"Do you often speak to Jeremy like that, Mrs. Oldman?" Harding asked.

"No. No," she said. She smiled, not knowing how to continue.

"Oh—come on, Mom. Why don't you just tell the truth?" Jeremy asked. Jeremy was about to explode. He was about to explode and tell all, and he even thought of telling his mother about Daddy's little play thing from the neighborhood. Jeremy never knew who that person was, but he knew that she existed. *Doreen knew too*, he thought. *Maybe Doreen knows who the woman was.*

"Now, Jeremy. Show some respect to your mother. Don't talk to her like that," Harding said.

Jeremy was brewing inside. "Mr. Harding," Jeremy said. "I was left out. Left out of everything that a boy growing up should be included in. I didn't go to kindergarten. My brother and sister did. I was never congratulated for good work that I did in school. It was like they hated me, sir. Maybe because I was ugly."

"Jeremy. One moment. Things in life go deeper than that, son. Your parents would not have socially abandoned you because of how you looked as a child. By the way, you're a handsome boy. And you're very bright."

"Thanks, Mr. Harding. I don't know about that handsome stuff. I do know that I'm bright. I proved to myself that I could succeed in school, but did I ever hear a word of appreciation for it? No. All I heard was Doreen this and Frank that. What is the matter with me, sir? Why didn't my parents love me?"

"We loved you, boy, and I still love you," Lana Oldman said. She began to cry. "It was—well—at first, we did think that you may have been—different."

"Why was I different, Mom? What? What was it that made you treat me differently?"

"It was us, boy. Your father and I were—well—weird. We grew up in very stern families. We were insecure. We thought you were mentally challenged, Jeremy, and we didn't understand it. I'm sorry, son. I'm so sorry."

"Well. That's rich. So—you thought I was retarded so you treated me like an animal in a cage? Speaking of cage. Remember my rabbits?" Jeremy looked at Mr. Harding with tears in his eyes. "When I was 8 years old, they cooked my pet rabbits. They didn't even warn me about it, Mr. Harding."

Mr. Harding was very upset about what he was hearing. He knew at that point that this boy was a very troubled boy indeed. He was unsure of what to say next, but knew that he must say something. "That was wrong, Jeremy. Very wrong for your parents to do that."

"It was his father's idea, Mr. Harding," Lana said.

"So—you just went along with it. Is that right, Mrs. Oldman?" Harding asked. He rubbed his right forefinger down alongside his nose staring at her, waiting for an answer.

"He—James. He always had the final say. I told him that I didn't think it was a good idea, and that they were Jeremy's pets, and he would be very upset, but…"

"But what, Ma'am?"

"He said that he didn't care. He went on about how he and his dad used to hunt, and rabbit was his favorite wild game to eat. He said something like 'the hell with what that boy thinks. I'm hungry for rabbit.' Lana, looking down while she spoke, glanced up quickly at Mr. Harding afterward.

Harding's look was intense. He looked at her with squinted serious eyes. "I see," he said. He looked at Jeremy. "Jeremy. How long did it take you to get over this—event?"

Jeremy was mesmerized by Harding's acumen in his questioning and had a great admiration for him as a counselor. He had also noticed that Harding's use of his mother's first name had ceased. "Well, Mr. Harding. I don't remember. I do know that I decided that I hated my parents that week. I guess they began to treat me somewhat normally, and I finally got over it. It's like—I don't know. I was used to terrible treatment by my dad. It was like my reality. I didn't know why things were the way they were, but I started to accept it."

Lana broke into the conversation. "James. My husband was abused as a child. I think it made him kind of—crazy."

"I can see the pieces of the puzzle fitting, Mrs. Oldman. Jeremy's treatment is not justified by any means. But—it does make sense. I mean—it's a classic case of repeat behavior handed down a generation. Are you, Mrs. Oldman, willing to try and make things right between you and your son? As far as I'm concerned we've made a tremendous breakthrough today."

"Yes. Yes. I will. I will try and make things right," Lana said with tears in her eyes. She looked at Jeremy. "Come here, baby." Jeremy rushed to her and hugged her tightly, also with tears in his eyes. "I love you, Jeremy."

"I love you too, Mom," Jeremy said.

Mr. Harding had a difficult time holding back his own tears. His eyes were glassy. "Great. I see no need in further therapy." He spoke to them both. "Remember though, Mrs. Oldman. If Jeremy's behavior does not change, and his grades don't improve considerably, I'll have to call you both in again. Is that understood?"

Jeremy and Mrs. Oldman had unraveled from each other's embrace. "Yes. I certainly do, Principle Harding," Lana said. She wiped tears from her face with her hand. "I think we'll be okay. And I'll offer any help that Jeremy needs in his studies, that is, if he needs help. He's a pretty smart kid."

"I'm sorry," Mr. Harding said. "Take some of these." He handed a box of facial tissues to Mrs. Oldman. Both Jeremy and his mother grabbed a few, wiped their faces, and started blowing their noses.

"Sounds like a duck farm in here," Jeremy said, and laughed. They all laughed.

"Now that's funny, Jeremy," Harding said, as he shook his head back and forth in amusement. "Okay, Mrs. Oldman. I'll hold you to that promise." They all stood in unison.

"I thank you, Mr. Harding," Lana said. "I just want you and Jeremy to know that I claim as much responsibility in this matter as anyone."

"That is wonderful to hear, Lana. Do you see how it's always a two-way street? We've helped you also. Jeremy wasn't the only problem to solve, and I believe that you have to admit that you were more of the problem, Mrs. Oldman, than Jeremy ever was. His antics are a cry for attention."

"Yes. You are definitely right," Mrs. Oldman said. "I now hold full responsibility."

"Jeremy," Harding said. "You are now responsible also for your actions. There is a time when you must allow the past to be the past and move on."

"Yes, I know, Mr. Harding," Jeremy said. He held his hand out to Mr. Harding. Harding shook his hand.

"Oh. Must remember my grip," Harding said as he laughed.

Lana Oldman hugged Mr. Harding in respect and then released him. "I'm sorry, Mr. Harding. I hope that wasn't inappropriate," she said.

"No. Not at all. We're adults. I wouldn't have expected anything less. Now--you two go and have the good life that you both deserve." They all said their thanks and goodbyes. The Oldmans left the office.

Epilogue

Jeremy looked in amazement at the set of train cars that circled around the track and through a tunnel built by Mr. Brian Sawyer and his son, Ted. There were patches of greenery, buildings, and a station that were neatly placed around the corners of the oblong set up that stretched about twenty feet in length. Jeremy remained very good friends with the Sawyers over the next several years. They had taken Jeremy to a Chicago Cubs game when he was eighteen years old. He thought that Wrigley Field was the most beautiful place that he had ever seen. The Sawyers were some of the catalysts that helped to set Jeremy's future into motion. He could never forget Principle Harding. He was the one that changed Jeremy's life forever. Jeremy graduated with honors.

In the spring of 2010, Jeremy received a scholarship to attend college. He began his college career at Princeton University where he furthered his studies in English. He was accepted without question due to his S.A.T. scores. He graduated from Princeton at the top of his class. He attended Graduate School at the University of Southern California where he also made impeccable grades. His thesis was entitled "The Direct Influence of 19th Century Literature on Human Direction." The catalyst that influenced the creation of his thesis was the book that he had discovered on that lonely afternoon in the grade school library. *Mary Shelley* had taught him much about human distinction, inhumanity, and suffering. It was still his favorite piece of literature of all time. Jeremy had learned to love life and what it had to offer.

The catalysts that began to make Jeremy's life unbearable at such an early age were obvious. His parents, peers, and his own weak state of self-esteem had nearly sent him into an inevitable realm of self-destruction.

Thank God that most people are loving by nature, Jeremy thought at the time he received his graduate degree. As Jeremy had stated in his thesis, *'There is no room in this world for inhumanity; and the creation of monster from man is devised only by those who wish to change the world for their own personal gain or because of their own personal loss.'*

230

Printed in the United States
By Bookmasters